Advance Praise for *Take*

"*Take Me There* is a smokin' hot sampling of sassy smart smut that took me where I'd never been before in print—this is the most gender-diverse erotica collection I've ever seen anywhere."

—Susan Stryker, author of *Transgender History*

"As someone who is androgynous-identified, it feels positively monumental to hold in my hands an erotica anthology where trans desire is not the token, but the topic! In making our desires visible—within our own communities and beyond—our gender expressions, our fantasies, our very lives are made real. *Take Me There* brings us HERE."

—Jiz Lee, genderqueer porn star

"There are multiple theories of desire out there; many histories of sexuality; lots of studies of sexual practices, but, until now, there were few accounts, fictional or otherwise of the multiple ways that queer people eroticize gender-variant bodies. This collection is hot and steamy, boiling with new lust, bubbling with new languages of desire, new ways of naming the body, different modes of telling each other 'I want you.' Ask what you need from this book, it will take you there. I promise."

—Jack Halberstam, author of *Female Masculinity*

"Finally, a satisfying resource that more of us can offer, with a sly smile, when they ask us what exactly we *do* with one another."

—Scott Turner Schofield, author of *Two Truths and a Lie*

TAKE ME THERE

TAKE ME THERE

TRANS AND GENDERQUEER EROTICA

EDITED BY
TRISTAN TAORMINO

Published in the United States by Cleis Press, Inc.,
2246 Sixth Street, Berkeley, California 94710.

Printed in the United States.
Cover design: Scott Idleman/Blink
Cover photograph: Ron Chapple/Getty Images
Text design: Frank Wiedemann
First Edition.
10 9 8 7 6 5 4 3 2 1

Trade paper ISBN: 978-1-57344-720-1
E-book ISBN: ISBN: 978-1-57344-740-9

Contents

INTRODUCTION: GENDER/ FUCKING

Where are the representations of the erotic identities, sex lives and fantasies of transgender and genderqueer people? In mainstream media, they are oversimplified, sensationalized or mostly invisible. Some occupy a niche in mainstream pornography: the so-called "chicks with dicks" genre. Although transwomen are the objects of desire in these films, they are still stigmatized for their difference and portrayed as secret keepers, circus freaks or evil dommes for a straight male viewer. Transwomen without dicks (or who don't consider their genitals *dicks*), lesbian transwomen, and transmen of all kinds are absent from the traditional adult industry. There is one exception: Buck Angel, a successful FTM porn star and self-proclaimed "man with a pussy." Angel has made tremendous strides to increase the visibility of transmen in porn. Plus, there is a small but growing body of independent porn that features trans and genderqueer people on websites like nofauxxx.com, by studios like Pink and White Productions and Trannywood Pictures and from directors like Morty Diamond and Courtney Trouble.

But what about depictions of transgender desire in erotic writing? For those of us who appreciate the written word's power to not just get us off but bring nuance and complexity to erotic storytelling, we don't have all that much to choose from. As the spouse of a person who identifies as trans and genderqueer, I believe it's time for transpeople to be the authors and central characters of a book of their own, to be enjoyed by other transpeople along with their partners, admirers, allies, fuckbuddies, friends and lovers. I want to see folks who challenge gender norms as leading men, ingénues, crush objects and sex symbols on the page. That's why I put together this collection. So, what exactly is transgender and genderqueer erotica? It's erotica by, for and about transfolk, FTMs, MTFs, genderqueers, gender outlaws, as well as two-spirit, intersex and gender-variant people. It is about people who like to genderfuck and fuck gender.

Among the diverse array of voices in the book, one theme that emerged is the power of seeing and being seen as beautifully illustrated in Patrick Califia's story about a gay transman longing for his identity and desire to be not just acknowledged, but treasured. It's not simply about passing or not passing, which is an idea often explored with transgender characters, but about being acknowledged and desired in a sexual context. Being truly seen for who you are by a lover is where affirmation and want collide, as in Andrea Zanin's story of a baby butch dyke and the transwoman she picks up in a small-town café. Likewise, the main character in Helen Boyd's "All-Girl Action" longs to be touched as a woman by other queer women. Amidst a neighborhood blackout in "The Visible Woman," by Rachel K. Zall, two women leave behind how others perceive them and focus on how they see each other. In "On Hys Knees," Evan Swafford's narrator articulates this hunger for recognition but also safety as he looks at his boi: "The naked female sex, which this boi usually hides under baggy jeans and men's clothes, is uncovered for Daddy. I warrant this trust and take it seriously. Because I see my boi as hy truly is. And hy knows that I'll protect hym, keep hym safe. It's what we both need." It is this recognition and trust that allows the boi to surrender to his Daddy in a scene full of fisting, sadism and love.

Throughout the stories, no one is all that surprised about anyone's gender, which bucks the trend of having a transperson's "real" or former gender revealed. But there are revelations of other kinds. Jack tries to have what he calls The Conversation with a trick at a bar, but his pants are down before the talk actually happens, in Michael Hernandez's "You Don't Know Jack." In "The Therapist and the Whore" by Giselle Renarde, Manny is a butch dyke struggling with her identity who can't seem to talk honestly about it to her therapist; she feels most at ease fucking a transsexual sex worker whose comfort with her own identity creates a space where Manny can be Manny. For Ivan Coyote's narrator in "Hold Up," too much talking and processing is an absolute boner killer: "I would rather be fucking or fisting or tangling tongues or pulling each other's hair and deciding by willpower and whim just who is going to suck whose what, and when and exactly how."

Most of the characters in these stories don't fit into neat little boxes and those that appear to fit, do it not-so-neatly. A lustful homecoming is full of sacred tradition and modern queerness in "Tel Aviv" by Jacques La Fargue: "I go from fresh-faced yeshiva boy to breasted bride as the layers come off, and I don't care. It's your cock I want." In Kiki DeLovely's "Taking the Toll," a femme describes her genderqueer lover: "She has this edge about her—not completely hard yet deeply masculine. This is the edge where my lust resides." That lust takes them both all the way to the confession booth. Anna Watson wrote to me before submitting her piece, "Femme Fatigue," inquiring if femmes as main characters were part of my vision for the book. I welcome her contribution since we both agree that many femmes consider themselves genderqueer, because they consciously choose to fuck with female and femininity norms. There are femmes throughout this book, including one who surprises her boyfriend when her gender changes mid-fuck in S. Bear Bergman's "Payback's a Bitch."

In her story "Dixie Belle," Kate Bornstein imagines Huckleberry Finn transformed into Sassy, a prostitute at a New Orleans brothel. Before there were identities like transgender, there were struggles and longing like those of the characters in "Sea of Cortez" by Sandra McDonald. Both of these pieces are the imagined histories of prototypical gender radicals grounded in the sights, sounds and language of their time periods. Considering the recent controversy—about NewSouth Books' decision to release a version of *Huckleberry Finn* without the words *nigger* and *injun* in response to the removal of the book from public schools and libraries—Bornstein's piece is especially provocative. It also speaks to the power of language to define and redefine cultural identities over time.

As befits an anthology about genderfucking, there are several pronoun variations you'll come across in the text, including *ze/hir/hir* (which some readers will be familiar with) and *hy/hym/hys*. Slowly, these new words are beginning to seep into our consciousness and people are using them more frequently in conversation and writing. Although this departure from *she/her/her* and *he/him/his* may distract you at first, I challenge you not to get caught up in their newness and miss the depth of these stories in the process. The writers who chose to use these words have done so deliberately, because they best describe their characters. In the process, they push the language about gender-variant people to be more descriptive and less binary. And those who use he/she pronouns, do so in wonderful ways; there is something deliciously dissonant about reading about his clit, her dick, his tits and her scrotum. What all this reveals, of course, is just how limited our language is for describing people of other genders.

Our language is also severely limited when it comes to describing the bodies of transpeople, bodies that don't conform to norms and may not look like other bodies. How do we eroticize these bodies, talk about them in dirty ways, worship *and* respect them? In several of the pieces, there is a tension between body image and the bodies we imagine. The spectrum of bodies we were born with, bodies we live in, bodies we want and bodies we create is present in some way in all of the stories. As characters work to quiet discomfort and shame and embrace acceptance, it's clear that the body is a place of much more than simply pleasure. It can be a site of self-doubt, pain and memory, but it's also one of craving, fantasy, transgression and, ultimately, freedom. In Julia Serano's "Little Blue Thing," when the narrator's body betrays her, she finds a humorous way to overcome it. The couple in "Somebody's Watching Me," by Alicia E. Goranson, shape-shift into different bodies as they have sex. With a nod to both a narcissistic phase of gender transition and transdyke desire, the woman in Tobi Hill-Meyer's "Self Reflection" has the opportunity to explore the body of her future self—and gladly takes it. The main character in "Face Pack," by Penelope Mansfield, manages to turn a misogynist Japanese porn trope on its head—rolling a celebration of her smooth skin and an empowered filthy girl fantasy into one surprising scene. The Daddy in Toni Amato's "That's What Little Girls Are Made Of" rides a dangerous line, as he takes a sharp blade to a cunt that has seen a different kind of knife.

Be prepared for *cock* to have multiple delicious meanings in these stories. Get ready for what you might think is a pussy or a cock to be called something else entirely. Some cocks are strapped on then thrown off to the side, as happens in one guy's beach adventure in "The Hitchhiker," by Sinclair Sexsmith. Some stay put no matter what. Others are always there, but not always accessible, as in Dean Scarborough's "Shoes Are Meant to Get You Somewhere," where a submissive gets a taste of a new kind of cock. "He had never, ever heard that tone in Hayden's voice before—sometimes the man had moaned and whispered dirty things to him before when Oscar had sucked Hayden's cock, but never this cock, and his voice had never sounded like this before."

Speaking of cocks, I worked diligently to represent a diversity of genders, sexual orientations, identities and bodies in the anthology. However, I want to acknowledge there is one group that feels the least represented: transwomen who've had bottom surgery. I can speculate about a number of reasons why this might be, but I want to challenge writers to tell the erotic stories of these women, and editors, including me, to seek them out and publish them.

Many of the people who populate these pages consciously invent, reimagine and play with gender during sex. The names they give themselves or call each other—cocksucker faggot, bad boy, bitch, Daddy, good little girl, filthy slut, gangsuck cumshot facial whore—can taunt or tease, but they always signify the presence of gender among sweaty bodies, lube bottles, latex gloves and leather harnesses. Gender is always there, usually front and center. Some of the pieces illuminate how gender can complicate sex, as when Rahne Alexander's narrator struggles with anxiety about revealing herself to a new lover in "Now, Voyager." Gender can also simplify sex—like it does in Gina de Vries's role-play fantasy "Cocksure," where a virgin teenage boy is seduced by his friend's older sister. He straddles a sense of sureness and shyness, and ultimately his gender frames his desire: "He's breathing that heavy way he does, the way he gets sub-verbal and breathy when he really goes under; becomes nothing but his hard cock and hungry mouth, big eyes and smooth hands."

On the other hand, there are some compelling examples of how sex complicates gender. In "Canadian Slim," Shawna Virago's trans narrator is discouraged by sexual partners who treat her like a fetish object: "I was both a source of desire and shame, and it didn't feel good." But sex can simplify gender, too, reduce it to its base of want and need. In Zev Al-Walid's "From Fucktoy to Footstool," a transboy gets to fuck his Daddy for the first time. Put in very compromising bondage and a hood, his body is whittled down to one single hand.

Bondage isn't simply rope and knots: passion and pleasure reside at the intersection of gender and power. Nearly half of the stories in this anthology feature some kind of BDSM. Two trans guys embrace their masculinity through masochism and submission in contributions from Arden Hill and Rachel Kramer Bussel. At the other end of the kinky spectrum, Skian McGuire's sadistic narrator spins a dark, unrelenting and revealing tale that takes us on a wild ride as he conjures up "The Boy the Beast Wants." Laura Antoniou wrote an original story for this book that stars Chris Parker, one of the main characters in her S/M erotic novel series *The Marketplace*. Whether you're a fan of the series or not, you'll enjoy tagging along as Parker undergoes a series of visits to a tattoo artist to mark and transform his body, while his longtime lover Rachel experiences a different kind of pain, potentially both physically and emotionally scarring.

Where are the stories about the erotic identities, sex lives, and fantasies of transgender and genderqueer people? Well, twenty-nine of them are here. This collection will take you from San Francisco to Israel, from heartache to lust, from stranger sex to a ten-year anniversary, from a pair of ballet shoes to a butt plug bondage table, from fumbling teenagers to leatherclad bears, from M to F and F to M—and in between and beyond. These stories celebrate the pleasure, heat and diversity of transgender and genderqueer sexualities. The thread that runs through each of the stories is a glimpse at where our sexual imagination can take us.

I chose the title *Take Me There* for several reasons. Bodies can be tricky territory: minefields or playgrounds or both, and the power of giving and taking is a gift. I want to acknowledge that moment of surrendering a part of your body, a piece of your sexuality that may feel scary, but through the fear owning it, asking for it, even commanding it, as in, "Take me *there*." Throughout the book, people harness their desire and imagination to go places that transcend bodies and language. They craft new worlds, rituals, and experiences beyond borders. I love all the fantasies these authors have designed, and I want to visit more of their worlds, as many as our sexual minds can create. My bags are already packed. So take me there.

Tristan Taormino
New York

COCKSURE

Gina de Vries

He's so nervous, this one. Fidgety. Tapping his hands against his denim-clad thighs, then playing with the worn cuffs of his plaid shirt—plaid like the early '90s grunge boys', I note. A good touch. I'm wearing lip gloss, a very short skirt with fishnets, a disintegrating halter top with layers of lingerie underneath. The more clothes I have to take off, the more I can fluster him. I'm playing bigger and older, but not by much. Seventeen to his fourteen, punk to his nerd, slut to his virgin. As soon as I get him up to my room—all it took was the line, "My brother's not home yet. Come listen to music with me while you wait for him"—I pull the halter off. His eyes flutter to my tits, then back to his hands. I can literally smell him getting uncomfortable, the scent of piney boy deodorant and sex entering the room. He shifts his eyes around to everything but me. He takes in the posters on my walls, the three overstuffed shelves of books. He clears his throat when he gets to the dildos on my nightstand, the whips hanging on the wall above them. Looks down suddenly again. I'd considered putting them away to make my room look more like a teenager's. Then it occurred to me that the kind of girl I'm playing just might be bold enough to sneak into stores where she's not wanted, pass for older, buy sex toys with her allowance and leave them out in plain view.

He's clearly spooked by it all. But he's polite, this one. He asks where he should set his stuff. "Oh, just throw your bag and your coat anywhere and sit on my bed." He stills at that. "I...can't just sit at your desk?"

I choose my next words carefully. I'm gentle, coaxing, "No, no, no, peach. Sit on my bed." I try to say it like sitting on my bed is a special honor, but he's dubious. He pauses, not at all sure of what he's gotten himself into by accepting my invitation. He sets down his bag and coat very precisely in the corner by my bookshelf and walks over to my bed.

"On the bed?" he repeats, hovering, not sitting down yet.

"Oh, the bed's way more comfortable than that hard desk chair. Have a seat." I notice that he flushes a little at the word "hard," and I smirk. He's extrasensory when he's turned on, responsive to the tiniest of stimuli—a single word, a light touch. He sits down, and I join him, just a little too close for comfort.

When our hips touch, he jolts a little, and my heart begins to race despite myself. Something about this feels so real; suddenly, it feels like now or never, like I could make the wrong move and he could bolt. I swallow my fear. Slip a hand onto his thigh and another under his chin. Turn his face to meet mine.

"I felt how you moved just then, honey. You like sitting next to me, don't you?"

He doesn't speak. Just shakes his head up and down very slightly, a barely perceptible nod, a lot of blushing and blinking his eyes. "No, baby. Keep looking at me." I hold his gaze. His eyes on mine are wide. Wild. He gulps, a movement that I feel because my fingers are tracing the muscles of his mouth and neck.

"Sitting here with me makes you feel good, doesn't it?" A nod, again. I feel him let a breath go. Feel his throat open up and expand to push air out and suck it back in again. "That's right, honey, breathe. Relax." I reach up and stroke his hair, and he leans his face into my neck, makes a noise somewhere between a sigh and a moan. He shivers just a little in my arms.

"I really want you to feel good, peach. That's why I invited you up here."

I have a thing for these boys. The ones who are sure of themselves at one moment, but awkward, nervous the next. I like extremes, opposites, contradictions. I like a boy supercool but painfully uncertain. Bold, then timid, then bold again. I like him unsure and breathless. Wet and hard, blood simmering, breathing heavy. Eyes and hands and mouth and cock all over me. But only how I want it. Only when I say so.

He becomes bolder as the night goes on, asks for more, timid but surefooted. I've gotten him out of the worn plaid shirt. His binder is the one thing that never comes off, and he's still in his jeans. I've convinced him to unhook my bra and coaxed him on top of me, *Like this, honey*. My skirt is hiked up around my hips. He's pumping instinctively, getting a rhythm going on top of me, and I swear, I swear I can feel his cock. Even though he's not packing, even though there are layers of denim and cotton and lace between us, I feel his cock like I would feel any boy's cock. It is there, it is real, and it is hard, grinding through his jeans, through my lingerie right down into my cunt. I feel so fucked, so good, and he is not even touching my naked body, just rubbing up against me through clothes and kissing me like his life depends on it, moving his hands all over whatever bare skin he can get to. He moans, over and over again, into my mouth, my neck, my tits. He pulls his mouth away from me suddenly, and I have to keep myself from whimpering at the loss. "What do you want, angel?" I say.

"I..." He giggles then, buries his face into my neck. "I...I want to be doing my homework."

Brat. He's only saying it to get a rise out of me, I know, but it works.

"Oh, really? You really want to do your *homework*?" I hiss that into his ear, bite his neck hard, and he shrieks. "You wanna be doing your *homework* when you're lying on top of me, and my bra's unhooked, and I can tell how much you want it from the way you're moving your hips? You wanna be doing your homework *right now*?" I thrust my hips up at "right now" so they hit his cock just right. He moans again. He's breathing that heavy way he does, the way he gets sub-verbal and breathy when he really goes under; becomes nothing but his hard cock and hungry mouth, big eyes and smooth hands. But I'm not letting him sink there so quick. I pull his hair and he yowls.

"You really want to do your homework right now?"

"Uhhh... Well, I mean, I mean"—I pull his hair again—"OW! I mean, I guess your brother won't be back for a while. I guess I can't do the Social Studies project with him till he gets back. I guess it's okay that I'm in your room with you, right?"

"Yeah, sweetie, he won't be back for a really long time. Now, why don't you slip your hands up under my skirt?"

He's only a year younger than me, but in some lights, at some moments, he really does look teenaged. Doe-eyed, scared like a deer in the headlights, but wild like a deer, too. Shy and cock-sure at the same time, just like he told me he was when we met. "What kind of boy do you like to be?" I'd asked. And he looked right at me and blinked those big, dreamy eyes. That's how we started. One of my hands at the nape of his neck, holding him there with me, coaxing it out of him. "Cocksure," he said. "But kinda shy."

He has a good mouth, this boy. He is good with his words, even when he's bratty, and he is good with his lips, and this is what I tell him as I slide in and out, murmur, "Good, good, you're so good, smart-mouthed faggot, sweet-talker, cocksucker, pretty boy..." He devours my fingers, sucks almost my whole fist down to the back of his throat, does the same with my cock after I hastily fasten the harness on over my lingerie.

I am so close to undone from this. The very look of his mouth on me, his hand wrapped around the base of my cock, those hot, fast gagging noises he makes when he takes me all the way to the back of his throat. My hand is fisted in his hair, pushing him just a little, but he doesn't need much force. He is the kind of boy who can take it, all of it. When he looks up at me from his knees, spits on his hand and lubes up my cock with his fingers, I murmur, "You've done this before, haven't you, gorgeous?" And he grins at me with pride, and this once shy, scared boy? He starts to talk.

He spins a story that is just a little over-the-top, but no less effective, stroking me all the while—about an older cousin and a vacation in New York City and a porn theater, walking in and seeing all the men jerking off.

"And I saw this guy, and he was *so hot*, and my cousin nudged me and told me to go over to him, and I totally sucked his dick and..."

"Did he suck yours?"

"No, he just rubbed his foot up against my crotch—he couldn't really reach me..."

"Has anyone, ever?"

And he replies sheepishly, his cheeks flushed, "No."

"Well, then. I'd love to be the first."

He all but leaps up from the floor. Shucks his jeans and socks, grabs his other cock and the harness from his bag, pulls them on over his briefs. When he approaches me, breathing hard, his rigid dick curving up from his body, I grab him and kiss him. I want my mouth all over him at this moment, wish for just a second that I had two mouths the way I have two hands and two feet. Instead I settle for kissing him again. Kneeling down, guiding his hand to his cock, taking his fingers and cock together into my mouth.

His cock is absolutely something to be sure of. I love him inside me, and I love his hands all over my body, and I am no less in control when his cock is in my mouth, no less in control when he is touching me.

He's slipped my panties off my hips, and he's on top of me again, his hips battering into mine. I could almost come from this, I'm so wet, so far gone from everything, his mouth on my cock, mine on his, the sweet tender teenage way he keeps asking things like, "Like this? Touch you like this? Like we were doing before, or different?" I thrust my hips up to meet his.

"Do you feel how wet I am for you?"

"Yes," he moans, and nods.

"I want you inside me. Have you done that before, honey?"

He whimpers back, "No."

"Do you want to?"

"Oh, please."

I reach down and guide the head of his cock between my lips, and he thrusts to meet me, fills my cunt in one long stroke. "Just slide it in, yes, that's it, like that, yes, yes," and I lose my words for a minute; I mean, I know I am saying words, but I don't know what they are, *yes* or *good* or *boy* or *God* or *fuck*. I am lost in the feeling of his cock in me, his breathing harder and hotter and his hips moving faster, mine moving up to meet his, to take as much of him inside me as I can. I love the look of him completely shattered above me, absorbed in every movement of his cock, my body the only place he wants to be. "Are you going to come inside me?" I ask, and he nods yes.

"Tell me when, honey," and the only words he can manage through his moaning are, *"Now, now,"* and I rise up with him, feel my cunt spasm around his cock before I even realize it's happening for me, too. "Oh, fuck, I want to do that again," I laugh, and he laughs above me, thrusts himself into me again, and again. His cock is the kind that stays hard inside me, and he keeps fucking me for a long, long time.

I am no less in control when he is fucking me, his fingers deep in my cunt or sucked back right to the edge of my gag reflex, his cock pumping inside of me slow and hard and dreamy. I am at my most powerful when I am open to him, and he, he is at his best inside me, the best boy.

After, he asks if he can curl up in my lap. He's that specific, he doesn't say "lie" or "sit," he says, "curl up," and it is this specificity that I adore about him, one of the things that drew me to him in the first place. He is so good with his words, this one, so good with his words and his cock and so good in my lap. "Yes," I say, touching the dark curls that frame his pale face. He blinks his big, dark eyes, and the curls of his eyelashes flutter. I open my arms and he leans his head into the crook of my neck, murmurs, "Mmm. Thank you." I pull my softest blanket around the two of us, the big fluffy maroon one; cocoon him in it. He wraps his arms around me, and he says it again: "Thank you. I just wanted to be sure of you."

NOW, VOYAGER

Rahne Alexander

All anyone seemed to be able to talk about at work was the Christmas cruise, this big annual event where the bigwigs rented a party boat and invited all their favorite clients to get three sheets to the wind while they sailed around the bay in a lazy circle. It was hard to believe that any of these people knew the first thing about having fun, but they were all full of hysterical reminiscences of cruises past.

My department was going out of their way to remind me about it, because they still all felt so guilty for having forgotten to invite me to last year's party. Mindy, the office manager, told me I was gonna love it and then danced, mouthing the words *open bar* while my boss stomped past. The same VP who brought me flowers on administrative assistant's day left his cruise photo album at my desk next to the business magazines on display, presumably for visiting dignitaries.

"So are you gonna break down and go? Is Jonas going?" Wendy asked. She was a copywriter who had gone to my same college. We hadn't known each other well at the time, but she was one of a very few people who knew me while I was still getting by as male. She took my transition in stride and that turned our acquaintance into friendship.

"I don't know. You know me; I just don't like being that far away from home without my own transportation." Wendy was already going to be up in the city; she was going to tear herself away from big family holiday plans for the night.

"Dude, I'm not gonna have any fun unless you're there. You should ask Jonas. He'll totally drive."

Jonas was sort of an impish teddy bear whose grin never seemed to fade. He had the curliest blond hair that I'd ever seen. I'd only known him a year or so, and I had no idea what he did for the company. He was one of the few geeks in town who seemed to prefer not to talk about work in his off hours.

He had shown up on my radar a few weeks before when he chatted me up at the coffee shop where I went to chew on pencils in solitude. He distracted me with lilting conversation for a couple of hours. He learned that I'd never eaten sushi and offered to treat me to Sushi Boat. Two nights later he invited me to happy hour after work with some of the engineers. A habit began to form—I'd bus to work, drive with Jonas to happy hour, bus home, repeat. Sometimes he'd drop me off at home after, but since he lived more than half an hour in the opposite direction, I always felt like it was an imposition.

I punched in his extension and waited for the outgoing message. He almost never answered the office phone. "I don't like interruptions," he'd say. "They're very disruptive." I got his voice mail and said, "Hey, Jonas it's me, and I was wondering if you were planning on going to this cruise thing this weekend. They're laying it on thick over here. I was thinking, well, if you get this just let me know if you're going and if you're going maybe we could go up together?" I hung up. Wendy grinned. "You just asked Jonas out on a boat cruise," she sang. My phone rang back, and of course it was Jonas. I waved her away.

"I haven't been on the Holiday Booze Cruise in yeeeeears!" Jonas said. He was excited to go with me. We made a little plan: I'd change into my cruise clothes at work and then head to the city.

I hung up feeling queasy. I had asked him out on a date. We had been *dating*. I wondered if I were prone to seasickness. I'd never really been on a boat. We were going on a date on a boat with our whole company. I had no idea what to wear.

In those days, if I wasn't wearing a tent, I was in turtlenecks and pleated slacks. For such a special occasion I really only had one outfit, in mondo velveteen: a tight, floor-length black skirt and a maroon cowl-neck top.

We drove up the coast, stopping off at his house to pick up his pipe and smoking jacket. His beat-up two-seater had a great sound system and CD changer stocked with Wall of Voodoo, Nick Cave and Front 242. We smoked and bitched about work. He told me jokes. He asked me if I'd ever heard the one about MacPhee the carpenter, which he told in faux brogue.

One day, Jonas said, he went down to the pub where he met an old man named MacPhee who was terribly drunk and looking quite glum. He asked MacPhee, "What's got you down, old timer?" MacPhee replied, "Do you see this bar? I built this bar with my own two hands. I went into the woods, cut down the tree, cut it into boards. I planed and polished the wood, and I've been drinking at this beautiful bar for forty years! But do they call me MacPhee the woodsman? Do they call me MacPhee the carpenter?"

MacPhee continued to list his accomplishments. This was

Jonas's favorite joke, and he reveled in the embellishment.

"That wall?" MacPhee continued. "I built that wall! I carried each of those stones from the quarry. I mixed the mortar, and by hand I built that wall. But do they call me MacPhee the stone mason? No, they do not!" MacPhee exclaimed, as he drained another pint. "But fuck one goat...!"

While he joked, I worried. I hadn't exactly had a conversation about my being transsexual yet. I didn't know how to work it into conversation with the people I met post-transition. I hated the way that coming out always seemed to trump any other conversation. I didn't feel like I needed to be in the closet about it—in most cases, I preferred people to take me at face value and draw their own conclusions. In those early years of my transition, I had successfully avoided situations that seemed to require that I confirm my gender and thus skirted the need to learn how to do so with any sort of grace. Jonas joked and puffed his pipe, I smoked cigarettes and laughed, and before we knew it we were on the boat.

It was pretty much exactly what I expected: puffy men in company-logo polo shirts clutching bottles of Corona Light and tensely-coiffed women dancing to the nostalgia cover band. It took forever to find Wendy, whose date was already drunk. The four of us decided to head to the upper deck, where we could maybe escape that still-beating Heart of Rock and Roll. We found deck chairs and settled in for a bit. Jonas packed his pipe and pushed it toward me. "A little of the homegrown?" he smiled, and initially I declined. Mostly, I didn't like feeling both sleepy and paranoid in public. Wendy and her date hit it, and Jonas warned me that I didn't know what I was missing, so I had a small puff. Some polo shirts found their way to our deck, and Jonas suggested that we find higher ground. Wendy and her date agreed to meet us up top after drink refills, but that was the last we saw of them for the evening.

The Golden Gate Bridge loomed over us like a Spielberg set piece, glowing brightly in the chilly night air as the yacht cruised underneath. Ever the Southern Californian, it hadn't occurred to me to bring—or own—a coat or a wrap to match my outfit. I was shivering. He took off his jacket and put it over my shoulders; he pressed into me from behind, pinning me between his considerable warmth and the cold deck rail.

He nuzzled into me. His breath felt amazing against my neck and I melted between him and the railing for a moment. Then I caught myself; I didn't want to be his tranny surprise anecdote. I wished I didn't have to tell him. I wished one last-ditch wish to magically change on the spot. I wanted to not feel like I was lying to him when, in fact, I was finally living true to my gender.

He slipped a hand around my waist and up my top; he brushed his fingers against my boobs, then massaged a little bit. He kept kissing my neck, my cheek. He turned so he could kiss my lips and my mouth. I felt my girdle stretch uncomfortably and he kissed harder. His tongue flickered against mine. He bit my lip softly as he pulled back from the kiss. Clearly, I had to stop this.

"I'm really dizzy," I said, because I was. I teetered on my heels and groped for the railing. He swooped in and before I knew it I was airborne; he lifted me across the deck and placed me on a deck chair. I asked for a water and he scooted off to the bar, telling me to stay put. I wasn't going anywhere; stars and birds were still circling around my head.

None of this made sense to me. How could he know I was transsexual and find me desirable? Was it possible for him to not have figured it out? Was it possible that such details were irrelevant to him? I stared at the receding Golden Gate and wondered if I was going to be able to get off the boat before my form-fitting outfit outed me to my entire company.

Jonas returned with water for me. He sat next to me and puffed his pipe and sipped his cider and told jokes. I felt sober again by the time we docked and we took our time descending the stairs. When we finally disembarked, the parking lot was nearly empty. We saw no one we recognized. We held hands from the dock to the car.

We were much less chatty on the way home; for me it was the pot and the booze and my fear. I worried what was on his mind. I chain-smoked and listened to Einstürzende Neubauten blend into Skinny Puppy; I couldn't find a foothold in all this urgent, unfamiliar music and I marveled that a man with such a sweet disposition could enjoy such dark, heavy music. He didn't seem violent, but I had no idea what I *could* tell him or how he'd react. I wasn't sure if I was attracted to him emotionally or sexually or what.

When we stopped for gas, he started to try to convince me to stay over. He had a point; if we stopped at his house we could be in bed soon after 2:00 a.m. If he drove me home and then back, he wouldn't get to bed until 3:30. He offered me a grilled cheese with brie before sleep and a trip to the finest brunch in the galaxy in the morning. While he cooked I curled up on the couch and flipped through the channels. When the sun woke me, I was dusted in crumbs and he was snoring on the opposite side of the couch.

We went to brunch in our disheveled cruise clothes; he dropped me at home and we went off to our various Christmases.

The office shut down between the holidays, so almost everyone spent that whole week traveling. I stayed around, though, and hung out a bit with Wendy who totally scolded me for not coming out to Jonas on the cruise.

"Dude, I'm sure he already knows. He's totally into you and it's not exactly like you're the only tranny in this town. You're not even the only one who works at this company."

"I just don't know how to bring it up," I said. "There never seems to be the right time."

"You could do it any time. You've got his cell phone number. You should do it right now," she said. "The longer you wait the more you're going to fuck this up. He's into you, and I bet that at least part of why he's into you is that he knows you're trans. But there's only one way to find out." Wendy pushed the phone into my hand. "Call him now."

I called. I got his voice mail. I left a message: "Hey, Jonas, I was just wondering how your holiday was and what you're doing for New Year's. Let me know—I'd love to talk again. There's something I wanna tell you." I still felt like a chicken, but Wendy said, "Well, at least it's a step in the right direction."

He didn't call me back for another couple of days—family had kept him busy. "So what's up?" he asked as if he was expecting a casual conversation.

"Well, I sort of wanted to apologize for the other night. I didn't expect to get so tipsy and all, but I wasn't sure if you knew that I was, well, that I *am* transsexual. Pre-op." There was a long pause on the other end of the line.

"Yeah, I thought so," Jonas finally said. "I mean, people gossip and all and I figured that if it was true you'd say so. It's okay with me, but honestly I think I prefer you as a woman."

His tone was so dry that I didn't get that he was joking until he started to laugh. He asked if we could get together after he got back on the second. He offered to pick up sushi and bring it to my house. I counteroffered: I'd cook. Maybe I'd make a pesto lasagna. We had a date.

He arrived in a bolo tie. "Posies and a present," he said. "It smells amazing in here." He'd brought a lily bouquet, a bottle of wine, a pint of gelato and a gift box.

"I know you're not big on Christmas, but I got you a little something" he said, smiling and pushing the gift box into my hands. "But don't open it yet. Maybe after dinner." He ate generously, praising my culinary skills with the same elaborate flourishes he gave to his jokes; I watched while he helped himself to seconds. He finished, refilled the wineglasses and requested that we retire to the parlor.

"I think it's time to open presents," he said gleefully. He sat on the couch while I opened the box and shook out a white negligee; a shimmering nylon skirt with a scalloped lace bodice.

"It's custom," he said. "I have a friend who's starting to sell vintage recreations through her website. That's her *Cat On a Hot Tin Roof* model."

"I don't know what to say."

"You can say you'll let me see you in it," he said. "I'd really like that."

I just stared at him, barely feeling the cool, soft material in my hands; I dropped it back into the box. "Like, right now?" I asked and he nodded eagerly. I stood up, feeling terribly light-headed. I drained my glass, took the box and said, "Why don't you find some music while I slip into something more...comfortable?" He was pouring more wine as I closed the bathroom door behind me.

I was tipsy and the bodice was a little loose; I hoped he wasn't going to feel disappointed that I wasn't quite yet capable of filling it out on my own. I'd have never chosen to wear white and was surprised to see that it looked kind of pretty on me, and that the cut of the gown seemed to be giving me curves I knew I didn't have. I posed in the mirror, gauging my ability to disguise any telltale bulge beneath my waist. I primped my hair, touched up my makeup and took a deep, cleansing breath. I felt sexy and delicate; I felt scared and vulnerable. I still felt that I wasn't enough of a woman to be in this position, and I was still skeptical that he didn't harbor similar doubts. "Relax," I told my reflection. "This is what you've wanted your whole life. This is a dream coming true."

I opened the bathroom door to find that he'd doused all the lights except for a candle and the music videos on the television. The candlelight somehow made his eyes look more sparkly than ever. He offered me a refilled wineglass as I perched on the couch, and quoted *Cat On a Hot Tin Roof*: "Be careful, Maggie, your claws are showing," he said. I froze up, worried that my slight costume had malfunctioned. He pressed the glass into my hand, apologizing: "Sorry, no—I was just quoting the movie." I sipped and said, "I guess I just don't get a lot of guys quoting Tennessee Williams at me anymore." He kissed my mouth. "You are even prettier than I imagined." He traced his thick finger along my shoulder blade and asked, "What would you like me to do for you?"

I hadn't prepared for that question. I'd been so wrapped up in worry about what he wanted from me that I had no idea what I wanted. I said, "I really don't know. Can I do something for you?" He shook his head no. "I'd really like to explore you," he said. "Let's figure out what you like." He kissed me and asked me questions.

"Do you like men?'

"Some."

"Do you like me?'

"Yes."

"Do like women?"

"Some."

"Do you like penetration?"

"It's never really worked for me."

"Can I see your pussy?"

"I don't really have one yet."

"Let me see." He pulled at my girdle until I pushed him away so I could slide it off. I sat up; I was shivering. I couldn't believe I was letting this happen. I tossed the girdle to the floor and pulled my legs up on the sofa again. He pushed my knees apart.

"I've been doing some reading," he said. "Since you told me I've read up a lot on what they're able to do these days for girls like you." His fingers traced a line up my leg until he reached my crotch. He stroked lightly on my scrotum. "Like this here, this is your labia, right?" His fingers rolled in small circles around the soft tissue until his middle finger came to rest on the underside of my penis. My stomach rolled; I didn't even like to touch my genitals.

"You're shivering," he said. "Do you need a blanket? Do you need to stop?" We'd gone this far; I shook my head no. He continued: "Good. Well, this, this is what everyone seems to have an issue with. I can see how everyone wants to think they know what this is and now that I've seen it for myself, I gotta say that it's sort of penish, but when all is said and done this—" He stopped talking and pushed his finger up into me and held it there while I writhed, pressing down with my hips until I couldn't take any more of the pressure. He pulled his hand away, and I said, "Not yet." I grabbed his hand and pushed his fingers up, beneath my scrotum/labia, up into my pelvis. "There," I said. "Fuck me there." He rolled his fingers around inside me and my mind splintered. Everything felt electric—his fingers burning deep trails into me; the fabric of the couch scratching out messages against my arms and my back. I felt like I was howling.

Later, Jonas would tell me that I was hardly making any sounds at all apart from soft, short gasps for air. He told me that he found that all it took was one small circle of his finger to send tremors all through me; he couldn't believe how little it seemed to take to send me into the stratosphere. I didn't feel like I could get enough. I had no clue what he was touching inside of me, but I didn't want it to stop. Surely he was going as deep as he dared; we were both in new territory. I felt him pull his fingers out of me and with that came jolts of energy, great muscular contractions. Jonas told me that I writhed for almost a full minute after he'd pulled out, and that he'd never seen anyone come with such intensity. My mind was blank; I remember feeling exhausted. I had no idea how long I lay there, dazed; soon enough I came to and I found him sitting opposite me, smoking his pipe and smiling.

"Was I out long?" I asked him, and he shook his head no. "Just five or seven minutes. Long enough for a bit of a smoke. Do you need anything else?" he asked, and I said, "How about dessert?"

HOLD UP

Ivan Coyote

She was hot and so was her friend. I had pissed her friend off about an hour before, back at the bar, by confessing that I really didn't like a lot of spoken word poetry, but out here on the sweltering summer sidewalk it seemed like all had been forgiven. They were sharing an American Spirit cigarette and flirting with me and my buddy with the suit vest and bow tie and slicked-back hair. It was one of those dress-up nights. Minutes ago she had had me by the necktie up against the wall in the hallway that led from the dance floor to the bathroom, her hand sliding mine up under her skirt to the soft smooth place where the curve of her asscheek met the top of her stockings. Now all four of us were halfway up the block from the bar, swaying and smooth talking and suggesting naughty things.

Somehow all four of us ended up back in my king-size hotel room bed, shirts off but pants still on, all eight hands meandering and mouths mixing lipsticks and cigarette-bitter and warm whiskey breath, spit-shined black boots and high heels all a-tangle. I remember her nipple hardening between my first finger and thumb, and her friend's fingernails biting into the sweaty skin of the dip in my back above my ass, and then she said it:

"So nice to have hormone-free beef in my hands again."

Her friend moaned in agreement just as my friend unsnapped her bra.

I froze; shook my head to get her words out of my ears, but they stuck there.

I didn't jump out of bed and ask them all to leave or anything drastic, but my heart just wasn't up to the mission after that, and a couple of minutes more of midnight groping later when she raised one expressive and delicately manicured eyebrow and tugged at the top button of my fly, I shook my head and stopped her hand in mine.

No sense letting her into my pants if she was just going to stumble around in there, knocking stuff over and scrambling for the light switch. I already knew she wouldn't know her way around without a detailed map, and I didn't have the energy to draw one for her. Not at this hour.

She thinks I am her type, but she only sees what she wants. She doesn't really see me at all.

Minutes later, my buddy started to snore like a puppy, her once-slick hair falling in a greasy curtain over her eyes, one hand tucked into the back of the BFF's black panties.

I didn't sleep at all that night, watching the light turn blue then gray then white on the hotel room wall, this almost stranger with her head on my chest, smelling like foreign shampoo.

A couple of months earlier I had a totally hot four-day fling with a not-so-straight woman with crazy hair and a heavy Quebecois accent. One of the things I loved about fucking her was her total and complete lack of processing my gender or my body or its desires. We were both staying in the same hotel and attending the same conference, and nobody at the morning round-table discussions had any clue whatsoever that the two of us had been up all night fucking, largely because she was so apparently heterosexual. No one suspected that she had rug burn on her ass and shoulder blades. She had invited me into her suite the second night to drink wine and listen to music, and the two of us had slept for a combined total of about fifteen hours since then. She never touched my breasts, she touched my chest only ever with an open flat hand, usually for balance while she rode my cock, oblivious to the fact that my tits even existed, uninterested, hungry. She never once put her hand in my boxer briefs, never once asked me, was it okay if she touched me like this? We would leave the dinner table separately, five or ten or fifteen minutes apart, and I would go back to my hotel room and put on my dick, bend and tuck it into my pant leg, pad down the hallway in my boots and leather jacket and knock quietly on her door as soon as the hall was empty. She would open her door just a crack and grab my sleeve, drag me into her room and bolt the door behind us. She was about ten years older than me and confessed that she usually dated older men; all she ever said about my silicone dick was that finally she had met a man who could stay hard long enough to tire her out, pour faire changement.

I don't think I could sustain a fully straight relationship like this over any length of time, but she sure was fun for those four days, and she sure beat out the hormone-free beef lover in the hot-for-me category. I remember thinking what did it all mean in the airport lounge in Oakland the day after the fumbled four-way in San Fran. What does it mean exactly when a predominately straight fifty-year-old woman who speaks another first language sort of gets me more than two twentysomething Bay

Area femmes did? I pushed the thought from my head because it depressed me.

I know I can be a complicated creature. I know this. I know it cannot be easy for a trick to figure out my body on the fly, and I understand that often the kind of tiresome questions and trepidation and fear that a femme feels when feeling me up for the first time is born from a desire to not trample where she shouldn't, and to step lightly through possibly painful territory, but that doesn't make it any hotter for me to discuss do's and don'ts in the dark, when I would rather be fucking or fisting or tangling tongues or pulling each other's hair and deciding by willpower and whim just who is going to suck whose what, and when and exactly how. I have always been a pay-as-you-go kind of guy, a trait that has landed me in trouble at times in the past, but more often led me to just right where I wanted to be as well, so I have resisted the urge to try to tame myself in this matter. I have always been more of a doer than a talker, when it comes to fucking. What is that old saying? Better to ask for forgiveness than permission? Dangerous, maybe, but definitely hotter. Nothing kills my boner faster and for longer than a good old-fashioned lesbian sex process. If you have to ask me whether or not I can be touched like this, or here, or like that, usually the fox has flown the coop. The cat is no longer in the cradle, or whatever. Just read my wet-and-hard-o-meter and listen to my breath. My body will always tell you the right next move. Stone butch? Only if you talk my dick out of its hard-on.

Last week I landed in the Vancouver airport after a long stretch of road and packed my suitcase up the three flights of stairs to my apartment. I opened my door and there she was, stretched out and sleepy in my clean sheets, blinking and smiling. She slipped from under the covers and met me in the bedroom doorway, smelling like her good perfume and the unmistakable odor that is her neck, and only her neck.

She kisses me and reaches around to grab one asscheek.

"Long road, cowboy?"

I nod, let my carry-on bag slip from my shoulder and to the floor. She pushes it to one side with a stockinged foot. She is wearing the new garters and stockings I got for her when she finished her PhD, and nothing else, her small pink nipples saluting me through my button-down shirt when she presses herself against me. She grabs my cold hand and leads me to her pussy, slides her warmth and wetness against my numb fingers. Her breath catches in the back of her throat.

"I was just thinking of you, right here, inside me," she whispers. "Cold outside. I am going to run you a bath."

I nod again, slip two fingers up and inside her, grab a handful of curls in my other hand, kiss her hard.

She slips out of my grasp and flits into the bathroom, lighting candles and filling the tub.

She washes my back for me and then leaves me alone in the tub for a minute. I hear music come on in the bedroom and will myself to sit up and get out of the tub and towel off, my skin now pink and clean and pulsing warm with my heartbeat.

She is in the bedroom, now wearing stockings and garters and black five-inch heels and nothing else, except for a cherry-red harness and dildo that matches her fresh coat of lipstick. She smoothes the covers out on the bed next to her.

"Get over here and lie down on your belly. We are going to start out with a little back rub and then I am going to take it from there." She winks. "I am going to take you from here."

How did she know? I am never quite sure, but she always does.

ALL-GIRL ACTION

Helen Boyd

She was convinced her body wasn't feminine enough, or sexy enough, to turn a woman on. Men weren't so picky, and chasers—well, chasers were after the cock she didn't like as a cock. We called it The Hugest Clitoris Ever. Eventually, that is, once she let me near her.

As estrogen softened and sensitized her skin, anything rough or hard was out of the question. She had always preferred women, but as her body feminized, the divide between how she felt and how her female lover felt shrunk and eventually disappeared. She had always preferred women, even when she was living as male, and it was all about the soft: soft skin, soft fabrics, soft smells.

I'd washed "his" hair for years and watched as it got longer and longer. I asked, and she joked that she was trying something new, but over time, she confessed that she was transitioning. She asked us to use her new female name, Sharon, and cease using the old one. It wasn't hard to do. She was a long-legged brunette, beautiful from the get-go: fashionable, femme and fierce. I'd been confused by my crush on her delicate, androgynous masculinity, but once she started transitioning, it all made sense: I was in lust with the woman she was about to be.

I offered to go shopping with her, even though I hated shopping. I explained her to our nail tech and got my nails done with her. I'd never had a pedicure in my life and she'd had plenty, but still she wanted my "real girl" guidance, and I admit, I didn't mind because I was also not-so-secretly hoping to guide her into my bed.

I'd asked a few friends—current lovers and past—if she could come to one of our parties. I told her she would be desired. I told her I would not touch her unless she wanted me to. I told her I could wash her in softness.

When the evening came, she dressed in a translucent nightgown with a half-slip underneath. She didn't want to be seen as a transwoman—just one of many women but new to playing with queer women. She didn't know what to do, how to flirt so that things happened, so I made a game of it. I stood her in a doorway and tied her wrists gently with velvet to the chin-up bar I'd found there. I blindfolded her with silk and lit the room she was standing in front of brighter than the one she was facing so that the outline of her svelte, curved body was clear. She insisted on thigh-high stockings and pumps, and I'd washed and perfumed her long hair for her—it was just approaching nipple length, blunt cut like a punk rock Bettie Page. The tattooed pinup on her arm just made her queer in a lovely, new way.

She bought me fancy lingerie, the likes of which I'd never worn, and it felt delicious on. Tanga panties rubbed their seam against my own slick parts in exciting ways. I felt like I could lean my chin on the rack her bra had given me. On top of those, I put on my suit, white button-down and cuff links. I opened the collar just enough to see my own cleavage. (She told me later she could see it too: a tall woman in tall heels has too many advantages.) I straddled a straight-backed wooden chair so I could make the most of that lace seam.

As I watched the rooms of the party fill up, and I watched people find others to play with, I looked over to see her leaning on one hip and then the other. As the noises of people kissing hotly nearby got to her, she rubbed one foot up against the other leg; she pulled on her soft restraints; she tried to rub against a door jam and couldn't quite reach. I reached for the stack of cards I had prepared in advance, which said things like:

Kiss her mouth
Kiss the space behind her knee
Gently scratch her upper arm with your nails
Suck her belly button
Bite her upper thigh gently
Lick her nipple through her nightgown

I had another set, too, but it wasn't time for those yet.

I watched women watching her. One kinky-haired blonde sat in an armchair across the room and stared for a while, licking her lips. I gave her the belly button card. Another card went to a genderqueer couple whose "to" and "from" genders I couldn't name; ze cupped her breasts from behind while hir partner bit her thighs. She pulled away from hir hands only to land in the other's mouth. She gyrated, twisted, pulled her long legs up to try to relieve the tension in those parts she'd hid under that half-slip.

The action around her—and in the room behind her—got hotter and more vocal as the night went on. One woman pushed her lover up against the door jamb behind her and fucked her slowly and passionately; once, the lover reached out for her girlfriend's arm and got Sharon's instead; I watched the gooseflesh break on all of her skin. When they were done, I gave them cards to suck her earlobes and to pull off her half-slip. She'd actually worn panties, so I scribbled up a few new cards, and eventually we got those off her too. She'd had the testosterone-producing bits removed long before but still had her *ladystick*—it was the term she used—but there was nothing phallic about it anymore.

By then her skin was hot to the touch and so was everyone else's; there were no toys left on the table. Some people, exhausted from multiple partners and multiple orgasms, were napping in the back rooms reserved just for that purpose. But she was still on those heels in that doorway, her wrists still sliding against velvet. She had one person's lubed finger in her, followed by someone else's baby dildo. At one point she had three different trans guys rubbing their chin stubble on her legs.

She was having a very good time when I pulled my chair in front of her and took her into my mouth and licked her. I found her own natural seam and sucked it, fucked her with patient fingers and held her thighs in my hands until I felt them twitch and gestured to someone else to free her—except of course she was perfectly able to get out of the restraints herself and did. Pulling off the blindfold, smiling, she straddled me on the chair, hung her head over my shoulder so her long hair tickled my back, and sighed a thank-you softly in my ear.

THE THERAPIST AND THE WHORE

Giselle Renarde

Last week we left off talking about gender identity," Liesl said, scanning the scribbled sheets of lined paper in her tattered manila folder. "Has that been preying on your mind at all?"

Manny took her usual seat. She preferred the ratty leather armchair to the pristine sofa. It was *her* chair now, a signifier of their relationship prior to Liesl's move to the big office at the fancy address. Manny had been seeing her since Liesl was a wannabe-therapist heading up the LGBT support group in the basement of the University Health Center.

"On and off, I guess," Manny replied. "But ultimately I have to ask myself, *Would I rather have a cock than a pussy?* No. *Would I ever give up my big tits?* No. *But do I want my share of the power men hold in this world?* Yes."

Nodding, Liesl said, "Sounds like your masculine style of dress and appearance is derived more from a desire for social standing than an attempt to align gender identity with presentation."

"Gawsh you talk awful purdy, Doctor Liesl," Manny replied, slapping her knee in her best Aunt Jemima impression. "How long have you and I known each other? I'm not one of your snooty Yorkville clients. You don't have to impress me."

"Sorry," Liesl chuckled, closing her manila envelope and setting it on her lap. "It's like Tourette's with me—sometimes big words just slip out at inappropriate moments."

"But, you know, the way I walk and talk and dress and act isn't only about achieving the social status a man is born into. No black girl's ever going to have that; it's useless trying. I think it's who I am now."

"Yup, you've mentioned that before," Liesl replied with a nod.

"And I really don't attach gender to it. I'm female—this I know—but I'm no girly girl. I'm butch and that's just...me. I think there are different ways to live your gender, and this is how I live the experience of being a woman. I don't see myself as any less of a woman just because I don't wear dresses and perfume."

"That's a good point," Liesl said, still nodding. "There are as many genders as there are individuals."

"Exactly!" Manny smacked the armrest with her palm. "Exactly! See? You're the only person in the world who can read my mind."

"I don't know about that," Liesl demurred. "I think sometimes I'm just able to clarify your thoughts."

"You must be so bored with me, talking about the same dumb issues since university." Sliding from her chair, Manny walked over to the window overlooking the greenery of Hazelton Lane.

"Not boring at all," Liesl said encouragingly. "It's obviously a matter you still think about from time to time."

"Are you ready for something new?" Manny interrupted. She'd been trying to get this out for months, and she hated being messy about it.

"I'm ready for anything you've got on your mind."

Was she ashamed of herself? Is that why she couldn't look Liesl in the face to tell her? Christ, it would almost be easier to tell Danica first, except that Danica tended to throw things. "I'm seeing someone on the sly."

"Another psychologist?" Liesl mocked. "I'm hurt."

"Oh, so now you're the joker?" Manny said with a smile, turning around to gauge Liesl's reaction. But Liesl never reacted to anything. "Her name is Star. Well, I'm sure that's not her name, but that's what people call her."

"And when you say you're *seeing* Star..."

"Yeah," Manny replied, leaning against the windowsill. "I mean, not *seeing* like we're in a relationship or anything. Christ, I can't believe how hard it is to say this word."

"What word?"

"Whore," Manny blurted. The hand of death took her throat in its skeletal grip, but Liesl's expression remained unchanged. "Star's a hooker...a prostitute. I don't know what to call her. I mean, I guess that's what she is. I pay her for what she does, but I don't see her that way. Not anymore."

Nodding her head slowly, Liesl opened the manila envelope and clicked her pen into gear. "How long have you been seeing Star?"

Manny wasn't sure if she was in the doctor's office or the principal's office. She didn't want to answer, and that made her feel like a sulky teenager. "I don't know. Awhile."

When Liesl looked up from her scribblings, she only nodded. She said nothing.

"Danica can't stand to see me naked anymore," Manny went

on, partly in justification and partly to change the subject. "She darts from the bedroom the second I start taking my clothes off." It occurred to her she sounded like she was blaming her girlfriend for her own indiscretions, and she didn't want to leave Liesl with the impression she thought that way. "I know it's not her fault. Shit, you must think I'm a total asshole."

"Do you think you're an asshole?" *Classic therapist move.*

"Kind of," Manny said with a shrug. "I'm cheating on Danica. She wants to look at buying a house, and here I'm spending our hard-earned cash on sex with another...woman."

Nodding, always nodding, Liesl asked, "If you don't like what you're doing, why are you doing it?"

"That's what you're supposed to tell me. I don't know!" Manny cried, for the first time this session feeling exasperated. "Why am I paying a hooker to do everything Danica won't? To kiss me and fuck me...you know, with a strap-on...and just fucking *look* at my naked body."

"I think you just answered your own question," Liesl replied with a nod.

All lies. Maybe next session she'd admit the truths.

Everybody recognized the Beach as the prettiest, most family-oriented area of the city. Who would ever have guessed the woman in the upstairs apartment of the mint-green semi was what they would term a *lady of the evening*? With flowerboxes along the balcony, it looked like a little old grandmother's home.

"There's my lover!" Star cried in a cheery lilt when Manny arrived at her door. "Amanda, honey, you look like you could use some love. Come in and tell me all about it." Pulling Manny inside by the shirtsleeves, she drew her into the kitchen's sunny breakfast nook. "I'll put on the tea. Would you like some tea? I would. But we can get right down to business, if that's what you want. It's whatever you want, sugar." Pressing the switch on the electric kettle, she turned to Manny and the feathers at the base of her pink vintage peignoir swished against her legs. "Do you want some sugar, sugar?"

Manny smiled. "You mean in my tea, or...?"

"Or..." Star repeated, shuffling her low bedroom heels across the kitchen tile. Setting her fingertips against Manny's shoulders, she planted a luscious kiss on her lips. When Star tore herself away to gaze adoringly into Manny's eyes, she tasted berries. Star's shimmering, waxy lipstick always tasted sweet.

"Gosh, you're handsome," Star gushed. "Did you know that? You are very good-looking."

"You're the only one who's ever thought so," Manny replied, trying not to laugh. She recognized Star's sincerity. "Even when I was a kid, it was my brother who was the handsome one. I was the dark one. Can't be both."

"Well, *you're* both," Star replied, kissing her nose.

Her gaze was so giving, Manny searched for something to give back. "Did I ever tell you you're the only person in my life who's allowed to call me Amanda?"

"Yup!" Star replied, hopping away to pull teacups from the cupboard. "You tell me that all the time."

"Well, it makes you special."

"You're the special one, lover." Star poured boiling water into the teapot. "We'll just let that steep while you tell me about your week."

As Star sank into her lap, Manny paid close attention to the sensation of Star's ass on her thigh. She hated that she did it, but she was just so astounded never to feel anything. She wasn't perfectly clear on how it all got packed away down there. "I had an appointment with Liesl," Manny said. "I told her about you."

"Aww," Star cooed, kissing her cheek. "That's sweet. What did she say?"

"Nothing. She just listens. She never makes judgments."

Setting her head on Manny's shoulder, Star went uncharacteristically quiet. Times like these, Manny tried to assure herself this was just a job for Star, but she knew that wasn't the highest truth. In the silences, Manny worried. She was always afraid Star would make some comment about dumping Danica and moving in together. One day, Star would slip. Manny was sure of it.

"Tea should be ready," Star said in her most shimmering tone of voice. When the tea ran clear, she grimaced and lifted the lid on the pot. Star laughed hysterically, slapping her thigh like a country music singer. "Would you look at that? I didn't put any teabags in it! Boy, I'd lose my head if it wasn't attached." Leaning against the counter's edge, she asked, "Should I try again, or should we head to the next room?"

Rising from her chair, Manny placed her arm around Star's waist. "I love your use of euphemism. *The next room.* Is that sequential? The kitchen is the first room, the bedroom is the next room..."

"And the bathroom is the last," Star giggled, trotting across the kitchen floor in her heels. She slipped into the bedroom before Manny and hid behind her closet door to take off her panties. After all this time, Manny'd stopped wondering why Star was so mysterious about it. Manny used the opportunity to take off her trousers. She left on her buttoned-up shirt despite the heat.

Star emerged in her peignoir and lace bra, absently stroking her cock as she looked Manny up and down. "You're binding every time I see you now," she reflected.

Shrugging like it was just a big coincidence, Manny said,

"I guess so." She tried to sound casual about it. "Why, does it bother you?"

Strange question.

"Of course not," Star chuckled, approaching at snail's pace, and all the while encouraging her erection with her fingertips. "Does it bother Danica?"

Manny breathed in sharply. It just seemed wrong when Star said her girlfriend's name. She had to be honest. "Yeah, I think it bothers her a lot. It really bugs her when we're out at a restaurant and the server calls me sir and I don't argue. She pouts through the whole meal."

"Does that happen often?"

"When I'm binding especially, yeah," Manny replied, pulling her shirttails between her legs to cover over her wide-open snatch. "It's an easy mistake."

Star gave her a generous smile. "Mistake?"

Manny couldn't keep herself from staring at the cock surging from behind Star's robe. She watched its shimmering head pop out from between Star's fingers as she pumped it with her fist. She'd always thought its flesh looked much pinker than the rest of Star's bronze body, especially when all the surrounding flesh was so neatly shaved. Star had the gentlest-looking penis she'd ever seen. Not that Manny had a lot of experience with penises.

"What do you feel like today?" Star asked. "Anal or..."

"I don't know yet," Manny interrupted. She didn't want to hear the word that would come next. "Can I just suck it?" She slid to her knees at the foot of Star's bed and waited for feeding time. "Let me suck it. Please."

With a chuckle, Star said, "Of course." She drew near, smelling of flowers and soaps. Taking the back of Manny's head in her hand, she held her cock by the base and ran its drooling tip side to side across Manny's lips. Manny opened her mouth to suck it in, and salty precum fell like white clouds against her taste buds. She couldn't explain to herself why she loved the sensation of cock firming up between her lips. Would Liesl ask about the sex, if she made a full confession? No, she never dug that deep. But she might. The chance was there.

As Manny plowed her head back and forth, Star guided her motion with both hands. She sucked the shaft. She released, leaning back, back, back until just the tip of Star's cock remained between her lips. As Star looked on like a fairy godmother from above, Manny held her cock steady with the tips of her teeth and tickled the slit with her tongue. Star giggled and ran her pink fingernails down Manny's neck. "Ooh, that feels nice."

For a butch dyke, she was pretty damn good at sucking cock. Star didn't have to say it for Manny to know what she was thinking. She swallowed the shaft, right down to the base. Her throat wanted to gag, but she wouldn't let it. She sucked and it settled. Cooing words of love, Star wrapped her peignoir around Manny's head until the light of day was gauzy and pink. She grabbed Star's ass and squeezed her firm cheeks. Manny let her thrust her hips a bit, even though she preferred being in control of the motion.

Enough.

When she rose to her feet, Manny found herself trapped in Star's arms as well as her robe. Until she stood with her thighs closed, she didn't realize how wet she'd become. Who'd have thought giving head would be such a turn-on? Manny stepped back, but they were closer to the bed than she recalled. She fell back on the plush mattress. As she kicked the quilted coverlet to the floor, Star plucked a condom from the side table and tore the packet. Holding it wide open with long glittering nails, she asked, "Would you like to do the honors?"

Manny plunged her fingers inside and pulled out the slippery condom. Every time she squeezed the tip and slid the slick latex down the length of Star's firm shaft, she thought of green bananas and Ms. Kensington's health class. Little did that saucy teenager know she'd be using these things with her transsexual whore while her girlfriend worked extra hours at a retail franchise. *Whore?* Why did she always use that word, even inside her own mind? It was unbearably crass and it certainly didn't do Star justice.

"What are you thinking?" the girl in the pink peignoir asked.

Danica liked that question too. Manny hated it. Inwardly, she refused to answer. Gripping the base of her rock-ready cock, Manny pulled on it until Star eased herself on to the bed. Straddling Manny's half-naked body, Star took back ownership of her sheathed erection. She unbuttoned the bottom of Manny's shirt, exposing her wet cunt to the sunny bedroom air. The mound was no longer fiction. Kneeling close, Star grasped the base of her shaft and smacked her with it. Manny leapt at the sensation of smooth latex flogging engorged pussy lips. Star smacked her again and again, aligning her cockhead with Manny's clit. Manny's whole body surged with adrenaline and desire. She needed a good fuck. *God, did she ever need it.*

Slipping her fingers between her thighs, Manny pressed Star's slick cock down until the tip sat in waiting at the entrance to her slit. Everything seemed inconceivably wet. Manny couldn't believe it was her body creating all that juice. Star must have slipped some lube up her cunt when she wasn't looking.

"You want it?" Star teased, pushing just the tip of her cock inside Manny's eager slit.

With so much juice, a cockhead was meager offerings. Manny thrust her hips hard to feel Star all the way inside her. "Aw, yeee-ah!" There was no other feeling like this one. She loved taking Star's firm cock in her snatch. Some days she couldn't do it. Some days she took it up the ass. Today she wanted the classics—penis-in-vagina sex. "Give me your tits," Manny cried, anxious, like she wanted to do everything quick before she came...like a man...

One by one, Star lifted her tits out of her bra and tucked the lace off to the sides as much as she could. "Gimme!" Manny urged like a child. With Star, she was selfish.

Leaning forward, Star set her tits on either side of Manny's face. When she shimmied left and right, they slapped Manny's cheeks. This is where their height differential came in handy. While Star grasped Manny's hips and fucked her from on top, Manny pressed her tits together and licked them from below. Sucking nipples in alternation, Manny pressed her feet flat against the bed and drove her cunt upward to meet Star's raging erection. She sucked so hard Star squealed as she thrust. This was good. This was *so* good. It never felt like this with a strap-on. *Cocks rock my socks.* Manny laughed.

Star offered a breathy but distracted chuckle in return. "What?"

Manny shoved a tit in her mouth so she wouldn't have to answer. Her mind said stupid things, at times. As Manny sucked like a banshee, Star yelped. She held tighter to Manny's hips and pumped in double time, but she obviously couldn't fuck fast enough kneeling. She flipped Manny on her stomach. As she grabbed the good lube from the side table, Manny eased her knees underneath her body and stuck her butt in the air.

Smearing a good lot of cold lube up and down Manny's asscrack, Star shoved her cockhead in Manny's hole and held tight. Manny looked back as Star ran her long fingernails down her asscheeks. She loved the contrast of Star's tan thighs against her dark rear.

Leaning way down low, Star grazed Manny's clothed back with her erect nipples. Manny's asshole pulsed like it was trying to suck her cock in deeper. When Star rose up and flipped long, dark hair behind her shoulders, Manny watched the pink feathers at the base of her sleeves shiver with delight. Star pressed her cock farther inside, pouting her full pink lips. Everything about Star shimmered. Even her skin glowed in the late afternoon sun filtering in through lace curtains. Manny eased her ass toward Star's hips as they picked up speed. God, she loved a woman who could give it to her. She wished she could give it right back.

Star rammed her. She went in deep. She fucked Manny hard until her ass burned at the razor's edge of pleasure. Manny reached below and smacked her clit. She slapped it with her fingers to fill in Star's expressions of bliss with shouts of her own. Even after Star pulled out, filling the room with Manny's characteristic stench, she continued spanking her cunt. Orgasms were weird for her these days. She never felt fully spent until she'd beaten herself up a bit.

They showered together while Manny's shirt dried out. As predicted, the pits were soaked with sweat. It felt nice to be soaped up by Star, naked skin to skin. As Star ran suds down her asscrack, Manny mulled over her compounded lies. "I told Liesl Danica won't look at me naked. I don't know why." She stared at the faint reflection of her dark skin in the white tile.

With a lilting giggle, Star rubbed the soap from Manny's cheeks. "Classic case of shifting blame. You feel guilty for hiding your body from your girlfriend. You feel guilty for being here with me. If you pretend it's Danica who won't look at you, you have your perfect excuse."

"But I know it's not true."

"It becomes true the second you tell Dr. Liesl. You believe everything you say to her. When you lie to her, you're lying to yourself."

As warm water coursed across her flesh, the sudden insight brought Manny to a new level of nudity. Star washed and dried her, bound her tits and helped her on with her clothes. After setting the kettle to boil, Star retreated to the bedroom to take care of her own binding issues. Manny opened the tea canister and threw two bags in the pot just as Star reemerged in black capris and a flowery sleeveless top. As they sipped from matching mugs in comfortable silence, Star nibbled on arrowroot cookies and dried apricots. Manny reflected on her desperate attachment to these three women in her life—wise Liesl, stalwart and silent Star, her glimmer of hope on the horizon, and Danica, simply her girlfriend. She saw their faces, Star's across the table, Liesl and Danica's in her mind's eye. "I can't keep juggling like this. I can't keep lying to the people I care about."

With a slow nod, Star snapped a baby cookie in half and dusted the crumbs from the table. Her eyes were diamonds as she explored Manny's gaze. "Do you bind when you visit Liesl?"

The question brought bile to Manny's throat. Rising from the table, she took her wallet from her back pocket and pulled out Star's fee in cash.

Manny took a deep breath. "I'm sorry to leave like this, but things aren't working out for us. In the beginning everything was good. You understood me then. To be honest, I've been lying to you a lot lately. I don't know why. It could mean a lot of things, I guess. Anyway, there's no sense in getting deep into it. I just wanted to say good-bye. I hope you don't think I'm a total cunt."

Liesl nodded slowly. "Do you think you're a total cunt?"

SHOES ARE MEANT TO GET YOU SOMEWHERE

Dean Scarborough

Most people were surprised to hear that pointe shoes had not always been a feature of ballet and had only come into common use within the last century. Oscar had plenty of feminist education under his belt (which, he said, was the proper place for a man to keep his feminism) and knew that it was not a coincidence that such grueling footwear had historically been reserved only for women. Upon women were placed the most extreme requirements for grace, poise and ethereal beauty at the cost of the physical body.

Oscar's ballet shoes were not real ballet shoes, of course. No dancer could ever fly in patent leather and heels. But the ballet wasn't what was important—what was important was the dance that played out when he wore them. One person led, the other followed—more like waltz than ballet, really.

Something he felt in the bones of his hips and the darkness behind his eyes told him that wearing this was *right* for him. He was not a woman, but who he was leaned close enough to it that he thought he could understand.

His stockings were held in place by six garters, which were held in place by the corset, which was laced tight. The shoes were strapped on tight, as was the collar, to which was attached the bar, and the cuffs were attached to that. The lacy underwear Oscar also wore had not been designed for someone with balls, and his genitals were pressed close to his body in a small high lump. His inner thighs brushed together as he moved, the freshly shaven skin plumping out over the tops of his stockings.

He did not feel very ethereal. Supporting his weight in the shoes for more than five minutes at a stretch was painful and made him feel anything but weightless and airy. Hayden was watching him carefully, Oscar knew, though he couldn't see the other man. The only thing assuring Oscar of his presence were the gentle tugs on the reins attached to his wrists.

Oscar knew he looked stunning. The corset and lace and shoes and blindfold rendered him into a sex object. Every part of this outfit reinforced the fact that his comfort did not matter and his pleasure was meant to come from how much he provided to others. He did not even get the privilege of looking at himself.

It felt perfect.

The shoes were the last item to be put on. Oscar had been sitting on the floor, tailbone aching, waiting for orders, when fingers had grabbed him by the hair and pulled his head forward. Something cool and smooth had pressed against his mouth.

"Lick," he had been commanded, and Oscar immediately extended his tongue. What it touched tasted like plastic and smelled like leather, and Oscar knew it was one of his ballet heels. The phallic shape of it as he slid his lips down it made him think—a shoe designed for women that was shaped like a cock and yet hobbled its wearer was a brilliantly cruel joke. He had smiled, still obediently licking.

"You like that?"

"Yes, Sir."

The spike of the heel pressed against his lips and he obediently took it in his mouth, sucking the tip before he dragged his tongue up the eight inches of smooth black plastic. He could feel the other man's eyes on him.

"You like sucking that?" Hayden asked in a low, throaty murmur.

"I wish it was your cock, Sir," Oscar replied immediately, and his face burned. It had taken months of training to get him to respond to such questions quickly and directly, but he wasn't sure any amount of training could make him stop blushing. Then he corrected himself—*I wish it* were *your cock*. His embarrassment deepened, even though he was sure Hayden didn't care if his grammar was correct, especially not right now.

"That could be arranged."

Oscar swallowed as the heel was used to push his chin up.

"Your...your *real* cock, Sir."

The silence that greeted this just made Oscar's face even hotter. What if that had been the wrong thing to say? What if Hayden was turned off by the idea of letting anyone near him like that? What if the strap-on *was* what he considered his real cock?

A hand wrapped around Oscar's chin, forcing his face up even higher, and when Hayden spoke again, his face was so close that Oscar could feel the other man's breath on his lips.

"You don't know how." He didn't sound upset. He sounded smoking hot; suggestive.

"I know," Oscar whispered. "I want you to teach me. I w—wuh—wuh—" Here came the stutter. He switched words, trying to avoid it. "I imagine you coming in my mouth. I'd...like that very much, Sir."

Oscar didn't know the mechanics of this. He had heard that

some men like Hayden ejaculated and some didn't. He knew that even if Hayden did come like that, it wouldn't be like the semen Oscar was used to. But that didn't matter. The only thing that mattered was that it was Hayden, and whatever his body did, Oscar wanted it.

The hand disappeared from his neck, as did the warm breath, and for a moment Oscar truly feared that it had been the wrong thing to say. He worried that Hayden was offended, or worse, disgusted.

Oscar startled when something touched his foot and then recognized the feeling of one of his heels being slipped on. Quick fingers laced it into place and then did the same to his other foot. Oscar bore it in anxious silence, heart pounding in his chest.

"Stand up."

A hand grasped each of his upper arms to support him as he rose in increments, getting his legs underneath him first, then planting one toe and pushing all his weight on that and the hands to rise till he could plant the other foot on the floor. The bones of his toes protested, but Oscar didn't care. If Hayden wanted him up, then he wanted to be up. Whatever it took to please him.

"I'm putting the reins on."

Oscar nodded obediently, and tried not to wobble as the leads were latched into the rings on each of his wrist-cuffs. Then Hayden backed away, his boots audible on the hardwood floor, and Oscar felt the gentlest of tugs on the bar, urging him forward.

"Walk for me."

He walked, and in the near-silence and the darkness, he thought. His motions were slowed to a crawl by the heels, the corset, the bar. Every movement had to be carefully considered, and he was painfully aware of his whole body, as every motion put him in danger of falling. There was no way he could walk a mile in these shoes, but with every inch he thought he could begin to understand.

He wondered if Hayden had ever worn heels before he'd been Hayden. Oscar wondered if this was what Hayden's whole life had felt like, before—so careful, so measured, so constricted that breathing or moving or even thinking of anything other than what everyone wanted him to be became impossible. His body and mind narrowed down to hard points that told him *You do not belong to yourself, and you do not get the luxury of choice. Who you are and what you do is for others to decide.*

Oscar had chosen this willingly, eagerly—had lifted his arms with a smile so Hayden could wrap the corset around him like a safety blanket; had nearly cried with relief when the blindfold went on, the cares of the week falling away—the fight he'd had with his mother, his boss's endless complaints and catty emails, his worries about paying the phone bill because he'd run over his allotted minutes. Here, all that fell away. They weren't his worries anymore, because Hayden was taking care of him. Someone else was in control.

And these heels: these ballet heels he loved, that had taken him so long to find in his size and even longer to save the money to buy. This was his freedom. He wanted nothing so much as to belong to someone and to give up, for a little while, the burden of choosing for himself.

"Good boy, you're walking so well," Hayden reassured him, voice warm and solid in the dark behind the blindfold. Oscar bit his lip in relief, unbearably glad that he had earned approval. But then he wobbled—and a hand was instantly on his shoulder, steadying him. He smiled nervously.

"Thank you, Sir."

What's the difference between you and a woman anymore? his mother had once asked him, when he had told her he would be performing in a drag show. *You sleep with so many men, you wear women's clothing and you let people do the most revolting things to you, I'm sure. For God's sake, you're not a tranny too, are you? What happened to the little boy I raised? I don't even know you anymore, and I'm not sure I want to.*

Oscar struggled for breath and balance.

"Do your feet hurt too much to keep going like this?"

"I think so. May I rest, Sir?"

"Yes, you may rest. Get down on your knees." A hand grasped each of Oscar's arms, supporting him as he eased himself down. The shoes prevented him from moving in anything like a normal way, and it was only the other man's help that kept him from crashing down instead of kneeling.

He panted in the tight corset, head spinning. A calloused thumb stroked over his mouth.

"You're such a good boy, and so beautiful. Do you believe me?"

"I think I do, Sir."

"You think you do? I already told you what to believe. Yes or no, do you believe me?"

"Yes, Sir. I believe you. I trust you."

"You really *do* want to make me happy, don't you."

It wasn't a question, and it wasn't delivered in a voice of command.

"*Yes*, Sir," Oscar replied. The hand left his face, and he waited to find out what this meant. Rustling noises told him something was happening in front of him, but he didn't know what. Rope? Hayden donning a bigger cock?

A hand slipped around the back of Oscar's head, cradling his skull gently.

"You really want to suck me?" Now his voice was rough, predatory.

Oscar's mind went blank with desire.

"Yes, Sir. *Please.*"

The hand curled into his hair, gripped and urged him forward. Oscar's nose contacted warm, hairy skin. His face was turned so his cheek lay flat against it; the hair was coarse. Hayden's stomach? He hoped so. The man had a treasure trail that made Oscar's mouth water.

Then Oscar caught the scent: musky. It smelled like sex, both familiar and not quite what Oscar was used to when he went down on men. He could feel his pulse in his chest, his neck, his wrists, his knees and his tightly bound feet as the anticipation rose inside him.

I've never made him come before. Please, let me do this for him, just once.

He panted, trying to get enough air and knowing that his breath must be warm on the other man. When he moved downward, just a little, asking for permission, Hayden let him.

More hair against his lips, spreading out even thicker than before, and then the flesh in front of his mouth sloped down away from him. In his panties, his cock started to stiffen, and Oscar extended his tongue.

There was just hair for a second, and then he slid past it, and—oh. There it was. Gloriously soft skin on his tongue and the taste of salt, and Hayden tilted his hips upward to meet Oscar's mouth.

"Suck it between your lips."

Oscar did. It fit so perfectly, sliding between his lips so the hard tip settled on his tongue. He wrapped his teeth automatically and began to suck like he would on any cock. The motions were smaller than usual, that was all. And usually they didn't make his blood hammer in his ears from fear and arousal and joy. Usually it was just sucking cock. But this, this was Hayden.

He wiggled his tongue over the tip and was rewarded with a groan that made him twitch, shift his stance, lower himself stiffly in the corset and curve his neck upward so he could take the other man better. He wondered what would happen if he extended his tongue, but didn't dare try. He hadn't been given permission, and he had no idea what he'd find.

Pins and needles prickled his fingertips and he realized his hands were going numb where they hung limp in the cuffs. Oscar flexed them into fists, squeezed; sucked; bobbled his head; heard Hayden's breath speed up, grow shallower and turn into a sigh of "Ahh—*ah*—yes, yes, *just* like that—such a good boy...."

Oscar had never been harder in his life. He could do this all day, and wanted to; had never wanted anything so much as he wanted this now. Hayden had both hands in his hair, clenching and unclenching them and rocking his hips into Oscar's face. Oscar couldn't count the number of times he'd fantasized about finally, finally being able to do something for Hayden.

"You've always been such a good cocksucker—so good—Jesus, Oscar—"

Oscar whimpered. His prick curved along his left hip, caught under the lace so he couldn't even rub it between his thighs. Not that it mattered—he didn't have permission. This was for Hayden, not him. He moaned again, tightened his mouth and gave it everything he had. And it was so easy, so natural, so right.

He had never, ever heard that tone in Hayden's voice before—sometimes the man had moaned and whispered dirty things to him before when Oscar had sucked Hayden's cock, but never this cock, and his voice had never sounded like this before.

The grip in his hair became painful, and Hayden cried out, harsh and loud, and Oscar knew; knew he'd been a good boy, that he was beautiful, and that for the first time, he had made Hayden come.

The grip loosened, but he was pulled away from the other man. There was a second of his mouth being empty, till Hayden kissed him and held his face like he was precious.

"So good. You're so good."

Oscar was flying in his beautiful shoes.

ON HYS KNEES

Evan Swafford

On hys knees, yes, on my lap, yes, but what I really want is hym spread naked before me, on hys back; lying back not quite all the way, eyes wide, nipples hard, as they always are, ready for me—always ready for me. Palms pressed against the bed, fingers together, in invisible bondage. So calm. Anticipation, but calm, trust.

I would be hard, stroking my harnessed cock, kneeling over hym, staring down at my boi. I would tell hym, "Spread your legs for me…farther apart." Hys dick would bob as hy slid hys heels across the bed, giving me a better view of hys pussy.

The color might rise in hys face: dusky skin becoming flushed. Hy would press hys lips together, perhaps moan a light protest, a quiet, "No, Daddy." But at the same time, hy would raise hys hips and I know that if I let myself touch hym, hy would be soaking wet.

I want to rub the head of my cock against hys wet hole, sliding around while hy whimpers. I want to spread hys wetness, rub it around hys hole and over hys swollen cock, but I know that I would lose my patience and shove in, right away. I want hym on my cock, for sure, but I try to take it slow.

Maybe it's because I know that it's hard for hym to be exposed like this: parts hy keeps hidden lie bare before my eyes. No fear; hy knows that I accept hym, desire hym, feed off of this. Still, the naked female sex, which this boi usually hides under baggy jeans and men's clothes, is uncovered for Daddy. I warrant this trust and take it seriously. Because I see my boi as hy truly is. And hy knows that I'll protect hym, keep hym safe. It's what we both need.

Hys submission makes my power surge, my dominance, my patience, my steel. Maybe the way hy submits to me, surrenders hys will to me, is what got me hooked. It's a feeling in my gut, not just in my cock: a safe, satisfying, steady feeling: Clear. Clean. I become calmer, steadier, stronger, more myself, when we're like this. It's like I could never fail. I'd never drop hym.

I'd never hurt hym, not really—just in the way hy needs. And when hy cries for me, hys tears are precious. Hy is strong enough to allow this vulnerability, strong enough to let me hold hym for a while. And I am strong enough to make it all right, to keep hym safe, to soothe hym as I hurt hym, to fuck the pain away.

Hy's tight, muscled, toned. Hy pushes hys small frame to its limits. Hy's ready for a fight but doesn't want one—not on the street.

Hy tries to push me off, but I hold hym down. Sometimes, hy needs to be held down. Hy tries to be a good boi, but it's hard to take, to submit completely. So, hy has to be held and pushed and pulled and forced. I take hym where hy needs to go. Hy struggles, fights me but never denies me.

Hys tattoos tell stories, etched across hys skin: some about hys past, some about hys future. Who hy is, what hy desires, is spelled out across hys skin in symbols. There is a double woman turned trans symbol on hys forearm. Those who understand see the evolution of the tattoo and know it means that hy once identified as a dyke but now identifies as a trans man; outsiders see an interesting design. A black band permanently encircles hys right bicep, marking hym as a bottom. Scars hy bears signify rites of passage; visible reference of past pain endured, rituals of healing, marks of ownership.

When hy is dressed, hy wears leather cuffs and flags right black, hunter, and red. Hy packs a cock: soft for daily, hard for action. Hy dresses boi: all male clothing—boxers, jockstraps, dress shirts and ties, hats, schoolboy uniforms, black leather. Hy keeps hys head shaved or cropped short, like Daddy prefers, and hy feels natural this way. Hy's been told that hys septum piercing "distracts from hys pretty face" and that's just the way hy likes it. Hy would rather look tough.

Hy's on hys knees, head bowed. I grasp hys chin and trace hys mouth with the head of my cock, running the slick silicone tip across hys shiny lower lip. Such a pretty mouth. I savor the anticipation, the moments before I enter hym. My cock throbs as I brush against the perfect silky mouth. I thrust inward, pushing past hys teeth.

Hy opens hys mouth to receive me like a benediction. Hy receives me on hys tongue like the host. I see the reverence in hys eyes, wide and innocent. And I worship hym with all my spirit.

I feel hys throat, hys tongue, hys mouth working at me. Hy opens to me in seemingly impossible ways. Hy gags and hys eyes tear, but hy swallows and continues sucking, with renewed vigor. Hy can't take the entire shaft, but hy gives it hys all, opening hys mouth and throat to my assault.

I attempt to hold off on having the first of many orgasms.

I close my eyes, because the sight of hys sweet mouth on my cock is too much stimulation. My hips move involuntarily as I fuck hys mouth, clutching at hys head, lodging my fingers in what I can grasp of hys short-cropped hair. I cum in hys mouth, spewing ejaculate down my legs.

And because I'm a cock-hungry queer, as well, I haul hym up onto the bed and onto hys back. I swallow hys rod with one breath. Hy gasps and moans. Between licks, I tell hym hy's a nasty boi, a horny fag, a dirty cocksucker. Hy arches up to meet me as I suck hym.

I slip my hand underneath hys harness and feel the wetness streaming from hys front hole. The large hands I once thought too big for a girl, serve well to stretch hym open and fill hys need. I shove three fingers inside hym and hy moans and clenches, as my hand becomes my cock, Daddy's cock, pulsing inside hym. I push on, deeper inside, closer to hys core, and I feel it all in my cock.

I like to use my strap on hym, especially hys faggot ass, but in hys hole my hand is the best cock. I can feel hys pulse, breath and heat; feel hym opening to me. I can feel hys need and where hy needs me to touch; push deeper, harder; hurt hym, love hym, giving hym exactly what hy needs.

I stop and yank off hys harness, uncovering hys flesh cock—swollen, attentive. I plunge my mouth down onto hys cock, as I continue to fuck hys hole. Hy swells in my mouth, grunting and thrusting against my face. Hys hole opens to me, as I thrust deeper and harder. Hy takes more of my cock, and I make a fist and enter into hym fully, making hym howl. Hy bucks and I can no longer keep my mouth on hym.

Vowing to tie hym down next time, I move forward over hym, between hys splayed legs. I grab and push hys legs up onto my shoulders as I begin to fist hym deeper.

"Deeper, Daddy, I need your cock," my boi begs, face so sweet and full of longing.

"Please, Daddy, hurt me."

How can I resist? I begin fucking hym as hard as I can, with the full force of my arm. Hy yells and screams, as I slide deeper and deeper into hym, burying my fist: my cock, my psychic cock, my actual cock, my real cock.

TEL AVIV

Jacques La Fargue

I will meet you in the small park on Shenkin in Tel Aviv.

It's a summer's evening, the air is cool with a breeze that has flirted across the Mediterranean before kissing our faces, which is a welcome relief from the heat of the day. Shenkin is closed to cars and the street teems with trendsetters in their finery out for the evening. Gay men are the majority of the crowd, but it is hard to tell for certain here: gay or Euro-trash? Of the two young men in uniform sitting on a bench across the park I have no doubts. They are obviously off duty, their fingers entwined, legs touching, their eyes on each other, their cigarettes abandoned beside them, smouldering on the bench.

You come to me direct from the airport, from the harsh scrutiny of Israeli security, from the cramped cabin of some crowded plane. Your name, your sex, your belonging have all been thoroughly questioned by a young woman in a uniform so tight it may as well have been painted over her pert breasts and tight ass. You were not supposed to enjoy her absolute power over you quite so much, nor her confusion. You were not what she expected when she was paged to the little grey room in the women's area of customs. You tell me that she bent you over without a word, one hand firmly on the small of your back, the other pushing into your ass, like she did not want to see your bearded face, but that she redeemed herself taking her sweet time with your front hole. Like she wanted to remember, like she wanted her hand hot with your heat, like she could not believe how sweet you are right there. I promise to make good use of any lube she left.

You are happy to be here, but not at home; you're on guard against the newness of this place. I have already *benched gomel* for your safe passage and am savouring your discombobulation, your lack of familiarity. I, with oh so slightly more experience, get to show off places I have known and celebrated. I have spent the day basking on the beach, being slapped around by the salty surf, and now it is your slapping I want, your salt water I want on my face, your glory I bask in.

"Meet me in Tel Aviv, fully loaded," I had commanded into the phone and here you are. My cock is hard and pressed against the inside of my pants, fully loaded and fit to burst with your touch. There is Hebrew in the air around us, G-d's language being used to seduce married men, to inquire as to how another likes to be fucked and to ask directions to the nearest leather bar. Tradition says that after death, G-d will ask if we have tasted all the pleasures of this world, and with a smile on my lips I want to be able to answer, "Ken, ken, ken, ken." You are one of these pleasures that at this moment I have but tasted, but I will gorge myself on you—eat without devouring, offer myself without being consumed. And I, the cocky bastard, am torn: do I take you out and show you off, or do I take you back to where I am staying and fuck North America out of you? I might tease you first, lingering here, steeping in this mixture of gayness and Jewishness all at the same time, but tonight I'm going to fuck coarse Sinai sand into your precious big-man's ass.

I have rented a room in a small hotel at the top end of the street. It's on the third floor of the building, up tight narrow stairs, and I lead you through the crowds in that direction. We stop to buy halva and ruggalah, sweet things that will melt on the tongue and further sweeten this already delicious occasion. I have in my room a small bowl of figs, dates and pomegranates, fruits of the land with which to welcome you.

While you are tired after the flight and the stairs and seven time zones out-of-place, I will make you say the *braha* before I feed you, every time. I will make you wait, learn the new blessing, press your lips to mine and G-d's before every bite. I will tell you this is how it is done here. I will bite the tops off the figs and open them with my hands before presenting them to you, open and juicy, like a woman's sex spread wide by knowing hands. I will spill open the pomegranate seeds, their bright red juice staining my hands, their turgid forms shining and glistening in the light off the street which enters through the open door to the balcony. I will feed you just enough to revive you, before I offer you my fingers, wet with my juices and not the fruit, for your pleasure. I will sit on your lap, my cunt pressed against your cock, pressed through our clothes and ride you gently as I strip off my shirt and binding. I go from fresh-faced yeshiva boy to breasted bride as the layers come off, and I don't care. It's your cock I want. I will unpack it from your suitcase and let you settle it in place before dropping to my knees before you to clean it with my mouth. You told me that you knew I was gay by my blow jobs, and I won't disappoint.

Your belt undone, your fly open and your cock released to the air, my need is too dire to take things slowly, too desperate to wait. My fingers play at the base of your cock, and my lips take you in. You lean back in the chair, your head rolling up; a deep throaty roar escapes your lips. "Welcome to Israel, brother," I say, keeping my lips so close they brush your cock with every word. "Welcome home."

You're watching me as I work your cock. I know I have you when I feel your hands on my throat. You bring my face up to yours and my attention is torn between your moving lips and my need to breathe. You however are steady. I feel the heat of your words as much as I hear them. "If I had my knife, faggot, I would have slit your throat by now, but you're in luck." You pause and I wait for the threat I know will follow. "The cock-tease in customs took my blade—I'll have to split you with my cock instead." You keep one of your massive hands on my throat as the other strips my pants. You don't bother to get me out of my briefs, you just wrench the fabric aside. You raise the hand on my throat, drawing me closer, and you bring me down on your cock. "Now," you say, with your hot breath in my ear, "would be a good time for you to say the blessing for cum." I don't know a blessing for cum, but I also don't have air to breathe. I let you slam me down on your cock, and I take it, take it in me, over and over again, until your pants are soaked with your cum and mine, until I beg for mercy, and until you have made me cum a good seven times after that.

You won't break me tonight, and when you finally let me off your cock I strip you down. I open your shirt and kiss your chest, teasing your new nipples with my teeth, keeping them high, hot and hard with my fingers when my lips move else-where. Tonight I will fuck you, with my tongue, with my fingers, with my cock. Tonight I will fuck you until you cum dry, until you lose count, until the people outside go home and the street quiets and the night is still. Until the time that people stir in their sleep and husbands and wives whisper to each other, past the watch when babies cry and dogs bark, until the devout rise from their slumbers to say the morning *shma.* And when we are through and fully spent together we will say a *shekianu.*

Tomorrow I will tremble before you and make demands that you mark words on my flesh with your power, ask that you speak things into being and believe you Abel, but tonight is for fucking and fucking alone. Welcome home.

TAKING THE TOLL

Kiki DeLovely

My eyes flutter open immediately. No time for this gently waking up business—conscious thought pouring like honey into my leftover dreams, slowly mixing together until cognizance fully takes hold and I contemplate getting up. No, there'll be none of that. Today's Sunday.

10:37 a.m. Good. I have just enough time to get this started.

We may have been out late last night but now is no time to worry whether she'll be sleepy, cranky, too tired... No matter what, I will make this happen. Usually I insist on being dropped off on Saturday nights or at least fucking at her house and then going home to mine. Sleepovers can happen on Friday, Thursday; shit, even Monday, for all I care. Sunday mornings are mine—ever since I was a little girl. But we had reached that point—the three-month mark—and she requested a Saturday night stay.

Normally this would be met with an immediate and firm, "No," but this one might be a keeper, so I figured I'd have to let her in eventually. And there's something about her that has quickly gained my trust. Something about the way she holds me—my hand on the street, my body in bed—it's charming and chivalrous. Something about the way she makes her way through the world, whether alone or with me by her side: exuding inward confidence, outward audacity. It's all so comfortable and natural with her, even encouraging. She enjoys existing in a duality—challenging masculinity while continually tugging on the boundaries of the box labeled FEMALE—and I enjoy eroticizing everything that makes her genderqueer. I like this thing we have. I like her. And I want to see where we could be going, so I grant her this one wish, warning, "You know I'm a morning person..."

Slightly distracted by her raised eyebrow, I continue, "I don't like to sleep my Sunday away..."

I'm even more distracted by how she's checking off each of my points in the air.

"None of this lazy Sunday morning, brunch at two, got it?"

Her dark eyes shine. One last check mark. "Got it."

We'll see.

She said she got it. So now I roll over, look into her sleeping face, her expression fetching and proud, her brow furrowing even in sleep, and consider my possibilities. She has this edge about her—not completely hard yet deeply masculine. This is the edge where my lust resides. She is not exactly my opposite but rather my complement: thuddy biker boots to my strappy Fluevog heels, bien morena to my slightly lighter hue, the curve of her biceps to that of my hips. Her masculinity takes my high femme to greater heights. Our complementary natures play into each other, coloring outside of the lines. We look real good together. More importantly, we feel exquisite.

I start to go in for a kiss but just before disturbing her sleeping lips, I decide on a different tactic and roll over once again. I slowly back up, deliberately pressing my ass up against her boxers; gently at first, then with just enough pressure so that she'll start to get the idea. She grumbles a slight groan.

10:41. Shit, I've got to work faster. I take hold of her free hand, interlace my fingers with hers and draw her fingertips across my skin skirting the edge of my panties, gliding up my chest, grabbing one breast firmly, dragging her palm across my erect nipple and finally bringing her fingers up to my mouth. It's just two fingertips; at first my tongue teases them—I can tell she's definitely awake now but not quite yet there—then I lick down the crack between the two, tracing back up and sliding both into my mouth. I suck and work my tongue, all the while still pressing back into her, as she's now beginning to press into me, moaning as though it were her cock instead of her fingers that I've wrapped my tongue around.

10:45. I'm a little later than I'd like to be...but this'll work. I run her moistened fingers back down along my chest. Teasing time is over. I slip the thin strap of lace on my panties to the side and guide her fingers into my already wet cunt. As I inhale audibly, she positions herself to take control, her teeth digging into my shoulder and then growls, "Fuck, baby, what's got you going this morning? Still reeling from last night?"

Perhaps, but that's not what's made me quite so wet this morning in particular, though I don't dare tell her that. Instead of playing along with her game, I make it clear that I'm in no mood to talk, arch my hips and slam myself down on her fingers. She's quickly forgotten she ever asked me a question in the first place, scooting down to get better leverage, fucking me harder, deeper.

10:55. Perfect.

She knows exactly how to work my pussy—how to get me going like no other and get me off such that my mind stops its obsessive running and I practically forget my name. I'm getting incredibly close now—the timing has seemed to work out to my advantage...until I hear her say, "Baby, I need to fuck you with my cock...."

10:58. Fuck.

"N-n-n-n-no...keep going... Please don't stop please..."

She looks down at me with that half-cocked grin. "Darlin', you know how I love it when you beg, but Papi knows best and, trust me, I definitely need to fuck you with my cock. My hard-on is raging." She's already flipped her legs over the side of the bed and is rummaging deep into the pant legs of her jeans to find last night's discarded strap-on.

10:59. Fuck, fuck, fuck!

I flicker my eyes closed and take a deep breath just as she steals a glance back at me—did she see my eyes start to roll back? It doesn't matter now because the bells begin to toll and I try desperately to regain my composure.

Ding-dong. I bite my lip. *Ding-dong.* Squeeze my thighs together. *Ding-dong.* Suck in more air. *Ding-dong.* Bite down harder. *Ding-dong.* My hips involuntarily raise...just...barely... But it's too late—a slight whimper escapes my lips. *Ding-dong.* I'm greeted by her eyes penetrating me. *Ding-dong.* Shit, she's been watching the entire time. *Ding-dong.*

She cocks her head, taking in the sound in the distance; it's finally striking her what's going on. "You're getting off on this, aren't you?"

"I—I...what?" Fuckin' stammering—it's my tell. "No..."

"Yes. Yes, you are. You're fucking getting off on those church bells tolling." I see an explosion of thought as her eyes light up with a wildness, her brain going crazy with where she wants to take this.

This. My...secret.

Ever since the first time I faked sick (when I was not quite yet done with my morning session, my mother walked in on me, saw my face flushed, my forehead sweaty and hot, and, lucky for me, immediately decided that I must be coming down with something), I've eroticized those bells. In my bed, alone again at last ("We'll be home soon," my mother said, as she closed the door behind her), I started over what had previously been interrupted. It wasn't long before I heard those church bells tolling from several blocks away and I was coming harder than ever...Ridden with Catholic guilt, I thought of all the parishioners entering the church, dipping fingertips into the holy water, making themselves pure with the sign of the cross, finishing it off with a besito, first finger crossed over the thumb...all the while I was here, my hand down my panties, doing extremely impure things to myself.

I learned two lessons that morning: 1) Being made to wait (no matter the reason) for my orgasm made me come all the harder; 2) I was a very dirty girl. (I would discover later in life just how dirty I was, gain language and lovers to assist in the process and fully submit to my filthy role-playing desires. But I'd never before allowed any of said lovers access to this particular, very peculiar turn-on.)

11:01. Normally I'm coming right now, thrashing about in the sheets, my body a creature of habit; after so many years it's more than difficult to control. My lover is staring down at me, grinning wickedly as she reads it all over me—witnessing just how hard it is for me to stave off that orgasm. I'm her own personal open-fuckin'-book and she's enjoying the read just a little too much.

"Go put on your uniform." Before I can even protest, drop to my knees, do anything to distract her (she's getting to know me a little too well), she gives me that stern look that always makes me weak (obedient) and raises her eyebrows with the Am-I-really-going-to-have-to-say-it-again? look and I'm up, heading toward the closet.

She's creative as hell when it comes to this stuff and quick as fuck, I can tell her mind has taken off into a full sprint as she leaves the room to collect whatever props she can find that will help bring the swiftly mounting fantasy in her head to life. She looked into my mind through my body's divulgences, revealed my secret and immediately ran with it, didn't even hesitate for a second. If she had, I would have feared judgment; instead I feel completely at ease, protected and cherished. Her presence and demeanor make this place safe for me. Of course she wants to go there with me.

Wondering just what she'll come up with, I finish pulling off my red lacy thong (definitely *not* part of the uniform) and I'm about to switch it out with the white cotton panties when it hits me and I slide the more scandalous version back on. Sure, we've played around with the naughty schoolgirl fantasy plenty...but never before have we done any specifically Catholic play...and I have a feeling this defiance might just bring it to another level.

When my lover reenters the room, dressed in head-to-toe black with a white "collar"—Where the hell did she get that?—I'm taken aback and only slightly scandalized that with her short, dark hair slicked back like that and her confident, broad-shouldered stance, she takes on a surprising resemblance to Padre José Manuel, the priest of my childhood who insisted that we all call him Padre Manolo. This role-play wouldn't work for me if it weren't for the queer masculinity she brings to it. Never once had I thought of Padre Manolo in an erotic way, but because it is my lover playing at this, the role of priest is suddenly turned on its head, queered, and hence, exciting. Since she already looks the part, I decide to go with it, excitedly running up to her, calling out, "Padre Manolo! Padre Manolo!"

I'm met with a sinister grin. "No, my child. Your beloved Manolito is not here today. I will have to be the one who hears your confession."

"My...?"

"Yes, my dear, your confession. I noted your absence at Mass this morning and yet, here you are, standing before me in good health. I presume you have much to confess."

Dumbfounded and delighted, I struggle to find the words. "Uhh...yes...um, yes, Father," I answer finally, bowing my head, my face hot with shame. I can tell that for her this is surface-level fun, but it strikes a deeper chord with me. She knows her way around the traditions from her studies, whereas with me, this was part of my culture growing up. It's weighty and charged. And her detachment makes it all the hotter.

"Well, it's good that you came." She lays one hand firmly on my shoulder. "Let's go into my private study." I'm led into the office where she has created the desired scene, having cleared my desk completely. Suddenly changed, the room seems quite sparse. He closes the door, turns the lock and answers my questioning look, "So that we won't be disturbed. Have a seat." His tone, presence, his very nature contribute to how he queers gender, or any role he takes on, so delectably.

I sit opposite the desk and he pulls the bigger chair around, sitting down right at my side, such that he can look closely into my face. "Now tell me, my child, why you weren't at Mass this morning."

"Umm...well...my mom...she, um...she thought I was sick."

"And why would she think that? You appear to be a vision of health."

"Uhh...I don't know..." I mumble.

More forcefully he continues, gaining momentum with each word, "Now, that simply cannot be the case. Clearly there must have been a reason. She wouldn't just make up an illness to keep her daughter from going to church. Your mother is a devout Catholic woman, certainly she doesn't want her daughter to go to hell!"

Seeing that I'm practically cowering in fear by this point, he takes a breath and starts over, more calmly, "My dear, I know that you are a good, Catholic girl at heart and you wouldn't ever want to do anything to jeopardize your place in the Eternal Kingdom of Heaven with Jesus Christ, Our Lord and Savior, now would you?" I shake my head slowly. So he continues in a soothing tone, "Good. That's very good. And so you know, as a good girl, that you must confess to me, right?" While I nod my head shyly, he goes on, "And that means you must tell me everything. All of your sins. No matter how bad you think they are." I lower my eyes, certain he can read it all over my face. My mother did always call me a sinvergüenza—if only she could see me and my shame now. "And I promise you, no matter how bad, no matter how filthy dirty those sins are, I won't be mad at you. Okay?" Barely nodding now, he takes my chin in his hand, raising it deliberately so that I'm forced to meet his gaze. And ever-so-gently he repeats, "Okay?"

"Okay." I manage, barely audible. My eyes wide and sweet, I can tell he likes this innocent, slightly scared, little-girl look on my face.

"That's a good girl." And he gently rubs the back of his first two fingers across my cheek. "Okay then. We'll have a formal confession and then I'm going to do everything in my power to free your soul of these impurities. And you must not be scared, you must trust me with all your heart. You must know that everything I do is in your best interest. Do you trust me?"

"Yes, Father." I say meekly.

"Okay. Good. Then let's begin." And he waits for me to start.

The words rise up out of my throat and I'm surprised at how the memories flood back. Each sound comes to me as though this incantation was imbedded in the depths of my memory, has shaken free from the cobwebs and flows off my lips with ease. "Bendígame, Padre, porque he pecado. Bless me, Father, for I have sinned. It has been three weeks since my last confession."

Before I can continue, he breaks in and I can tell he wants to cut to the chase. "What are your sins, my child? Why did your mother presume you ill this morning?"

So I do my best to make haste. "Well, she walked into my room...and I...I was...well, my face...it was...all red and sweaty."

"And what had left you in such a state?"

"Umm...well...I was...I mean, I had been...well, I was kinda touching myself."

Some color has come into his face now and he's getting agitated. "Where were you touching yourself? Tell me exactly where and how you were doing it," he commands firmly.

"I...I was on my belly in my bed and I put my hand down there and"—I look up for a split second, long enough to know not to stop—"and I was rubbing my...my...mi cosita." (My mother never did teach us the proper term for anything.)

"Tu cosita?" He tries to hide his amusement. "And why would you be rubbing down there? You know it's a very naughty place that a young girl like you should never touch except to clean yourself, don't you?"

"Sí, Padre...Es que...well, it just felt so good. Like it was... tingling. Like...I had to."

"Like you had to." It's not even disguised as a question and

I think he's mocking me now. His face grows very grave and he shakes his head mournfully. "My child, I see now that this is much more serious than I had thought. We're going to have to take some drastic measures to save your soul. You clearly have the devil inside you and we're going to have to fill you with Christ. Now I need you to take off your panties."

"But...I..."

He cuts me off before I can get anywhere, his voice harsh, speaking more vehemently now. "This is not the time to question me, my child. Your soul is in danger. You have the devil inside you! Do you want to go to hell?" I shake my head nervously and realize that I'm trembling all over, yet I can't do what he's told me to do. "Come here." He pulls me toward him brusquely and yanks my skirt up, gasping once he sees my choice in undergarments. "I can't believe this! What type of little girl would be wearing such things? This is disgusting!" And he rips them off of me, pushing me back up against the desk. "Do you realize that you look like a whore, wearing this filth?" He shakes the panties in my face to make his point before sliding them into his pocket.

I look over and see him reaching for...what is that? And then a flash of recognition. He's grabbed my decorative cross that normally hangs on the wall and is rolling a condom over the long end. "My child, we're going to have to fill you with Christ..."

Now this is really getting somewhere.

I try not to look excited as he catches my gaze, walking the few steps back around the desk. He plants each of his hands on either side of me, inching closer and closer, breath hot on my face, until I'm forced flat on my back against the desk without the slightest touch on his part. I'm slightly startled yet simultaneously delighted at where this is going and not wanting it to show. He stares intimidatingly into my eyes with such intensity that suddenly I'm back in the role—a scared little girl, shaking ever so slightly, nervous about what's to come. "Please, Padre, please don't..."

"I'm sorry, my dear, I see no other way. We will fill you with the love of Christ and drive the devil out of you."

"I'm scared..."

"Don't worry, sweet child, it will only hurt for a little while..." he tries to reassure me as he's spreading my legs. I feel the chill of the instrument sliding up my thigh and a shiver ripples to my core. "You must take this like a good girl. I know you can..." And he's pressing the tip against my opening, undeniably wet from all that had come before. The cross slides in without the slightest resistance, but I don't want to make this quite so easy.

"No, no, no, please don't...Nooo! You're hurting me!" He continues despite my protests, going deeper and deeper unrelentingly. I can tell this is almost too much for him and it's taking everything in him not to shove it hard and fast.

"Hush now, mi cielita. We must drive out the devil. I can tell he has a strong hold on you." And he begins to pump the cross in and out of me with greater force.

I'm so there, I start to shout out, "No! Stop! It hurts so bad! Please stop! Pleeease..." And with each of my protests, his fucking gets more and more vigorous. He's thrusting in and out of me aggressively, each of my shouts fodder for him to give it to me harder.

"Can you feel it? Can you feel the Holy Spirit washing over you?" A bead of sweat drips from his forehead onto my thigh and it rolls down joining my dripping wetness.

"Ay, Padre! Ay-ay-I don't know...I feel...something..." I can barely get a single word out now.

"That's good, sweet girl, the Holy Spirit is going to enter and fill you, rush over you completely and wash away all your sins. Don't resist it."

"O-okay, Father. I'll do whatever you say."

"Yes, mi angelita, that's veeery good. You do just as I say. You're taking it so...fucking...well..." He's slamming into me with each word as punctuation.

I'm so worked up I hardly even notice that he's let profanity slip out in the heat of his passion. It's only seconds before I feel my orgasm mounting. "Padre, I-I...I feel like I'm going to... explode!"

"Very good, my child, don't resist it. Take it all. Let the Holy Spirit consume you." And with his final command I'm coming so fucking hard, shaking to the point of practically falling off the desk. But he collapses on top of me, trapping me there, preventing me from going anywhere. We breathe hard in unison for a few beats before I feel him shifting a bit, propping himself up a bit on his elbow. "That...that was...very, very good..." He pushes a few strands of my hair back off my forehead as he starts to jack himself off with his other hand. "Now I have to finish me off..." The whole scene has gotten him so excited that he too is coming hard, in just a matter of seconds, feeling only slightly guilty for taking advantage of such a sweet, young girl. He collapses on me again, his weight pinning me against the desk and we lie there for a moment, coming down from the high.

Suddenly she looks up at me with a wicked grin, kisses me on the forehead and says, "Next Sunday we'll further discuss your acts of contrition."

"Gracias, Padre."

DIXIE BELLE
THE FURTHER ADVENTURES OF HUCKLEBERRY FINN

Kate Bornstein

May 26th, 1865

My Dear Friend Tom,

It has been nearly two months since General Robert E. Lee hanged up his fiddle, and it's only today that the very last of the organized Confederate troops are turning their weapons over to Union soldiers. I am writing to you after so many years and on this particular day because for the first time since the war begun, there's a good chance there ain't no rebels in the hills to ambush the United States postal express, and so this letter may ackshully get all the way to your door.

I have addressed this to Tom Sawyer and I hope with all my heart it is Tom Sawyer who is reading this letter and that he ain't dead and buried out on some battlefield. But whether it's him reading or maybe some surviving relative, have you got any idea yet who's writing to you with such fancy, fine and dainty handwriting? It's me, Huckleberry Finn hisself! Not that anyone in the city of N'awlins has ever knowed me by that name. No, sir. I go by Miss Sarah Grangerford, of the Jackson, Mississippi Grangerfords, honey, such a pleasure to make your acquaintance. There are a very few folks know me as Elexander Blodgett, but the crawfish aristocracy and not a few soldiers and officers around town know me better as the Sassy Sarah from Madame Violet's Parlor of Elysian Delights and I sure would appreciate if you don't tell anyone that Huck Finn ever was my name.

Speakin' of names, the illustrious Mister Twain and I have crossed paths again, right here at Madame Violet's! I am sure you will see him soon yourself. He asks after you constantly. I am trying my best to persuade him to write stories about this new life of mine the way he done before, but he seems to have some misgivings, which doesn't make sense because I heard that "The Adventures of Huckleberry Finn" made him some good money, more even than "Tom Sawyer," how about that! I never read either of 'em all the way through. Have you? *You* tell Mister Twain to write us into another book of his. You was always the one who could sell arrowheads to injins and chains to niggers. Have you seen the old man since we knew him, Tom? He has the same tobacco smell and the same crow's feet about his eyes only much deeper now and his hair is gone all snow. He always tells me to send you his warmest regards and hopes for your well-being should I ever see you again alive. I certainly hope I am being successful in delivering his message through this letter.

Well, I am bustin' with all sorts of good stories to tell *someone* and they are the truth mainly with only some stretchers. So, if it ain't Tom Sawyer readin' this letter, then whoever you are, I hope you enjoy the tellin'. I'll start back when I took my leave of Miss Watson and the Widow Douglas. Much as I appreciate those two god-fearin' good women and all the charitable work they did on me, I reckon I was never cut out to be the well-behaved boy they expected me to be in return. So I let 'em kiss me good-bye and I set out down to the courthouse to collect the $6000 that you told me Judge Douglas was holding for me. You remember? My pap never did get his hands on it, you said, and the judge still had it? No hard feelings, Tom but it might've been better for all concerned if you'd hadn't stretched the truth quite so far. The day I showed up to collect my 'heritance, the good judge instead made me the gift of bein' a two years all expenses paid guest of the great state of Mississippi for what did he call it? Vagrancy and Public Noosance. He did it to self-improve me, he said, and if there ever were any $6000 I never did see a nickel of it. Sure enough though, I learned a great deal about life, liberty and the pursuit of happiness as a guest of hizzoner's sheriffs. Soon as I was fully rehabilitated from being a public noosance and released back I high-tailed it as far as I could from respectable society, and headed down to the river which is the only place I ever felt free. I spent a year and some workin' engine room on all sorts of steamboats, ferryboats and fish-boats. Tom, I was happy as any river snipe ever had a right to be. Did you know I love to tinker with engines? But when your time is up, your time is up or so they say, and I landed down here in N'awlins just three days before we heard that war had broke out between the States. From that time on, any sort of river travel got a whole lot harder to do without the Union interferin' in your business, and it was clear to me that I was stuck to death in the largest city of the newly constitutionalized Confederate States of America.

What little money I had saved ran out. I was a fine mess with not even two bits to pay a barber to cut my hair, which by thist time had growed down to my shoulders, as long as my pap's but nowhere near as greasy. I had the choice of stayin' in the city, or livin' out in bayou territory, shootin' possums and

Union soldiers. Well, I was never very fond of eatin' possum nor have I ever shot a human bein' in my life, though if I was to, it would be a Union soldier rather than a rebel. So I stayed in the city and took myself whatever slop jobs I could find on the waterfront where everyone worked long hours for not one penny, but for two tasteless meals and a sweltering bunk-room filled with too many hard-working newly 'mancipated niggers, Creoles, and no-account tars like me. I was beginning to reconsider my thoughts about possum.

Then came April, 1862, a dark month for the Confederacy but a darker month for N'awlins. The Union admiral Fraidy-Guts invaded the port like it was no more than a mud castle made by children. He fit an almighty battle, sinking eleven of our ships, and clearing the way for the soldiers to march in and take the city which they wasted no time in doing. The Occupation dried up most of the river trade and most of us dock rats found ourselves out of work. Both armies were lookin' for fresh meat for their cannons so they sent recruiters down to the waterfront every day. The Rebel recruiters were sly. They had to be. If they was catched, it was prison and certain death as traitors. Still, some niggers and bums sided with the rebs and resisted by all means the Occupation. The Union recruiters on the other hand were full of themselves and with good reason: they was holding all the cards in this game, and they offered us positions in their army like they was offering us a place in heaven, which is a place I have never been very anxious to visit.

Well, I reckon you are about all out of patience wondering what a boy like me is doing calling hisself Sarah and writing you with handwriting so like a girl's. Well, wait jest a minute more because I'm getting to that part.

I suppose I owe it all to the papists. There sure are a whole mess of 'em here in N'awlins, and most of 'em residing in the

Frenchy Quarter. A couple years back, they built themselves three entire new churches in that part of town. Well, I heard tell Our Lady of Perpetural Sorrows would feed the poor, and none bein' so poor as me and since I hadn't had a bite to eat for nearly two days, I saunters my way down to the Frenchy Quarter. It were a summertime sabbath morning. I never been inside a Catholick church and I didn't figger on spending so much time on my knees. I was beginning to wonder when that perpeturally sorry lady would make an appearance and start feeding us poor folk when all of a sudden this priest feller in skirts commenced ringing a bell and eve'body in the place gets up off their knees quick enough and marches up to a little fence they got inside the church, right up front. Then this fancy-dressed priest pours hisself about the biggest cup of wine I ever seen and I'm wonderin is he going to share it or drink it all hisself.

One by one each of them Catholicks dropped to they knees, turned up they faces, and opened up they mouths like baby birds waitin' fer worms. My turn at the little fence came soon enough and I dropped to my knees like I been a Catholick all my life. The Frenchy priest looked down at me and muttered something or other and it wasn't even in the French language, but I closed my eyes and opened my mouth. Durned if he didn't drop a insignificant crust of bread on my tongue which I chewed and swallowed even though it was dry and dint particularly taste much. Naturally, I opened my mouth for more.

"Move along, my child," says this priest to me.

"Well, sir," I say perlite as I can, "I'm still hungry."

"Well I ain't a-feeding you," he says, "I'm a-blessing you."

"Priest," says I, "ef this is a blessing, then I'd ruther have a curse as it would likely leave a better taste in my mouth."

He made to push me away and I think I took a swing at him. I'm not all that sure what happened next because I fainted dead away from hunger right there at the little fence. I know I didn't get any more bread. The next thing I do know is I'm flat on my back out in the middle of some dusty road in the Frenchy Quarter at high noon, and I'm lookin' up at the prettiest angel I ever did see. She was lookin' down at me and the sun was behind her head, all halo-like.

"Ma'am," I inquired perlite as I could, because the Catholicks had jest showed me how ornery they could be if a feller wasn't perlite enough, "Are you Our Lady come to feed me?" She jest tosses her head back and laughs.

"I may feed you, boy," she says, "but first you come with me out of that awful hot sun."

I was surprised to see that Our Lady was a quadroon beauty, tall, long of limb with skin the color of creamed-up coffee. I let her lead me across the road and through a pretty little wooden gate set into a row of nicely trimmed hedges and we come into a well-kept garden. A nice breeze springs up, so cool and fresh and sweet to smell on account of all the flowers. Of a sudden, I remembered my manners and tip my hat and out spills all my scruffy long hair down over my face and shoulders which I think is gonna put her off, me being such a bum.

She laughs about the loveliest, deepest, richest laugh I ever did hear and says: "Better and better," and smiles a smile like to break my heart she is so lovely. "Young man, you want to earn yourself a dixie?"

Well, that settled it for me: she was not Our Lady, for I had never met a Catholick willing to part with a nickel, let alone one of the famous ten-dollar notes writ on the back of them in French with the word "dix."

"Ma'am," I said to this beautiful woman, "I will do whatever it is you want for jest a little bit of supper being as how I haven't et a bite for nearly a week now."

She jest clucks her tongue and marches me into the house attached to the garden, and I find myself inside a cozy kitchen presided over by a fat, smiling Creole cook.

"Bon Mambo, please fix this boy a hot breakfast right away. I'll go fetch Madame Violet. She's going to like this one. Boy, my name is Miss Rosie, so how do you get called?"

"Elexander, Miss Rosie," I says, Elexander being a name that has served me well in the past. Then I add for good measure: "Elexander George Phillip Blodgett."

"Fine then, Elexander George Phillip Blodgett, you eat your fill and I'll be back with good news by the time you're done." And with that, Miss Rosie sweeps out of the kitchen through a fancy beaded curtain, leaving me alone with Bon Mambo who has already begun to crack a couple of eggs and turn up the flame under a pot of greens. Now in case you don't know, a Mambo is a lady priest of the voodoo people, whose priests ain't nothin' like the Frenchy Catholick priest I near brained over the street at Our Lady of Perpetural Sorrows. I heard tell that Mambos could turn you into a zombie ef'n they wanted to, and you'd have to do everything they tell you to. Bon Mambo set a plate of eggs and greens down in front of me, and I fell to it like a dog.

"Mistah Elexander," she says to me while I devours the victuals, "you ain't really no Elexander and if you stay in this house much longer, you ain't gonna be no mistah either. But they's good news for you, too."

Now, the short hairs on my neck were standing on end but I kept silent and went right on eating. It's best not to innerupt Mambo ladies who are tellin' your fortune so she kept on a-tellin' mine:

"Come tomorrow mornin', you gonna be not one but two dixies richer than you are right now. An' you gonna give Bon

Mambo one o' them two dixies as tribute, and fo' me keepin' you alive with these here eggs and greens."

"Yes, ma'am, Miss Bon Mambo, ma'am" says I, for her greens were perfectly greasy and mighty tasty and besides I had no wish to be zombified. "Soon as I get me two dixies, I'm giving one of 'em to you."

This was the rightest thing I coulda said, for she smiled real big and added some awfully good spoon bread and syrup to my plate and I fell back to breaking my fast. Bon Mambo and I had ourselves an understanding.

"Don't you be wasting all my profits on every rag-tail scalawag what sets down in this kitchen, Bon Mambo." And with that, the beaded curtain swooshes open and in marches the Madame of the house, followed close on her heels by my quadroon angel. Where Miss Rosie is tall and thin and long of limb, Madame Violet is short and stout and about as stubby a woman as I ever seen.

"Stand up, boy, and let's have a look at you," says Madame Violet. So, I do.

"Turn around." I do that as well.

"Take off your shirt and trousers." I don't do *that.*

"Boy, this is not the sort of house to be shy in."

I am at a loss for words, which as you know I am not often.

"Go ahead, Elexander," says Miss Rosie. "We seen it all before."

I finish chewin' the bite of spoon bread that's in my mouth, and look over to Bon Mambo who gives me a wink and a nod. So, I shrug my shoulders and in no time, I'm standing in this kitchen in my underwears.

"See, what'd I tell you, Madame Vi? Jest what the Major's been asking for: right size, right face, even the right hair. Ain't he perfect?"

"I wouldn't call him perfect," says the Madame, "and it depends how good he'll look in a dress."

The power of speech having returned to me, I reply: "Madame Violet, I look durned fetching in a dress, my hair cleans up real good, but I'm afraid nuthin' can be done for this pug ugly face of mine." All three women laugh out loud, and Madame Violet looks at me a lot closer then, pretty near to like a butcher who's inspectin' a not-too-rancid side of bacon.

"So you like to wear dresses," she says, "but did you ever lay down with a man before?" Well, it all fell in place for me right then and there what they wanted from me and what I'd most likely be doing to earn myself that dixie or two.

"My pap brought me to his bed more than oncet or twice, ma'am," I told her, "but layin' there was all I did. Ef'n you mean did a man ever love me and did I ever love a man right back, then yes'm, I have and I find it to my liking. Might I put my shirt and trousers back on now?" Did I ever tell you that about my pap, Tom? I don't think I ever did. I don't talk about those times all that much because when I do, I pretty near always start in crying which is what I started to do right there in the kitchen all over my greens.

Miss Rosie leans down next to my chair and wraps her long arms around me and squeezes and squeezes. When she'd done with that, I get myself dressed and set back down to eatin' and this madam lays out exactly what I am to do, with whom I am to do it, and what words to say while I'm a-doin' it. She has plenty of time to tell me all the details because I am eating a great deal of Bon Mambo's delicious greens and spoon bread.

What followed then was pretty near a day full of bathing and dressing and girl lessons. Pretty near every one of the wild women in that house took a whack at gettin' me ready. They fussed all over me like I was they little sister gettin' ready for her debyootant ball which in a way was what I was. One of 'em curled my hair all up, and I ain't never felt any thing softer against my neck 'cept once I spent a night with a cranky old tomcat who liked to suck on my ear. One of 'em sprayed me in parfum all the way from France, every part of me except my feet and my toes which they left all road-dusty and I'm sorry to say a bit ripe to the nose, but they explained that the Major perferred odoriferous feet. Next, a tall handsome nigger showed up. He is the piano player and barber of the house by the name of Perfesser, and he shaved me with a straight razor but he didn't stop at my neck.

By this time, I am feeling mighty fine. I am surrounded on all sides by scanty-clad women and they are touching me, stroking me, poking me and sponging me and soon enough, a part of me has come to attention. A skinny little thing named French Annie says: "Sugar-boy, you want me to take care of that little soldier of yours?"

"Miss French Annie," I replied, "I would be most obliged."

But instead of what I expected her to do, she flicks me across that very tender part of me with just one finger, and down I go to half-mast again and they bust out laughing all over again.

"You remember that move. It may come in handy some day."

They were pretty much all generous and good-natured like that. I was a bit embarrassed. Not shy, I wasn't shy. I was embarrassed I couldn't pay them for all the work they were doing making me pretty and presentable. Madame Violet was giving me just one dixie for the whole night. Looked like Bon Mambo wasn't that much of a fortune-teller, for with no second dixie, I couldn't pay her tribute. But ef'n I did good enough tonight, and this Major who was from Massychoosets liked me and all, well I could move into the house. I'd be a regular, and I could work there and get the same pay as the other girls.

That's what she said: "the other girls," like I might could be one of 'em. I didn't mind much the idea of lying down with the Major. Boys and men can be just as lovely as the ladies ef'n you're lyin' in their arms.

By now we was getting down to the finishing touches. Little French Annie places her palms just over my nippies and pushes 'em one toward the other, giving me little boobies. And while she's holding my new boobies in place like that, another of the girls applies a sticking plaster and some minutes later, I am the proud bearer of a fine set of womanly bosoms which shook like the real thing especially when I laughed. But then, they commenced to apply feminine underwear to me and this was truly torture. Tom, I have beared up with ticks and chiggers and fleas and skeeters. I have braved snakes and even once't I faced down a mad fox was fixin' to bite me. But I have never come to grips with any thing so diabolical as the womanly torture of hooks and eyelets. Hunnerts of them on one little piece of skimpy underwear and they helped me hook each and every one of 'em. I always been most comfortable with niggers, and these girls were just another kind of nigger so we all got along.

By now it is evening time and all the girls and women are in their finest frippery and Tom, I am one of them, waitin' down in the parlor, flirting with all the gentlemen callers. Miss Rosie, my tall quadroon, crooks her little finger at me and that is my signal to meet my Major in the parlor. He is the attashay to General Butler hisself! Taking the Major's arm like I was teached, I wait while he counts out the cash into Madame Violet's hands. Only then do I let him escort me up the stairs.

"What's your name, lovely lady?" he asks of me.

"Miss Sarah Elizabeth Amy Potterfield Grangerford, suh," I reply. "Of the Jackson, Mississippi Potterfields and Grangerfords of course."

"Do I detect a hint of Southern aristocracy, Miss Grangerford?"

And here, I lifts my chin into the air and squints my eyes at him like he was a bug, just like Madame Violet teached me and I say, "Major, Suh, there is no Southern belle as aristocratic as I and I will thank you to remember your place as the crude barbarian invader that you are." The fine Massychoosetts Major writ them words, not me, and now he turns all red and commences to sweat like a plow-horse. Did I mention the Major is easy on the eye? Well, he is. We reached the top of the stairs and we were standing in front of our room for the night, and the Major gives me a wink of his eye that makes me blush like a girl.

Inside the room, I remember the words I am 'spected to say, and I start saying them. I call him all sorts of worm and coward.

"You ain't even fit to lick my toes."

"Oh, Mistress Grangerford, ma'am," says he, "I am, I am fit to lick your toes."

"Oh, no, you ain't, you catawumptious weasel," says I just the way I been schooled.

"Oh, yes I am. Allow me to prove it to you."

"Oh, no, you ain't, you gritless varmint and if you push me one step further, I'm gonna whoop you with this here cow-hide like the monkey you are."

Now I should tell you that women in N'awlins are not in any way permitted to call Union soldiers monkeys, nor are they to spit on 'em in the streets, much as they may want to, for otherwise they are to be taken as common whores and subject to their whims and all this by the order of the boss general of my very own Major, General Butler hisself!

But here I am, calling this Yankee officer a monkey and then

I hawk a fine gob of spit right down into his face. Well, you woulda thought I'd fed the man a spoonful of sweet potato pie the way he slobbered it up. This was gettin' to be fun. Then I whoop him. I whoop him really good, and once I done that, I tell him:

"Now lick up my toes you chatterin' monkey. Clean up these here Southern belle toes of mine, you Yankee scum." I made that one up myself, and he seemed to like it. "Go on, use that ill-bred tongue of yours."

He goes down on his knees, and I'm afraid his smeller is gonna get more than he bargained for. But no sooner do I finish this thought when I feel that bristly moustache and his warm tongue of his working their way over my toesies. He pauses right there and looks up at me, and I'm afraid he's got himself some misgivings.

"Miss Sarah Grangerford," he gasps, "Your feet are the most delicate flowers of the South," and he falls to further lickings and suckings for the better part of half an hour. I have learned myself a good lesson and that would be that beauty is in the eye of the one payin' for yer services.

Then, just like the madam said he would, he starts workin on my ankles with that prickly, tickly moustache of his. I am biting my lip as I dasn't laugh; but then his moustache is ticklin' the calf of my leg; and next the back of my knees. Seemed like I'd die if I couldn't laugh, and all the time I'm tryin' *not* to laugh, he's shoutin' things like, "Long Live King Cotton," and "Ulysses S. Grant is the Devil incarnate!" and "I believe in States' rights!" which is the signal for me to pull his head up between my legs and say:

"Use that mouth of yours to show me how sorry you are for despoiling our gentile South with your oafish manners," which I say, but as I'm pullin' his head up, that troublesome moustache of his tickles me where I can't stand it one moment longer and I bust out laughing. And he's lookin' up at me, all astonished and then he busts out laughing hisself! But he takes me into his mouth anyways and I didn't know you could do that so good and be laughing at the same time, but that's what he's doin'. He's doin' it so good that pretty soon I stop laughing and commence in gasping. And then I'm not gasping but I'm jest cryin' out: "Oh, oh, oh! Oh! Oh! Ohhhhhh!" And without thinking and without being teached by Madame Violet, I ask him does he want me up between his legs with my mouth on him.

"Girl," he says to me real soft like, "I can think of nothing I would cherish more." No one's ever talked to me like that before. He ackshully used the word "cherish" and it wasn't 'til then I noticed what a nice smile the Major has. We spend the better part of the night wrapped up in each other's arms and legs and tongues and other parts.

The way he's treating me I think to myself maybe just tonight I am a little bit of a woman.

He has to get back to his barracks before the bugles blow revelly, so he gets outta bed just before dawn. I pretend to keep on sleeping, so's I can enjoy watchin' what he's like when he's not acting out the words he writ for us to use the night before. He gently tucks something in between my bosoms, which by now have come partly unstuck one from t'other, and then he walks out the door, pulling it closed real quiet behind him. I just watch the door through half-closed eyes fer maybe ten minutes. Then I remember to reach in between my bosoms to see what he left me. He had tipped me another dixie. Bon Mambo was gonna get her tribute after all.

Well, my Massychoosetts Major is uncommon fond of me, and I of him, so I been staying here at Madame Violet's since that night. A true adventuress, that's me. The war is over and he has told me he is returning to Massychoosetts where he has a wife and four chil'ren, the oldest is my age near exactly. But the city has been filling up with carpetbaggers and scalawags for some months now, and with the war over, it is sure to fill up more. So, there's gonna be a whole new crop of men who are gonna want to buy themselves some evenings with girls like me. I got nowhere in particular to go, and besides I sort of like it here.

Bon Mambo is ringin' the dinner bell, and I am uncommon fond of her cooking so I'm gonna close up this letter now. Write me a letter when you get a chance to, will you? It would be so very good to hear how you're getting along. Or better yet, come to N'awlins and allow me to show off our lovely city to you. That would be ever so much better. Jest make your way to the Frenchy Quarter and remember if you please to not ask for Huckleberry Finn. But you ask any kind stranger where is Sassy Sarah, and they will lead you right to my door.

Fondly,
(your) Sassy

THAT'S WHAT LITTLE GIRLS ARE MADE OF

Toni Amato

She likes it best when I shave her first. Not just because she is a good girl, and a clean girl, but because she wants as much of her Daddy's attention as she can get. She's a good girl and I love her dearly, so it's easy enough to give her what she wants. Once she's earned it.

She likes it best when I shave her, first, and sometimes she even asks for it nicely. Not just because she is a clean girl, and a good girl, but because she can't get enough of asking me to do that, to shave her. And I make her say the whole damn thing, with a pretty please on top.

"Daddy, will you pretty please shave my pussy after I get it all ready for you?"

She asks all sweet and big eyed and one hand on the crotch of my pants, where I keep her best surprise of all. And when she is good like that, and sweet like that, I take out my shaving kit and set up everything carefully and slowly so that she can see it. I sing to her while I set things up, because she is such a sweet and special girl.

"You're the end of the rainbow, my pot of gold," I sing to her as I lay out the heavy pewter shaving mug she gave me for Father's Day and the brush I bought for myself. "You're Daddy's little girl, to have and hold." She likes it best of all when I sing as I set up all the bright, shiny things I'll use to shave her, and I like to watch the way her eyes follow the cool smooth ivory handle of my vintage straight razor. They don't make them like that anymore, and she knows it. And I know she'd like to say it bothers her, just a little, that the handle is real and actual ivory, just like she'd like to say it bothers her, just a little, that the strop I'll use to sharpen the razor is made of leather, extra long and extra heavy, just like her grandpa would have used. The bristles on the brush are from a badger, and that bothers her a little, too. She likes the way they prickle her, though, just beneath the warm, silky smoothness of her favorite lather. The soap I'll use tonight is not my usual bay rum and bergamot, but ginger and orange scented, special made, because she loves Shirley Temples and I like it when she tastes sweet. The handle of the shaving brush is smooth, rounded wood. She likes the way it warms up in my hand, and I like the way she looks like a little velveteen rabbit, with it sticking out of her ass. She loves bunnies, my sweet little girl, just the way she loves all the animals, and that's why the bristles and the strop and the handle of the razor make her a little sad.

I could be a mean Daddy and tease her about how much she loves the bristles and the strop and the razor. But I don't. Because I love them too, because they show their age and because they are real things that don't break easily, just like the velveteen rabbit. Just like her. Bonafide. Made of skin and bone and bristle. I tell her that. I tell her that as I fill a white porcelain basin with steaming water and carry it over to where she has been sitting, very good and very still, on the edge of the bed, waiting for her Daddy.

I set the basin on a small table, beside a clean, white washcloth and towel, a pump bottle of lube, one latex glove and a gold coin condom. Everything is clean and bright and arranged just so, the way I know she likes it to be. And I wonder if she remembers the cool, professional precision of other bright and shiny things. I am careful and deliberate with her, my precious girl. I place one hand just below the hem of her skirt. "Now lift your skirt up over your knees for Daddy," I tell her, and as she obeys, I lower her panties to her ankles. When her panties are down, I tell her to lean back on the bed and to spread her knees wide apart for me. She used to be too shy to let me lower her panties with the lights on, too shy to let me shave between her pretty, dimpled knees. She is still shy, now, and I can see her struggle, but she's a good girl and she wants to make me happy. She spreads her knees and I pull up a stool, next to the table with the strop and the brush and the razor and basin. She spreads her knees and only hesitates for a moment when I tell her to spread her lips so that I can see what she has made and kept all ready for me.

She does that for me, getting ready. Less often, now that she has healed up, and now that she can take all of her Daddy. But still once or twice a week. I bought her a special set of dilators in her very favorite colors so she could always feel pretty. Four soft pastels, all in their own special pouch.

"But Daddy," she asks, even as her hands are doing as she has been told, "won't that be naughty?" She knows how to be good, when she wants to be, and she knows how to be naughty, when I need her to be, and that, I tell her, is how I know that she is my best little girl, made of sugar and spice and everything nice.

"Such a pretty girl," I whisper to her as I lean forward just close enough to blow a kiss and her thighs begin to tremble. "Such a sweet and special girl, all ready for Daddy to make her clean and smooth. Are you ready for Daddy to make you all clean and smooth?"

"Yes, Daddy. Please."

I gently lift her hands and place them at her sides. The water in the basin is still steaming and the brush makes a soft swishing sound as I work up lather for her. I work quickly so the lather will be thick and warm. I would never use foam from a can on my girl. When the brush touches her skin she jumps just a little and so I slap her thigh and tell her to lie still. She whimpers quietly, but does her best.

"Such a good girl," I tell her, and carefully brush lather across every inch of her pussy. With a swirling motion, I make soft peaks in the lather before I push the bristles gently between her lips and over her clit. She jumps again and I have to tell her, once more, to lie still. Better to practice now, I tell her, when the only thing next to her pretty little pussy is a soft brush. Better to get all her jumpiness out before the sharp shiny thing gets there. She sighs and I can see all the tension go out of her, starting at her shoulders and moving across her rounded belly and into her thighs. Her legs part just the barest bit wider and now I know that she is really and completely all mine.

The first long, slow stroke of the razor leaves a swath of pink skin. Her hair here is like corn silk and eiderdown, made soft where mine has become coarse and thick. We are marvels of change, my sweet girl and I, miracles of longing and intent. The second and the third passes of the blade leave only a narrow strip of lather down her center. I stop, then, to run my tongue along the edges of her mound. She is slippery and wet and she tastes like heaven. Her hips rise just the tiniest bit and I decide to be lenient. I blow more cool kisses on her hot skin before I place the edge of the razor to her slit.

This is the part that scares her the most, now, when all the cool steel sharpness is once again so close to all that is new and tender and freshly exposed. This is when she goes as still and quiet as a frightened rabbit, when she struggles the most to stay open and trusting for me, and this is when I love her the most, so sweet and willing and a little afraid. But she knows that I am a nice Daddy and that I know how much time she has spent being hurt and afraid. We are miracles of courage, my sweet girl and I, marvels of survival and strength. She knows that she is my special girl and that all I want to do is make her feel well loved.

The last of the lather is gone, finally, and I gently wash her clean with a cotton cloth.

"Now wasn't Daddy nice to you," I ask her, as I place the wide palm of my hand flat against her and hold it there so she can feel the heat. I press against her, first easy and light, then firmer and harder so that almost all my weight is balanced there. She's not a big girl, and my weight pushes her deeper into the bed.

"Yes, Daddy," she says. "Thank you, Daddy." The cool smooth of her shaved pussy against my palm is slick and delicious and I cannot wait any longer.

"Sit up, now," I tell her. "Sit up and do something nice for Daddy."

She knows, my good girl, exactly what I mean. She knows I need for her to be a little naughty. For her to unbutton my trousers and reach in for my cock. What she doesn't know is that tonight I have a new one, just for her. A new one in the same color as what she has used to make and keep herself ready.

"Oh, Daddy!" she says before she can stop herself, "what a pretty cock you have!" And then she flushes. She knows better than to call her Daddy, or any part of him, pretty. She knows how to say *handsome*, and *good looking*, and even *manly*, but this time she just couldn't help it. I knew she wouldn't be able to. And I am not a mean Daddy, but sometimes I do like to punish her. She knows this, too, and she knows she has been set up and she tries very hard not to pout and not to get herself into more trouble. I grab her ankles and use them to flip her onto her back, then spin her like a top, her head now hanging just off the edge of the bed.

"If you can't talk nicely, maybe you shouldn't talk at all," I tell her and step forward, the crown of my cock bobbing just above her lips. They part more easily than her thighs had. She's good at giving head, my girl, and she is eager to make me happy with her again. As she swirls her tongue along the ridge of my cock, I put on the glove and a dab of lube. I slide one and then two fingers slowly into her so that I can feel the deep groan in her throat.

"That's my good girl, sucking on my cock. Show me how good you can be, sweet girl, and maybe I'll fuck that tight little pussy of yours." I pump my fingers knuckle deep and turn my wrist in half circles so that she can feel me everywhere, inside, as she tightens her throat muscles around my cock. With her tongue, she presses me hard up against her palate while I push in and out of her. Slurping and sucking noises fill the air, and I am close to coming when I pull my cock out from between her swollen lips. She looks up into my eyes, tears brimming just at the edges of her own. My fingers are lightly strumming her clit, my thumb just resting on the edge of her need.

I push her back onto the bed and lift her knees, resting her ankles on my shoulders. My cock hangs long and heavy and glistening between us and she knows, now, that the time has come to ask nicely again. It's time to be the best little girl she knows how to be. I wait, with my hands against the back of her thighs and the head of my cock against her opening.

"Daddy, will you fuck my pussy?" she asks me, eyes locked to mine. Sugar and spice, and everything nice, that's what my little girl is made of. She reaches for the foil-wrapped condom and smiles sweetly, willingly and just a little bit naughtily as she rolls the latex over the head of my cock. "Pretty please?"

SEA OF CORTEZ

Sandra McDonald

The war is the best thing that ever happened to most of the guys on your ship—a wild storm of global upheaval that flung them out of the flat, dull prairies or gritty coal mines of Appalachia and dropped them right here, stranded on a floating oasis of two thousand men in the South Pacific, a goodly amount of them shirtless at any given time. Certainly the war's the best thing that ever happened to you. If it weren't for the Japs, you'd be freezing your toes off back in Iowa City, working in your dad's shoe store. Instead you're lying on this wool blanket on this steel deck, and Robbie Coleman's head is pillowed on your bare stomach. The sky is canary blue and cloudless, the sun smiling directly above the gun turrets.

"What are you thinking about?" Robbie asks, his voice low and lazy.

You're thinking that Paradise is the dozens of men paired up around you, smoking or dozing or reading dog-eared magazines. Most are bare chested, some are stripped down to shorts and some are casually buck-naked: acres of skin, tight and tattooed and smooth and hairy. The blue-green sea glitters to the horizon in all directions with no trace of land. One day the war will end and all this will vanish like a mirage. All the handsome men will return to where they came from. You will measure old ladies' feet and lace up winter boots on little kids trying to kick you. You'll live at home, the bachelor son. Once in a while you'll go out of town for a secret tryst, but your parents will never meet your lovers and you will die alone, lonely, unfulfilled, longing for the pretty boys of war.

"I'm not thinking about anything," you say.

Robbie arches his arm and pinches your thigh. Not hard enough to sting. "Liar, pants on fire."

He's told you before that you think too much. Which is silly, since he's the educated one, three months of college in his hometown of San Diego before he decided to drop out and enlist. He's read every book on the ship at least twice, and that includes two plays by Shakespeare. You hated every minute of high school and never met a book you didn't want to bury under stale gym socks at the bottom of your locker.

It's not that you think too much, it's that you can peer through time. You look at the ship and can see it in the Philadelphia shipyards, a frame accumulating pipes and wires and bulkheads, a vast investment of labor and material. You also see it rusting away on the bottom of the ocean, a habitat for fish and plants and ghosts. The beginning and the end of most things is yours if you concentrate hard enough. Two ends of a pole, like the ones track athletes use for vaulting. You see Robbie, who like you is nineteen years old, and simultaneously picture him also as a baby sucking on his mother's teat and a bald husk of a man in a hospital bed. He's surrounded by his kids and grandkids. He dies peacefully, quietly.

But right now he's alive and questioning so you murmur, "I'm thinking about the movie tonight."

"I'm on watch," he says. "Besides, we've seen it."

Everyone has seen it. A soldier goes to a cantina looking for love and eventually Carmen Miranda sashays around with pineapples and bananas on her head. It's the strangest musical you've ever seen. You knew already Robbie would find a reason not to go. On the last movie night you sat in the back, holding hands, little kisses of soft lips and raspy stubble, with the ship's officers just a few rows ahead, not noticing or pretending not to notice. Hands sliding beneath waistbands. Tongues between soft lips, hands grasping heat and hardness. Nothing the two of you haven't done before.

Later, though, you saw him clutching a photo of his girlfriend Nancy as reverently as a Catholic holds a rosary. Nancy, who is eighteen and honey haired, her penmanship round and blue on perfumed paper. Nancy with her pert nose and bright eyes and a smile so wide you could fall right in and drown in sweetness.

She's cute and all, but if you were a woman—and here's an area you definitely do not think about very often, a boarded-up hurricane cellar of cobwebs, rat droppings, and rusty nails that lead to tetanus—if you'd been born a girl, you wouldn't be sitting around in California writing love notes to your sailor boyfriend. You'd be working in a steel plant or shipyard, doing your part for the war. On weekends you would wear blouses the color of freshly churned butter, and ride a bicycle so that air flutters up under your skirt, and sleep in short cotton nightgowns with lace on the cuffs and neckline. You would keep your hope chest stocked and organized until the man of your dreams proposed with a gold ring and a long-stemmed red rose.

In the photograph that Robbie treasures most, he and Nancy are sitting on a beach blanket, laughing, his left arm casual around her shoulder, her head tilted toward him. Nancy's bathing suit has wide white straps and cones that make her breasts point out like cannons. He says they were visiting the Sea of Cortez. You think that's in Europe somewhere. Wasn't Cortez an explorer, like Columbus? If you ask, you'll sound like a dumb hick. You do know that Robbie thinks a lot about what Nancy would say about him kissing you, what his momma would think, what the chaplain would admonish over the rims of his square black glasses.

What exists between you is nothing unexpected on a floating prison of men who sleep, shit and work together twenty four hours a day for months without relief.

Or so you tell yourself.

It's not love. It can't be love. Robbie can only love women.

Here's what happens: a boatswain's mate named Williams has a fight with his buddy Lee, who is a cook, apparently because Lee has been spending time with two radiomen, Easton and DeRosa. Everyone calls them Fruit Salad or the Two Fruits, but not when officers can hear. A tolerant captain will look the other way but the fleet admiral has eyes everywhere and he won't hesitate to discharge a man for being homosexual. You've heard of sailors sent to psychiatric evaluation or imprisoned in the brig. They get kicked out with what looks like an honorable rating but is coded on blue paper, so that the Veterans Administration will deny benefits. Anyway, Williams and Lee broke up over Lee's too-obvious affinity with Fruit Salad. Williams isn't homosexual, or so he says. He's got a wife and two kids to prove it. But he needs a pal to blow off steam with, and he decides that pal should be you.

He's big in the shoulders, with anchor tattoos on both biceps and a thick corded neck, narrow waist and dark, slick hair. He has a dangerous look to him. He's the kind of man who might throw you overboard if you crossed him, or at least teach you a lesson in a filthy alley. You like that he's fierce. He asks around and finds out that you don't like books, so the first gift he gets you is an almost-new issue of a Hollywood tabloid.

"I'm done reading it," he says, brushing your fingers as he hands it over.

The next gift is a little flask of whiskey that tastes vile but gives you a warm glow on an otherwise bad day of combat drills and foul weather.

The third gift is a backrub late one night in the ammunition room, you standing upright against the bulkhead with your right cheek pressed against the cool metal and your arms splayed as if you are under arrest. His large, calloused hands dig into the tight muscles of your shoulders, blossoms of pain-relief-pleasure. In the secret hurricane cellar of your brain, you imagine yourself wearing a blue silk dress, sheer silk hosiery, a lace bra, black high-heeled pumps. You're a lady reporter come to do a *Life* magazine article about the war and he's lured you down here, is moving his hands down your hips, is thumbing his way into your secret passage. If you were wearing pearls, he'd pull them cool and firm against your throat, or slip them one by one inside you like exquisite gifts.

"Baby," he breathes. "Baby pie."

Which is maybe the dumbest endearment you've ever heard but you take it, you will take anything you can get. You know that people see what's happening. People always see. Robbie is a boatswain's mate like Williams and there's no way he can be oblivious. You want him to object, get mad, claim you, but he writes daily letters to Nancy and reads his Bible so much that the binding cracks open. You share cigarettes and go to the mess together and he slings his arm across your shoulders in the same familiar way, but if he's bothered about Williams, he's keeping it completely to himself.

Meanwhile there's a war to fight. You man the 16-inch guns. You fire at Manila, Panay, Leyte, Cebu; places you've never heard of back when you were failing geography in tenth grade. The roar of the weapons leaves your head ringing and makes your hands shake. The Japs dive out of the sky in suicide attacks. The antiaircraft guns shoot and shoot and shoot, ships sink on the horizon, you can't sleep, you can't eat, and Williams is the one who pulls you into tiny spaces, gets you to your knees, tugs on your ears, stuffs your mouth. There's no sweet kissing. This is not like cuddling on the deck under the blazing sun. He teaches you how to take him, his tattoos moving like snakes in the dim light, and he leaves you sore and addicted and craving more.

"Tell me what you want," he orders in the dark, but you can't even tell yourself the truth, how can you tell him? You want lace underwear that rides against your thighs, and a garter belt snug around your waist, and a bra to fill with breasts you'll never have. You want cherry-red lipstick and tiny bottles of perfume to spritz on your neck. You can see Williams home after the war, calling his wife "baby pie" as he nails her into a new white mattress in a four-poster bed. She will look like Robbie's girlfriend Nancy. She will swell with a new baby, a satisfied gleam in her eyes. You will eat your mother's meatloaf and listen to the radio with your father and go to bed with a pistol under your pillow, dreaming of the day you can shoot yourself in the head.

You lie and tell Williams that you want more whiskey. Any warm glow is a good one.

For three days, your ship is part of a task force attacking Japanese airfields. A dozen cruisers, battleships, carriers and destroyers assail Luzon. Their pilots dive out of the sky, trying to smash your decks and turrets. You can't even count how much metal is screeching across the sky. Your sense of the future starts to fail. Maybe the war will never end. It will simply stretch on forever, reeking of gunpowder and deafening with its monstrous noise, the sea tossing you up and down with angry swells.

There's a reason they don't let women out here, you think. To witness destruction is to take it in, like inhaling poison, and once inside you it can never be expelled. Your strictly imaginary womb aches for the babies who will never be born because their fathers have been wiped away from the planet by steel and fire. But eventually this battle does end, and you crawl into Robbie's rack because you're too tired to climb into your own. He finds you there a half hour later, roughly shakes your shoulder.

"It's not big enough for two," he says, even though men are double-racked all around you. Some are weeping with relief and being comforted, with small words and soft gestures, by their buddies. They have seen too much.

"Let me sleep," you plead.

Annoyed, he hauls you out. You land on your knees on the deck.

"Sleep alone," he says.

You go find Williams. He's upright, exhausted, his face dark with stubble, a cigarette burning unnoticed in his hand. He's talking to one of the Two Fruits. When he sees you, his face gets all tight. You think he doesn't want to be seen with you. But then he pushes you into his rack and crawls in right after you, an impossibly tight fit, his body crushing yours. You want to be crushed. You want to be held immobile and safe, a woman safe in the arms of her man.

"Close your eyes, baby pie," he says roughly.

The next morning, the seas are so rough that cooking is limited on the mess deck. You don't mind, because just looking at food exacerbates your growing seasickness. As you sip bad coffee you hear the ship's latest scandal. One of the officers found pornography and women's underwear in the boatswains' locker and there's going to be hell to pay. It's not regular pornography but "perverted" stuff—men posed in women's lingerie, men with fake breasts, men in long slinky dresses. Your face burns because you want to see it.

"The captain threw it all overboard," you hear Robbie say. "Rotten filth."

That afternoon a typhoon blasts through the task force, an unannounced guest at an already terrible party. Planes slide off carriers or smash into bulkheads. Three destroyers capsize and sink to the bottom of the Pacific. Your ship rolls so dangerously to starboard and port and starboard and port that men scream for fear you're about to go right down alongside the destroyers. This is what terror really is: knowing in your heart that you will drown entombed in metal, seawater rushing in to flood and trap and smother you. It will hurt. You will scream, but that will just let more water invade you. You will convulse and choke and scrabble for help that never comes. Then your body will hang suspended in dark cold water forever, a watery grave from which no one is ever rescued.

Eight hundred men die in the storm, every death frantic and painful.

You live. You're safe, you don't drown, you emerge onto the deck to a gray windy sky with the typhoon extinguished. The captain orders a shipwide muster and head count. Three sailors are missing and presumed to have washed overboard in the confusion of the night. The youngest is BM3 Robert Allen Soward, of San Diego, California.

You don't believe it—not when your chief tells you, not when the captain confirms it, not when everyone in your corner of berthing slaps your shoulder and tells you they're sorry. The sea is too big, the waves too choppy, the ship is almost out of fuel. There is no chance of recovery.

"But I've seen him," you tell them. "He dies as an old man, surrounded by his kids. I can see it right now. He's in a bed, and they're surrounding him."

Eventually the ship's doctor gives you some little white pills, makes you sleep twelve hours in the infirmary and sends you back to work.

Grief is a sword. It splits your spinal cord from head to toe, making you unsteady on your feet. You walk into bulkheads and trip over hatches. Grief is also a knife. It slices through your brain and makes you forget he's dead. You think you see him in the mess, in the showers, on deck when the sun breaks through. It's a finely honed razor that leaves a million tiny cuts on your hands and face. They sting when you touch his locker or turn your face into the pillow you stole from his rack.

When did your vision fail? What can you trust, if not the inner sight that points you to the inevitable future?

You decide that he's still out there in the water, swimming his way back to Nancy and sunny California. He will be rescued by a passing ship, swaddled in blankets, reunited with his one true love. He will die old and beloved, not cold and abandoned to the ocean.

This fantasy helps in only the smallest possible way.

It's the beginning of 1945. The Japanese are not yet exhausted enough or horrified enough to surrender. You still have Williams, but he still has a wife and he has secrets, too. He gets packages in the mail but opens them in private. He barters tobacco and chewing gum and candy but won't show you all of the bounty he earns in return. Every morning when you wake you see your bleak, gray future unfolding in Iowa City. You think, sometimes, that it would be easier to drop off the side of the ship and sink into darkness, let the whales and sharks and fish finish you off. Cortez explored the sea and so will you, your every cell scattered by tide and swell.

But then the ship puts in for repairs at Ulithi, an atoll with crystal clear lagoons and gorgeous long beaches and sunsets like blood oranges. There are beer parties and midnight movies and a lot of men sneaking off into the jungle for some private R & R. Williams takes you to a cove where the ocean washes in and out just a few feet away. He spreads a blanket on the sand and crawls all over you and takes you apart inch by inch. You participate as required, thinking of Robbie adrift on currents and calling for your help. His hands and voice grow rougher.

"I don't know what you want," he says.

You don't know, either.

More ships pull into port. The Seabees finish up a big rec center on Mogmog Island and there's a rumor that Bob Hope will be flying in next month with a USO army of singers and dancers. In the meantime, the Morale Committee is organizing a musical revue. Every ship will provide volunteers to do skits and numbers. The Two Fruits are first to sign up. They ask you to perform as well.

"Why me?" you ask.

DeRosa says, "Gets your mind off things."

"I can't sing."

Easton says, "It's a chorus. You can just mouth the words and let the stronger singers carry it."

You ask Williams if you should do it, but he has no opinion on the matter. Maybe he's losing interest in you. You saw him talking to his old buddy Lee the other day, Lee with the thick blond hair and bright blue eyes. You're disposable. Maybe you deserve to be disposed of. You tell Easton and DeRosa that you'll volunteer but when you get to practice you realize they left out the crucial detail that the entire show is in drag—grass skirts, coconut-shell breasts, wigs, makeup.

"Absolutely not," you say, and try to flee.

The Two Fruits grab your arms and turn you back. "It's just for fun. No one cares."

The other chorus members from your ship are a laundryman, a barber, a corpsman, a chaplain's assistant, a radarman and three yeomen. They know how to put on makeup. They argue about the costumes. Too late you realize that every single one is homosexual and you're probably going to be branded as one, too, but what does it matter? The world is ending in fire and Robbie is floating in the Pacific and Williams wants to put his hand down someone else's pants. This might be the only time in your life that you will get to dance on stage for the hundreds of drunk and cheering men. You certainly won't get cheered back in Iowa City.

"I want the blond wig," you tell them. "I want pink lipstick and a seashell necklace."

The night of the revue brings high winds that rock the Chinese lanterns strung outside. The lagoon is full of ships riding the high tide. Somewhere out there, the admiral and his captains are eating dinner in a wardroom full of brandy and cigars. In the auditorium, rowdy sailors drink beer and hooch, cheering for each act. The "Andrews Sisters" are three Seabees with pretty good voices. "Marlene Dietrich" has to retreat from an ardent fan who storms the stage. You're in the chorus for "Carmen Miranda" but she's late for her entrance. You and the others swing your four-foot-long wooden bananas and do the best you can, given that you're a little drunk and a lot worried that Williams will see you from the audience and walk away in disgust.

Robbie would have walked away. You know that.

But for these few glorious minutes you can forget Robbie. You can pretend you are the woman denied to you by biology. You are radiant and alluring and the men are cheering. They shine desire on you, they lust after your lithe legs and firm breasts, they are on their feet clapping—

Then you realize they're clapping for Carmen, who arrives like a Hollywood movie star. She's glorious. Six feet tall, black skirt, black top, bare midriff, bananas and oranges on her head, singing about how happy and gay she feels. She hasn't been to rehearsal all week long so you don't know who she really is. All you know is that you feel inadequate and small. Reduced to a sham, a weak imitation, while she struts and sings, and what kind of imposter are you?

Then she turns, and you see the anchor tattoos on her forearms.

The roar of the crowd becomes a sea of blood draining out of your head. Your vision dims to shadows. You make the fastest exit in the history of South Pacific musical theatre and a stagehand puts you on a chair before you faint entirely.

Ten minutes later, Williams exits to thunderous applause. He kicks off his shoes and tutti-frutti hat and stands before you as if waiting for you to strike him. You pull him outside, down a path, away from every prying eye. The full moon slips out from behind cloud and bathes you both in white light.

"You're insane," you tell him.

"I'm crazy," he agrees.

This time you're the one who drives him backward, you're the one who pins him against a tree trunk. He wriggles against you gladly. You suck on his lips and neck and leave your lipstick on his bare skin.

"Carmen got appendicitis," he mutters. "I owed Lee a favor."

Which is a good story if you believe it. In the moonlight of a tropical island, you're not too worried about the details. You're kissing him and he's pushing you to the ground and your costumes are coming off, your grass skirt a bed to lie down on.

This is wartime, this is the best and worst thing that has ever happened to you, these are his hands on your hips, this is the body you must live in, and in the morning you realize you can't see the future anymore. Your gift is gone, if it ever was a gift at all.

All you see before you is shimmering blue, the unexplored Sea of Cortez.

THE PERFECT GENTLEMAN

Andrea Zanin

She probably wouldn't ever have fucked me if anybody else had been available. But y'know, sometimes, "available" is hard to come by, and it was awfully cold out, and we were both more than a bit out of place in a small town in Northern Ontario. In any case, I sure wasn't about to complain.

My Nonna had just passed away—old age; she had a long life. Her parents had come across from Italy decades ago, found their place amongst the other Italian immigrants and French Canadians who populated the tiny silver mining town of Cobalt. And populate they did; most families had ten, twelve kids at least. She gave birth to three babies—my dad Leo, my uncle Giovanni and my aunt Rosa—and decided that was plenty. When the village priest came by, leaned over the garden fence and told her it was about time she had another baby, she told him exactly where to stuff it, and he never tried that again. That was the kind of lady my Nonna was.

She had been a hairdresser for most of her life, used to cut our hair when we spent a couple of weeks in the summer there. Every year my hair got shorter, until there wasn't much for her to cut when I visited, but she never made a fuss about it, just winked at me and said, "It's all those brothers you've got. Such a tomboy you are." And then she'd slip me a five dollar bill and pat me on the hand and say, "You go buy yourself some candy." So even though my dad just frowned and went silent, and my blue-blooded mom nearly had a conniption fit, I knew Nonna wouldn't mind when I showed up for her funeral in a dark suit instead of a dress. I felt like I could see her winking at me in the sunbeam that streamed through the church windows during the ceremony. I could almost hear her saying, "What's all the fuss about?" Besides, I did look awfully dashing, if I do say so myself.

I had never really fit in with my family. We tolerate each other well enough, but I left for university in Toronto four years ago, when I was eighteen, and found my way into the big-city urban dyke community not long after that. That's where I started listening to the Lesbians on Ecstasy and turned vegetarian and met the women who showed me how to get a suit jacket to fit properly despite my breasts—oh, the irony of perky 38Ds on a baby butch! I always did envy the flat-chested girls. Don't get me wrong, though, I have a healthy appreciation for the curve of a pair of beautiful big boobs under a tight sweater. I just wanted them on other people, not on me.

Speaking of big boobs, that's kinda where this story really begins.

After Nonna's funeral and the reception at her place that afternoon—endless gooey homemade brownies and baby carrots, endless relatives asking if I was married yet, endless vaguely disapproving comments about how much I looked like my brothers—I needed to escape from my family for a little while. So I took a walk in the sharply cold evening air of late autumn to what passes for downtown in a place that only has one traffic light. And lo and behold, what did I see but a vegan café.

A vegan café? In Cobalt? Well, times were a-changing.

I stepped in and instantly felt the warm air hit my chilled cheeks. My glasses promptly steamed up and my nose started running. Once I'd honked into a tissue from my pocket—still a bit soggy from the afternoon's emotions—I noticed the smell of homemade lentil soup and baked bread, layered over the scent of herbal tea and a touch of incense. The place had "lesbian" written all over it. I felt right at home.

I ordered a bowl of soup at the counter and then sat down in a creaky, threadbare velvet chair near a small table. I noticed a rack of magazines for sale on the wall nearby—*Adbusters*, *Bitch*, *Canadian Living*, *Macleans*. The juxtaposition made me grin.

"Kinda funny to see those all in the same row, isn't it?" said a deep, velvety voice near my ear. I jumped so high I knocked my glasses clean off my nose, and instantly the world went fuzzy.

"Oh, sorry, I didn't mean to startle you!" said the voice. "Let me get those for you."

My glasses were promptly handed back to me, and when I put them on, the first thing I saw was cleavage—deep, generous, tawny cleavage, to which a red sweater clung desperately. My eyes would have done the same, but instead I forced myself to meet the gaze of the gal to whom the cleavage was attached. Far be it for me to objectify a woman. I've taken my Feminist Theory 101.

What I saw next surprised me more than a vegan café in Cobalt or *Bitch*-meets-*Macleans*. It was no wonder I'd seen the cleavage first; the woman was well over six feet tall. And she was stunning: broad shoulders, narrow hips, legs that went on forever under a pair of slim black pants. Her face was all angles and lines—strong jaw, cheekbones that could cut ice, lips carved out in crimson (which, I noticed, was exactly the same shade as her sweater), a proud nose, all softened by a shoulder-length blonde hairdo with flatteringly placed highlights. I found myself blushing, and it wasn't from the warmth of the radiator.

"Mind if I join you?" she said, clearly amused, as she pulled up a chair without waiting for me to answer. "It's not often you see people like you in these parts. My name is Crystal. What brings you into town?"

I did mention that I'd taken Feminist Theory 101, right? Well, I also took a few other classes. And I must say I'm way more into Kate Bornstein than Janice Raymond, if you know what I mean. And I totally get that your gender is about what's in your head and not what is, or no longer is, in your pants. And I've read my Joan Nestle and my Leslie Feinberg too; I may be young, but I can recognize and respect a femme when I see one, regardless of the box that's checked on her birth certificate. But you know, all the reading in the world doesn't help when you're struck with an intense desire to nuzzle your face into the fragrant cavern between someone's breasts and then, maybe, lick your way south from there and...and, well, when you don't know how to do all that without saying the wrong thing and messing it all up.

So I decided it was best to let her do the talking.

She was probably about ten years older than me, and taking care of her aging uncle for a couple of weeks in New Liskeard, the next town over, as he recovered from gallbladder surgery.

"He doesn't really accept me, but I'm between jobs and nobody else in my family could make the trip, so he's keeping his nasty comments to himself," she said ruefully.

It was a test. I'm no expert at this, but at twenty-two I've navigated my way into bed with three women so far—well, two and a half, since that straight girl from my cousin's wedding last year chickened out partway through—and I've flirted with plenty more, and I can tell when someone's trying to gauge whether or not I'm safe.

"Is he at least getting your name right?" I ventured.

"Mostly," she answered with a slow nod, holding my gaze thoughtfully. "I correct him when he slips up. He doesn't apologize, but he seems to be trying, at least a little bit."

She gave me a small smile. I think I passed.

"Where are you staying while you're in town?" she asked.

I rolled my eyes and told her about the air mattress on the living room floor at my Nonna's tiny house, with my parents snoring through the wall in the master bedroom and my brothers playing video games in the basement until the wee hours. "Not exactly a great place to...uh, to bring someone," I said, my eyes dropping to the swell of her cleavage again and then darting back up with a pang of guilt. I felt the blush creep up my neck again.

Her little smile turned into a wide grin, and she laughed out loud, tossing her head back.

"Well, since we've apparently got the same thing in mind, why don't you come with me for a bit," she said.

With my heart beating too fast and my palms sweating, I paid for my soup and her pastry. I held her jacket for her to slip into. I held the door for her as we walked back out into the cold. I was trying my darnedest to be the suavest, sweetest, sexiest butch in town. It wasn't hard; there weren't exactly a lot of us to pick from. But listen, I'm not stupid. I know that under normal circumstances, a gorgeous older woman like her wouldn't look at a kid like me twice on the street, but this wasn't normal circumstances. We were both out of place, both relieved to not be the only ones, both hankering for a better way to spend the night than avoiding awkward conversations with our families. I was being handed a chance, and all I had to do was not fuck it up.

She took me to her car and drove us to the Silverland Motel just up the street. The clerk was too sleepy to do much more than grunt and hand her a room key.

And then we were alone, and I was terrified. What if I did something wrong? What if I touched her in a way that wasn't cool? Would it be okay to cup those gorgeous breasts in my hands, or would that make her feel like I was some stupid guy with a fetish for implants? I knew how to deal with girls, but she was a woman and not exactly your average woman either. Would she want me to get into her pants? Would she want me to leave her alone down there? Would I know how to make her come? Would I hurt her by accident? Would I need lube? Shit, I didn't have lube with me—the gloves I normally kept stashed in my coat pocket for just such an occasion were chosen with self-lubricating cunts in mind. Would she...

She interrupted my panicked inner monologue by tilting my chin up and bringing her mouth down to meet mine. My heart leapt in my chest and I kissed her back. Her lips were soft, aggressive, wet, hungry. I tasted herbal tea and a hint of raspberry pastry filling on her tongue, caught her bottom lip gently between my teeth and let it go, let the scent of her hair climb up my nose and into my brain, and all of a sudden I wasn't thinking anymore and we were just kissing.

Eventually we dropped our jackets on the floor and our bodies greeted the complaining old mattress. She pulled me on top of her and my breasts, flattened under a tight sports bra, pressed into hers. I opened my mouth and said, "I'm not sure I know...I mean, I've never really been with...well..."

A frown creased her forehead. I was going in the wrong direction, I could tell. I took a deep breath and let it out.

"Tell me what you like," I said simply, letting the end of the sentence trail upward, a soft question. Vulnerable. *See me*, I was thinking. *I so very much want to do this right. I know how women like you have been treated. Just let me be different. I want to be the one-night stand you don't regret. I want to be the perfect gentleman for you. That's what you deserve.*

And so she told me what she liked. She peeled off her red sweater, unhooked her black lace bra, pulled my eager face into the delicious space between her breasts. She told me just how hard to suckle on her dark, stiff nipples and, just when I was thinking I could do that forever and die a happy dyke, she told me just how softly to press into her super-sensitive clit with my thigh. She told me how to bite her neck in just that right spot, how to lazily trail my fingertip around the edges of her belly button. Eventually she stopped talking, and she simply took what she wanted from me. She clamped her thighs around me and gripped my wrist and guided my fingers beneath the waistband of her black lace panties—which, I couldn't help but notice, were a perfect match with her bra—and moved my hand exactly the way she wanted it, and she wrapped her other arm around my back and buried her forehead in my collarbone and then something gave way and she made a sweet sound and her body shook under mine, and I held her, and I kept holding her until she relaxed and curled into me like a kitten, all softness and silky strength.

We must have stayed that way for an hour or more. She breathed rhythmically, her spectacular breasts rising and falling, but I couldn't sleep. My arm went numb under her shoulders and I wouldn't move it for fear of disturbing her rest. Eventually she stirred and opened her eyes.

She looked at me. "What about you?" she asked quietly. "What do you like?"

My mouth went suddenly dry, and I had no idea what to say.

She looked thoughtful for a moment. "Let me find out," she said, and grinned, just like she had back at the café, and then she deftly flipped me onto my back.

She kissed me again, only this time she ran her hands over my chest while she did it. My chest, yes. Not my breasts. There was something about the way she touched me that made it clear that she was touching the body I felt I had rather than the one I actually had. There was no cupping, no squeezing together. None of that stuff that always made me feel like I had to tune out and wait for it to be over. Just a pressing and stroking and oh, my god, her hands felt so good. She unbuttoned my shirt and played with my nipples, one after the other, starting gently and pinching each one harder and harder, almost to the point of pain, before moving to the next and then back. My cunt swelled in response, my back arched, and I could feel my boxer briefs slowly soaking through. And then she started to whisper in my ear.

"Your cock," she said, "I can feel it getting so hard for me. I can see it through your pants, you're straining, you want me to take it in my mouth. Is that right? Do you want me to suck your cock for you?"

Her words were sending electric shocks down my spine. All I could do was moan. How did she know?

"I'll take the head in my mouth, I'll be careful not to use my teeth," she whispered. "I'll suck it slow; I'll let it fill my mouth and press on my tongue; I'll take it all the way back into my throat. I'll lick the shaft and I'll tug on your balls with my fingers and I'll let you fuck my mouth until you come. Is that what you want?"

She was unbuttoning my pants, unzipping my fly. And then she shifted down, and her warm, wet mouth was on me, and she was sucking my cock, and yes, it was my cock and not my clit, and as her head moved up and down I felt the tip of my cock press into her palate and rub against her tongue. And she moved faster, and drew me deep into her mouth, and spread her soft blonde hair over my hips and gripped my ass with her hands and I could feel her breasts squeezing into my thighs and my hips bucked as I desperately drove my hard cock into her mouth and as I came, I finally found my voice, and I was roaring like a bear and letting my jizz shoot into her throat and feeling her swallow it down.

When she felt me relax, she made a satisfied little "hmf" sound and moved back up to kiss me again. Then she rolled over, turned her back to me, and wiggled her little rump into my side. In moments she was softly snoring. And once again, I was wide awake as she rested, trying to process what had just happened. I know, I know, my friends always tell me I think too much.

I don't remember when I fell asleep, exactly, but I do remember awaking with a jolt when my cell phone beeped. It was three in the morning and the message was from my brother Dino. *Where R U?* it read. *WTF?* I texted back, *I'm OK. Hanging out w a friend, see U in the a.m.*

I slept again and had dreams about looking in the mirror and seeing a different face: a new version of me, one that was both frightening and familiar.

When I woke in the morning, my head was full and my belly was empty, and I could hear the shower going. In a moment it shut off, and Crystal stepped out of the bathroom, a towel wrapped around her like a short strapless dress, and another twisted around her hair. "Morning, sunshine," she said cheerfully. "Your turn in the bathroom. Then I'll drop you off at your grandmother's place."

My suit from yesterday's funeral was the only clothing I had. I felt awfully overdressed for a Saturday morning, but Crystal didn't seem to mind; she straightened my lapels and insisted that I tie my tie up just right, even if we were just going for a quick drive. I assented, too preoccupied to argue. Crystal was even more gorgeous in the daylight, but I felt a bit detached from things. I wasn't upset; I just kept replaying things in my head, wondering what it all meant.

A couple of blocks away from Nonna's house, we passed by the church where the funeral had taken place. I felt tears gather in my throat.

"Hey," said Crystal, sensing that something was wrong. "I'm sorry about your grandmother. Are you okay?"

"Yeah. I'm okay," I answered. And y'know, I was. I could almost see my Nonna winking at me in the morning sunbeams that streamed through the car window as we turned onto her street. I could almost hear her saying, "What's all the fuss about?"

Besides, I thought, looking down at my outfit, *I do look awfully dashing, if I do say so myself.*

PAYBACK'S A BITCH

S. Bear Bergman

You're all dressed up, still. She's just a little more dressed up than you are, like she so often is. Girls with four older brothers rarely get to indulge their dress-up fantasies as children, it turns out, so when an opportunity arises she takes a bath and then shines up. By now, when you hear her open the tap on the bathtub you get started ironing a shirt.

Tonight it was a dinner in honor of someone she works with having won an award for something hardly anyone understands; you in velvet pants that made the gay boy at the store stammer when you tried them on and her in a long skirt with a high slit and tall boots, your favorite. You're back at her office afterward, because she needs to pick something up and you follow her up there, the tall, dark office building reflecting something out of your porn star fantasies, and of course you have a plan. Of course, you have a big idea about how this is going to play out.

Up in the elevator, you admire her ass in the long skirt and free her hair from her coat and act like you're five kinds of good intention in nicely polished loafers. You're going to escort her to her office, yes you are. Good boyfriend, maybe a better boyfriend because you weren't born a boy and never learned how to disdain a woman's fears on one hand and feed them with the other. But then again, there you are with your cock hard in your pocket and a plan born in the pages of *Hustler* playing behind your eyes, so maybe you're not so far from your factory-direct brethren after all. Eighth floor. Everybody off.

She walks to her office and you follow, maybe a little close, maybe your breath stirring the short hairs on the back of her neck. She flicks the light on in her office and you reach out and trap her hand with yours on the wall, flick the light back off, grab her and pull her close to you, your hands full of her fine ass and your voice in her ear saying, "C'mon, now, baby, I know you want it." You chew on her neck and hold on to her tight, mutter all manner of dirty things in her ears, telling her how you like it when she struggles and that the smell of her sweat turns you on. You tell her she'll never get away from you; tell her you know she really doesn't want to, grind your hard-on into her and say, "Look what I've got for you, baby girl." You grab her hand and make her hold on to it until she knows how big a cock you're packing.

She groans. She slides to her knees, pliant and generous as a really good wine, and you run your fingers through her hair, admire the curve of her neck as she dips her head to rub her soft cheek over your bulge. You shiver when you feel the heat of her breath against your skin, through your pants. Before you quite know what's happening you're leaning back against the desk in her office, velvet pants around your furry ankles, getting a champion blow job from your girlfriend. If the lights were on you'd be able to see the smears of her lipstick around your cock, concentric circles of passion and carelessness. You can see, just barely, that her mascara is starting to run from taking your cock all the way into her throat, and you like that. You like it a lot.

In your secret heart you wish there were a coworker or a member of the maintenance staff around to interrupt, someone to see you starring in your first big-boy porn movie moment—tie flapping and belling as you pound your hard cock into the willing mouth of this brilliant girl, who is on her knees for you; on her knees in her own office, ruining her makeup on your cock. This is a beautiful moment, and you would love to be caught in this act, almost more than you hope nobody comes along.

The two of you find a rhythm, both easy and hard, speeding up and slowing down, you watching her gag on the thickness of it and feeling your cock jump in response. You grab her throat, hold her away from it, encourage her to cut off her own air to get to your cock, to show you how much she likes it and you almost come all over her face watching her work: mouth open, tongue out, eyes closed, reaching for you. You wish you could come, just like this, all over her face, the perfect ending to this hetero-style silhouette enacted by two of the queerer people for three counties, wherever you are. Your head falls back a little bit. You gasp with how good it feels and grin when you feel her hands slide up the back of your thighs, palming your ass and using that grip to pull you closer, farther into her mouth, to take more of your cock in. You're distracted when her hands close around the back of your belt, so close to coming, so close to losing your load and you start talking to her about how much you want to come in her mouth.

Suddenly, there's a cool breeze where your warm girlfriend used to be. Suddenly, you're being tugged, then yanked around to face the desk, off balance and off kilter. Did you come? You're not sure. You're still distracted and throbbing when her small, cool hand grips the back of your neck, pushes you down, bends you over the desk. The surface is hard against your cheek, and you realize that your ass is in the air, nearly naked except for the harness. She spreads your cheeks with those small, cool hands and spits twice, telling you that an ass like that is enough to drive even a strong man crazy. In your brain you know that this is your girlfriend, she of the long skirt and blown mascara and fourteen varieties of herbal tea arranged alphabetically in the cupboard at home but at the moment your gut, not to mention the point of the gut's natural conclusion, is telling you that a bad man has hold of you, and hard.

You stiffen and try to turn around, to stand up, but she smacks your ass with something that hurts like hell, so you lie still again—maybe when she's distracted, you think, forgetting who you're talking about. She leans into you and tells you to lie still, that it'll hurt you less if you don't fight. She says, "G'head and try, pretty boy—your hole tightens up real sweet when you try to get away." You flush a bright, terrible red and feel your knees buckle while she works a dollop of cold grease into your asshole with two fingers, making you open up for it. It's too much all at once, and when you try to say something she smacks your ass again. It's your belt, you realize. She's hit you with your own belt. That bastard.

What's happening in your ass is delicious and terrible, beautiful and profane, and she is fucking you slow but hard, those glittering red fingernails somehow silent and safe in your body, opening you up. When you can't keep quiet any longer you let out a groan, and she growls, "Yeah, faggot?" and fucks you harder. It's like she's possessed, and whatever's got hold of her is more than big enough to take you, too. You start to push back, start to fuck back against her, and she holds the end of the belt around your throat like reins and giddyups right into your willing hole, filling you up with her hand, telling you you'd better move for her. She instructs you to stroke her hand with your tight hole, tells you that you look like a hustler hoping for a tip, and you dimly remember having thought the word *Hustler* earlier and know it was nothing like this. She's banging into you, taking up space in your body with her hand and in your brain with her words, talking you right up to the edge of coming for her bent over like this, spread out under her, open and wanting nothing more than your high-femme girlfriend who is apparently also your dirty faggot boyfriend, and you had no idea.

You feel the edge of your come and tell her how much you want to come for her. You start to whimper, start to say please, and when she says, "Beg me, cocksucker," you do with more sincerity than you could have imagined while she plows you just right and you come, hard, yelling, conquered and redeemed under her hands.

You both slide to the floor in a heap of sweat and lube and rumpled clothes, and you have just enough wherewithal to tear her panty hose with the edge of your ring and rip them open, sliding three fingers into her like the hammer of a gun slides home. You spare her nothing, pumping her in time with the throb and grin of your own asshole until she's whining and clawing at you, gasping and howling, and when you say, "Payback's a bitch, baby," she says, "Just you wait, faggot. Just you wait," and comes, screaming into your mouth while you kiss like lovers do.

FEMME FATIGUE

Anna Watson

I was having a "Wind Beneath His Wings" moment. Again. It had been that kind of book tour, where people just kept smiling right past me, eager to get next to Mitch. Here in this big Chicago bookstore, on this crisp fall evening, my charismatic and famous husband had just wrapped up another standing-room-only reading in front of an adoring crowd. He was now sitting comfortably near the front of the bookstore at a table piled with copies of his latest memoir, *Elemental*, signing books for his public. His tie was slightly loosened, his suit jacket draped over the back of his chair, and the dress shirt I'd ironed that afternoon was far from crisp, but even slightly mussed, he looked good to me, and every inch who he was: a god in the high holy pantheon of spokespeople for trans rights and visibility. He radiated confidence and wisdom and people couldn't get enough of him.

I retrieved a couple of extra pens that had rolled under the table and poured him another glass of water. I was straightening a pile of books when a little chippie of a femme brushed past me and gave him a very good look down the front of her dress as she leaned over to whisper her name in his ear. Mitch enjoyed the view, knowing I was watching, teasing me a little, then began to sign her book. The chippie's hopes had been raised, no doubt, by the piece Mitch read that evening about our own special brand of monogamy; how we sometimes branch out. I knew, however, that she was bound for disappointment, as Mitch had nothing more on his mind than a long soak in the hotel bathtub and an early night. It had been a grueling book tour, and Chicago was our last stop before heading home. I would go with him back to the hotel, of course, but I wasn't really tired, just bored.

Mitch is an incredible writer. Even if I've heard something of his over and over as he works on it, when he reads it in public, it can still make me cry. He is so caring of queers of every stripe, so generous with a world that seems determined to fuck us over, so wise as he navigates through his own journey, which turns into everyqueer's journey which turns into everyone's journey. I support his work with my whole heart and believe that his writing has, does, and will save lives. I already know that it has, in fact, from the kinds of mail he gets from high school students in particular. His writing is filled with honesty and love as he writes about his childhood as a queer, abused kid; how he got from there to here, to the healthy, proud transman that he is; and he just keeps changing lives and hearts and minds and the guy should get the fucking Nobel Peace Prize, in my opinion.

I am proud of my husband, and almost all of the time, I am totally okay being in the background, keeping the home fires burning, being there to bounce ideas off of, hear endless versions of the same piece, cook nourishing, tasty meals, walk the dog and feed the cats, take care of the food shopping, make sure he takes his vitamins, keep up to date on any medical issues for transguys, keep the social calendar, iron his shirts and pick out his ties, hem his trousers and throw out his boxers when the elastic goes. I am almost always totally okay with being the odd girl out at the events he gets invited to, where, I understand, people of course want to get to know him, get his opinion on things, hear what he has to say and find healing in his presence. He and I laugh about it, sometimes, when people struggle with how exactly to include me; me, who obviously knows nothing about what it means to be born in the wrong body and to have to walk that road. I actually have a few things to say about that, but in general, I am almost always totally okay with not being a very big part of that conversation because I so completely believe in what Mitch does, so completely love his work, and, for heaven's sake, I fucking love the guy.

The day we got married absolutely was the happiest day of my life, and really, I am usually totally okay with being Mrs. Mitch. The whole femme thing, well, you know, I have a job I really love being a nanny, I have my book club and my quilting group, and Mitch and I have our real friends (as opposed to the sycophants who tend to flock around him), who know me and see me and love me, so what's a little invisibility when it's all in the service of a greater visibility for transfolk? I'm almost always okay with it. Except sometimes.

That night in Chicago, that night I was getting more and more irritated with the ho-hum looks people got on their faces when Mitch introduced me as his wife, all eyes snapping immediately back to His Nibs, the Touter of Trans, the High Scribe of Holy Sex Change—that night, someone was noticing me. And about the time I noticed her noticing me, she was beside me, holding out a plastic cup of warm white wine like she was offering me a chilled flute of champagne.

"Drink?"

I don't usually, but I took it from her and wet my lips without hesitation. She watched me sip.

"I like your husband's book," she said, nodding her head in Mitch's direction. We were over by the magazine rack, where I'd been hoping to have a quick flip through a couple of DIY glossies. I followed her gaze and caught Mitch's eye. He took in the situation and raised one eyebrow. *Yes,* I thought. *I think definitely yes. It's been a long time, and I'm a little out of practice, but I'd like to go—please, honey?* He nodded, winked his "go ahead" wink, and went back to scrawling out his name and answering earnest questions. I saw that the chippie had more than satisfactorily taken my place as personal assistant to the writer: she had put together a little plate of munchies and was carefully topping off his glass of ice water. Fine, she could have the job. I was off duty for the rest of the evening.

My admirer's name was Per, short for Persephone, another butch victim of cute and unusual baby girl names. We strolled around the bookstore, stopping here and there to browse, but really just checking each other out and offering up relevant bits of personal information. Adopted from Cambodia by her lesbian moms, one of whom transitioned when she was a teenager just coming into her own queer sexuality, she told me cheerfully that she had plenty of identity issues.

"Momdad's over there," she said, gesturing toward a shy, nerdy-looking older guy standing in line to get his book signed. He was also holding a couple of comics and a "Star Trek" magazine. "He's the one who told me to check out Mitch's blog."

Per had immediately related to Mitch's eloquent exploration of the ins and outs of coming home to your own particular place in the queer spectrum, and was, in fact, here tonight doing research for her thesis. She was a grad student in anthropology at the University of Chicago, and she made me laugh with her stories of the old-school professors who weren't quite up to speed with the hermeneutics of gender theory and the straight students who were desperate to be her friend because she was so "interesting."

By now we were in the deserted kids' book section, sitting close together on a miniature couch shaped like a fire truck. I put my hand on her sleeve and asked her to tell me more about her thesis. I was still in my supportive role, still bolstering up the man (or in this case, the butch). I knew I was supposed to be off duty, but I couldn't seem to help myself.

"Oh, maybe later," she said, smiling. "What about you?"

When I thought about it later, I realized that that was when the evening got really hot. That's when Per stopped being a simple distraction from my usual life and became something a lot more important. I used to have this self-help book called *Brief Encounters* that talked about how sometimes even the most fleeting contact with certain people can do for you what years of therapy cannot. Per was right there, fully present, looking at me, waiting. She was adorable in her version of metro modern, her hair mussed, wearing low-slung jeans with a wide belt, a plaid shirt with the tail hanging out and what were probably her momdad's scuffed old '80s Doc Martens. She was waiting for me to reveal myself to her, but better than that, she already saw me—saw me as a person of my own. It would have been understandable if she thought she already knew some things about me, since Mitch had read a long section that evening about our relationship, and he is so good at describing our marriage, making pithy insights about two people in love who have weathered a lot. I totally would have understood if Per had thought that Mitch's take on me (published in several books and a daily part of his blog entries) is really who I am. But the way she was looking at me made me think, *No, she really wants to hear it from me. It's me she's interested in, not the me on the page.* And I told her. I told her about my job, where I take care of three-year-old twins, and how all the other nannies and mommies at the playground think I'm straight and it can drive me crazy 'cause I hate not being seen as queer, but somehow coming out all the time when you're dealing with potty training and boo-boos and lost lovies just recedes in importance. I used to be such a fierce femme when I was in my twenties and me and Mitch were such a prominent butch/femme couple about town being all polyamorous and doing play parties, and then Mitch transitioned and we got married and there was all of that to sort through. Now he's working so hard writing and doing advocacy stuff and so when he wants to relax it's mostly watching some BBC drama about World War I where we both drool over the costumes and hairstyles and it's really cozy and not fraught with Identity Issues like the rest of his life and I really am just mostly cozy, like cozy has become my sexuality almost, because, really, aren't we more than who we fuck? Aren't your thirties a good time to explore those other areas? A lot of the people I hang out with now are straight, like the women in my quilting group—straight and a lot older than me and more concerned with material and patterns than anything else, and, I don't know, things get lost in the shuffle. I don't know if they're getting lost or if they're becoming integrated with all the other stuff, but all I know now is that sitting with Per on that tiny fire truck, my queer femme whipped up into tornado strength, and she just closed her eyes, relaxed, and let herself be sucked into the maelstrom.

As I talked, we leaned closer together. I pulled my foot out of my pump and traced the stitching on that old Doc she was wearing. I saw her admire my pedi, I saw her run her gaze up my calf and I could feel it like it was her hand, rasping over my panty hose. How can a femme walk out in the world and have people know she's queer when she looks to most people like she's just a regular straight girl? It's like I have a storehouse of queer energy somewhere in my belly, and it runs out—it runs out all the time. Mitch does what he can, but he's got so many of his own complicated feelings about queer and straight and man and woman—things aren't as straightforward with him as they were before he transitioned (although, as it turned out, they weren't even straightforward then, we just didn't exactly know it). Per queered me. She sparked my queer energy until I was flaming like the queer northern lights, and even if I'd suddenly been transplanted to the wilds of Alaska where no one knew me and the three other people who lived there were straight, they would have known that I'm so queer it's a force of nature. It was sexy as hell. Just when I thought we were maybe going to do it, right there under the watchful eyes of *Where the Wild Things Are* and *King and King*, Per put her hands on my upper arms and kind of pressed me down into the cushion. "Is your monogamy thing he writes about true?" she asked. I loved her all over again for asking, for not taking Mitch's word about me.

I leaned against her, breasts to breasts. I could smell her hair pomade and a hint of musky excitement. I nodded against her neck, and she let go of my shoulders to pull me closer.

"Let's go."

We walked to a girl bar near the bookstore, and Per's old-fashioned manners—opening doors, walking on the curb side—contrasted deliciously with her appearance. I expect these courtesies, but when Mitch performs them, as he does without fail, he does so as a man, as my husband, and that's what most people see, and poof, I'm gone. With Per, there was no question that my presence is a queer one in this world, and I felt so bolstered that I almost appreciated the few glares we got, which Per countered with an even more protective stance toward me and a glare of her own. At the bar, we slipped right into the pool of the anything-goes crowd: ultrafemmed-out girls fixing each other's outfits and feeling each other up, the bois and their Daddies, sporty girls dancing energetically, dykes in jeans and button-down shirts checking out their reflections in the mirror, middle-aged lesbians in work clothes sitting quietly holding hands. No one blinked or even for a moment questioned our right to be there, and I got off on it, that warm sea of women thing, caught that wave and dirty danced with Per like a wanton hussy.

As we were taking a break with long, tall seltzers in hand (I was done drinking booze, and Per kept right up with me), a few folks came up to say hi, and while I thought I saw a flicker of recognition in the eyes of a couple of them, they didn't ask about Mitch. For them, I was just another femme ensnared by their handsome friend for the evening, a queer among queers getting ready, without doubt, to go do unspeakably queer things in bed.

In the bathroom, I stood in front of the mirror reapplying lipstick and trying to do something with my hair, which had come undone from its chignon and was flying every which way. I used to always travel with a few emergency items in my purse—hair spray, clean panties, an extra toothbrush—but really, it had been a long time, so that all I had in there was a few tissues and a folded-up flyer for Mitch's reading. Never mind. I pulled out the hairpins and let my hair have its own way. I smiled at my reflection. I was glowing.

When I got back to our table, Per asked me if I was hungry, if maybe I wanted to check out a diner she and her friends really liked. In fact, there was a bunch of people heading over there now, if that sounded good to me at all. I'd been fantasizing about being naked with Per for hours, but when she named a couple of the women I'd met earlier in the evening, I found myself wanting to hang out with them more.

"That sounds great," I said, and Per looked relieved, probably having worried that I'd be put off by the suggestion, think she wasn't interested anymore. While the rest of the crowd was gathering itself, she moved her chair closer and stroked my cheek, moving my hair back out of my face, and kissed me for the first time that night, a sweet, slow, just-a-hint-of-tongue kiss that melted me completely.

Per's slow, sweet seduction continued at the diner, where the big flamboyant crowd of us took over, making the regulars grumble and shift on their stools and the straight college kids gawk, especially when one of the group, fresh from a drag king contest at another bar, got up and performed his whole routine for us using the sugar shaker as a microphone.

After we ate, Per and I left the rest to their coffee and went outside into the chilly air. Per's apartment wasn't far from the diner, but the neighborhood changed dramatically in just a few blocks, from lots of light and people to sedate, almost-suburban rows of houses with big trees and not very many streetlamps. Per held me tightly as we walked, and I could feel her protectiveness amp up. She told me there had been a queer bashing a few weeks ago, and now the whole neighborhood was on alert.

"See?" she said, pointing to a house that had a small rainbow sticker in the window. "That means it's a safe house and you can go there if you're scared or need help. We have a whole neighborhood watch thing going on, too."

I turned all shy when we got inside her place, and I could tell Per was feeling a little awkward, too. She rose to the occasion, though, clearing books and papers off of the tiny living room floor, where, she said, she studied best, then lowering the lights and putting on a little Al Green. She took my purse and my wrap, placing them carefully on a table teetering with more piles of books and papers, then wrapped me in her arms again and we danced through three songs until my knees were too unsteady to keep upright, undone by her kisses, her body pressed against mine, and the sexy ooh-baby vibe of the music.

"Where...?" I whispered, and she led me into another tiny room, almost entirely taken up by a futon. The sheets and blankets were tangled together and the room smelled slightly stuffy. I tumbled onto her, stretched out over her, grinding myself against the seam of her jeans, gasping as she rose to meet me. We kissed and rolled, giggling as she tried to get my skirt off and I squirmed away.

"You," I said, and obediently she skinned off her shirt, exposing a muscle tee. She wasn't wearing a bra and her breasts were small handfuls, dark nipples showing through the white cotton. I was all over them before she had a chance to take off the shirt, tasting laundry detergent and a hint of sweat as I mouthed the soft flesh. She arched and moaned, a hand on her belt buckle, which I began undoing without abandoning her breasts. She helped me get her jeans off and then her boxers, flopping back unselfconsciously, arms over her head, hands pressing against the wall. She smiled up at me happily. I reached down to cup her pussy, dusted with a sparse crop of silky hair, parting now at my touch, the lips slick and swollen. I lay propped up on one elbow beside her, still fully clothed, my mouth on her tits and my fingers dancing around her cunt as she sighed and moaned beneath me. I stayed on her tits for a long time, sucking them while she ran her fingers through my wild, flyaway hair, anchoring herself. Every time I came up for air, I noticed her legs were more widely splayed, and she got wetter and wetter. At last, I began kissing my way down her taut belly, moving the shirt out of the way so that it was askew on her chest, exposing her breasts, which I continued to work with both hands. When I reached her crotch, she shoved herself up to my mouth with such force that I bruised my lip, something I realized later, too turned on in the moment to notice anything other than how badly I wanted to eat her pussy and how badly she wanted me to.

Despite our mutual need, or maybe because of it, I went slowly. I savored her delicate aroma, sampled her taste with the most demur of licks. I covered her inner thighs with kisses; I reached down to massage her calves and slowly moved my hands back up to her hips. Her belly button seemed to require attention, and I gave it a thorough scouring with my tongue, allowing my breasts to fall against her pussy. She humped them tentatively, perhaps back to feeling a little shy, but obviously in need of some good, old-fashioned titty fucking. To accommodate her, I took a moment to slip out of my top, sitting up to let her get a look at my pink, lacy bra, before slipping out of that, too, and sinking my boobs right down on her cunt. I pressed my tits together, pressed against her, and let her slide all over them. My nipples were exquisitely tender by this point, and her wet pussy bumping against them felt fantastic. I didn't want her to come just yet, and she sounded close, so I rolled reluctantly away and sat up again. I am blessed with a big rack and can suck my own nipples, which definitely adds to an evening's entertainment. Per's pussy juice coated my tingling nipples now, and I lapped it off, pretending not to notice how closely she was watching me, her eyes wide and shiny with lust. She tried again, more feebly this time, to get my skirt off, but I just giggled, letting my breasts shimmy as I positioned myself between her legs again. This time, she was very docile, a very good girl, not pushing up so greedily, just letting her knees loll to either side, whimpering a little as I bent over her, inviting me in, giving it all up.

I buried my face into her, nose to chin. I slowly ran my tongue between her lips, flattening out when I came to her clit, exerting pressure. She was making really cute noises, little yips and gasps, her hands clutching the bedclothes on either side of her, her knees drawn up now, feet flat on the bed. The insides of her thighs were so sweet and soft, I took a break from my licking to get back to them, stroking first one, then the other, resting my cheek against her pussy, my nose full of the smell of her musk. I was thinking about how I would lick her until my tongue was exhausted, and then, when I knew her hole would be aching and ready, I would fuck her, see how many fingers she could take, how deep I could go, how many times she would come for me. Her thighs quivered as I stroked and she shifted her ass on the bed. I could feel every movement through the tender skin of my cheek and I made my own little noises of contentment and arousal. I reached around to the back of her knee to stroke her there, and she hissed with pleasure. She said my name.

Per dropped me off in the hotel lobby the next morning, early, on her way to the library to prepare for the class she should have been studying for last night. We had showered together after a brief, sticky sleep, and I knew the memory of her soap-slick body rubbing me up and down would be one to take out and linger over in the future. The whole evening was already feeling precious to me, restorative.

"I am under no illusions," Per murmured in my ear as we hugged good-bye. "I know you are a true and loving wife, which is, by the way, incredibly sexy, but if you ever need me, wherever I am, I will endeavor to be your girl in that particular port." Then she left me, hurrying to class, her hair still damp and her shirttail untucked.

Mitch was awake, the newspaper spread out over the bed, a breakfast tray from room service waiting for me.

"The coffee's really good," he said, pouring me a cup. I got all shy and just stood there for a moment. Mitch held out the cup.

"Now then, honey," he said in his deep morning voice. "You come and tell me all about it." I took the cup, holding it in both hands and letting the delicious steam wreathe my face. Today we would be going home, getting the dog out of the kennel, settling back in to our work and our routines. I mentally inventoried the contents of our freezer and decided to defrost some chicken thighs. Mitch chuckled.

"You're not getting out of telling me," he said, patting the bed beside him. "There was something special about this one, I think."

Right, as always, Mr. Observant. I sipped reverently at my brew as I regarded my husband, upright, expectant, bed headed. Oh, I would tell him, of course I would, because that was our arrangement. He would hear about the miniature couch shaped like a fire truck, the dirty dancing and the tiny room where I ate pussy for the first time in many years. For the first time, though, I found myself wanting to hold some things back; some personal things, like how Per made me feel when she was a girl for me, the way she coaxed my queer out of hiding. If I told Mitch all of those things, he wouldn't be able to stop himself from writing about them—I can hear him now protesting that this is the kind of information our queer people need to hear, but I don't care. He can talk about himself all he wants, even talk about our marriage, that's fine. But I am remembering what my grandmother says to me all the time: the man doesn't have to know everything, and he doesn't want to, not really. Keep a little something back, sweetheart, it adds to your allure. My grandmother is a wise woman, and I am thinking that I'll take her advice. Careful not to spill my coffee, I got in bed beside Mitch, snuggled up to my husband, took a deep breath and began.

SMALL BLUE THING

Julia Serano

Way back when, on many an occasion, I would get aroused, even to the point of orgasm, without my penis ever getting hard enough to properly perform penetration. And back when I considered myself a straight boy, I was embarrassed by this. And the women I dated—twentysomething het girls, trained since birth to burden male shame—tried to take the blame for my flaccidness, despite all my assurances that I was intensely attracted to them, that my lack of erection was not a reflection of them.

But by my late twenties, I had moved beyond missionary position vanilla sex. And I found myself with bisexual women who were into topping me while I played the femme role. And when their hands hiked up my skirt and began to flirt with the space between my legs, they didn't really care how hard I got, just as long as I was hot, squirming and breathing heavy.

But I did have one last fling with the whole penetration thing, and I shared it with the most kick-ass girl in the universe. For most of her adult life she considered herself a dyke, eight straight years of exclusively sleeping with women. And ironically, I first met her shortly after she had rediscovered her appreciation for men. She was trying the word *bisexual* on for size and, much to my surprise, I found myself ready, willing and able to rise to the occasion!

For about a month or two. Eventually, pretending to be a boy lost its novelty and I found myself once again imagining how wet my vagina was getting when I should have been entering her instead. And like I said, this girl was kick-ass and I didn't want to disappoint. So I did what any self-respecting semblance of a man would do: I set out to score some Viagra.

It was so easy to get! I just went to my doctor, told him I was impotent, and voilà—he wrote me a prescription, no questions asked; he didn't even take my temperature. But designer drugs don't come without a price, as I spent thirty bucks for three blue pills.

I wasted the first one on a necessary test run and it seemed to work just fine. So the second time I tried it with the kick-ass girl. After a date, we went back to her place and began to suck face, and before I knew it I had circled second base, and that's when the pills kicked in. And unlike most drugs I've taken, there was no buzz really, no giddiness or disorientation: just a reliable hard-on.

Afterward, I let the kick-ass girl in on my little secret and she thought it was hilarious. And my little blue pills became our little inside joke that no one else knew about, although I only refilled that prescription twice before we both got bored with straightforward sex and began to explore more sordid acts.

So here comes the happy ending: I married the kick-ass girl, transitioned to female, and we were together for ten years, living as lesbians. And on the rare occasion when one of us had a hankering for penetration sex, I no longer needed Viagra. I just used my strap-on.

THE VISIBLE WOMAN

Rachel K. Zall

I'm staring out the bus window and Natalie is taking off her clothes. Her long, slender fingers delicately work each button on her plaid flannel shirt through its hole, popping one button at a time out, slowly, patiently, inch by inch of skin revealing itself, and I've missed seeing this so much while she's been away. I wish she was here right now.

As I'm lost in that dream the bus bounces over a bump in the pavement where new asphalt was recently laid, and the bottle of wine I'm bringing home leaps out of my hands. "Shit!" I yelp, snatching at the air just above it as it continues on toward the floor. I can't get another one—I spent my last ten dollars on this one, a special treat for Natalie who'll be home when I get home, and who'll need cheering up after being dumped by her other girlfriend in Seattle.

Just as the bottle is about to crash, a hand with well-manicured nails and just a hint of black fuzz near the watch-band appears from nowhere and snatches it from the jaws of death. “Got it!” a deep, even voice intones.

As I take the bottle from him, I look up into the face of my hero. The first thing I notice are his eyes, so dark brown that they’re almost black to match his ever-so-slightly shaggy hair. He smiles and I smile back and thank him.

“No problem,” he says, righting himself and turning back to his book.

He’s dressed unusually well for this bus route: white business shirt, carefully ironed khakis and polished black shoes. He looks so out of place I can’t help but wonder if he’s knocking on doors to talk about his religion. Do I want him to be a missionary?

No. No, I think I’d rather he was a bright young staffer for a conservative politician. I want to be his dirty secret, the queer girl he knows he shouldn’t be around, the one he’s always trying to end things with, except every time she comes around and gives him that sexy little smirk he gets weak and sins again. The girl who shows up at the worst possible times, knocking on his door just because she saw his priest sitting on the living room couch. He’ll answer the door and try to shoo me away, unable to pull his eyes away from the shadow between my breasts, the little edge of lace poking out above my shirt. I’ll smile down at the outline of the stiffening cock inside his khakis and say, “You don’t want to go back and speak to the padre with that sticking out for all the world to see, now do you? Tell him you have to step out for a minute, and I’ll take care of that for you,” punctuating the word with a gentle tap on its rounded peak. He’ll hesitate, quivering with excitement, voice tangled in his throat, and then at last he’ll turn to look back up the hall and say in a hoarse voice, “Eh-excuse me for a moment, Father...”

I realize I’m staring just as he looks up from his book at me and I try to look away like I’m staring out the window. Stupid, stupid, god, he’ll think I’m a total creep now.

I look away just in time to see a pudgy man with greasy blond hair staring at my tits. He looks up and tries to cover: "Uh, I love your shirt, ma'am! What's the picture mean?" I get asked this question every time I wear my super-trans T-shirt—a red and yellow trans symbol on a blue background like a Superman T-shirt. I feel like I should just start handing out FAQs.

Q: What's the picture mean?

A: It's a transgender symbol.

Q: Yeah? What's a "transgender?"

A: It's an umbrella term that includes folks like transsexuals and cross-dressers and—

Q: So, like, men who become women? Like gay guys who've had the surgery so they can do it like women, right?

A: Uhh…kind of…um, I guess…

And for the first time he looks at my face in earnest, rather than just politely diverting his attention from my breasts, and something in his eyes changes and I can see the usual follow-up question condensing on his lips for a long moment before it finally emerges as he points at my chest.

Q: Those ain't real, are they?

A: No, you're imagining them.

He squints at me and puckers his lips skeptically, looking from my breasts to my face and back again. Then he turns to the dark-eyed man and taps him on the shoulder. Dark Eyes lifts his handsome face out of the book. The creep leans in close and stage-whispers, "Hey, man, hey…lookit that over there. You wouldn't do it with one of those, would ya?"

"Me? Oh, no, I'm straight."

That's the way it always is: no I'm straight, no I'm gay. Lesbians who only like cis women and trans men, or straight men afraid that touching me will mean they can't call themselves straight anymore. There's always only one meaning: whatever it is you are, I'm not into that. Natalie and I have an open relationship, but because she passes for cis and I don't, her end of the relationship tends to be more open than mine.

She swears the difference is that she's butch and I'm femme, and I'm what people expect to see when they see a transsexual woman. "Take my word for it," she teases, "we shave off all that pretty red hair and no one will ever read you as trans again." She's only messing with me when she says that, of course. She wouldn't say that if she thought I'd do it.

She's not afraid of not passing like I am either. I remember one time when some teenage boy leaned out the window of his car and shouted "Hey, trannies! Show me your cocks!" And I just wanted to sink into the bench we were sitting on and disappear, but Natalie rose to her feet, raised her middle finger and screamed, "GROW ONE!"

Coming home to her is a joy, coming home to her is a relief. She's fierce and fearless and tender and sweet, and with no family left after I came out, no hometown that I'm welcome in, my home is wherever she is. Home is the woman who knows I'm beautiful, the beautiful woman who loves me.

I walk through the door to find her waiting for me in the dark on the couch. All the windows are open and the air conditioner is off. The air is so thick you could reach out and pull off big, soft bites of it. Everything is electric; the sky is getting ready to open up and give us all relief. Three little white candles are lined up along the top of the television, and she's in the shadows just at the edge where the shivering light turns into darkness.

She's wearing jeans—how can she wear jeans in this weather?—and a white tank top, both stained and streaked with paint. *The Collected Poems of Pablo Neruda* and a tube of lubricant are on the floor by the sofa, neither of which was there this morning.

I set down the wine, cross the floor to where she is and curl into her, my head on her shoulder. I brush my fingers through her short, spiky hair and kiss her cheek. "No power?" I ask, though I knew the electricity was out as soon as I stepped off the bus. You can always tell when the electricity in our neighborhood is out, because all the people who never see or speak to one another spill out into the street all at once as if some invisible hand pulled a lever that raised one end of every floor in the neighborhood, dumping all of them out their front doors.

The Puerto Rican family next door had been having a party when the electrical fire started at the fast-food franchise around the corner from us. The parents are all leaning over the porch rails holding onto dripping beer bottles while their children run back and forth across the pavement, chattering excitedly and pointing at the fire trucks and police cars. The elderly man across the street who shakes his head and murmurs, "Homosexual sex freak," every time he sees me is ignoring the incident completely, standing in his front yard with his son staring up at the enormous American flag stretched across the front of his house, and not talking. The college students are downstairs smoking on the steps and debating whether to stay here and wait it out, or go to someone else's house and see if they can catch the end of the football game.

"No power," Natalie shrugs. "Hope you weren't planning to cook anything fancy for dinner." I think of the steak marinating in the fridge and wonder how well cold Spaghetti-O's go with merlot.

"Well, I'm glad you're home. I missed you a lot." I reach up and kiss her on the cheek. "I'm sorry things didn't go well out west."

She looks away. "It's fine. She's marrying some cis dude and they're going to be monogamous, and I'm sure she'll be very happy with a house and kids and whatever. She'll probably never say the word 'bisexual' out loud again." She runs her fingers idly through my hair and sighs. "Whatever, I don't really want to talk about it. I'm just happy to be home."

"Well, how do you want to spend your first night back? I had a steak and a Humphrey Bogart movie all ready for us, but I guess that's not happening."

"I appreciate the thought," she says. "But now it's all dark and we'll have to entertain ourselves some other way." She looks down at the floor. "Hey! Did you notice that there was conveniently placed lube by our feet?"

I laugh and kiss her cheek. "Babe, you are so corny."

"Oh, okay. Well, if fucking you silly is corny, I guess I could read you my thesis on Jackson Pollock. Hang on, I'll go get it," she says, rising slightly from the couch.

I leap across the sofa and grab her around the middle. "Hey, hey, hey, get back here!" I kiss her and say, "You're lucky I think corny is cute."

She laughs and sits back down on the couch. "You're lucky you think corny is cute. Do you know how boring my thesis is?" She gives me that cocky smile like she knows I can't resist her, and when she gives me that smile, I can't. I straddle her lap and lean in to kiss her. She reaches up and runs her nails back and forth across the back of my neck. She lays her palm across my left breast and gently pushes me away, her wrist covering the bottom fork of the transgender symbol.

She leans up and kisses me on the ear and whispers, "Take that silly thing off."

I roll off and lean back against the arm of the couch, coyly defiant. "I didn't hear a 'please.'"

She wraps her hand around my wrist and pulls my hand in close to the stiff bulge in her jeans.

"Silly girl," she says. "'Please' is your line."

"Oh!" I gasp crookedly. My mouth is suddenly dry with desire; I want her so much it's hard to speak. "So it is." My fingers creep up the little hill to the prize, the brass tag of her zipper peeking out of the front of her jeans. My index finger just barely touches the little hard piece of metal before she jumps backward and up, plopping herself down on the arm of the couch and crossing her legs.

"Excuse me," she says, scowling over the top of her little round glasses. "I'm pretty sure I told you to take your shirt off, young lady." Too excited now for coy denials, I grab the bottom hem of my T-shirt and pull it off so hastily that I smear a pale streak of foundation makeup down the middle of the transgender symbol. I toss it away and it vanishes into the darkness. "Good girl!" she smiles. "You don't need that here."

Outside, four news vans pull up at once, and four camera operators with their hats on backward leap out in sync. They begin setting up as close as they can, but the street near the fire itself is clogged with emergency vehicles and police are keeping them back while the firefighters work, so they set up across the street from our apartment. I can see them out of the corner of my eye, pulling off their lens caps and looking around at the crowd, deciding which neighbor to talk to.

I reach behind myself to unhook my bra, and Natalie, who doesn't wear one, tugs off her white tank top. She uncrosses her legs and I rise to my knees between them, pressing my mouth to the tiny curves of her breasts. "Mmm, good girl," she murmurs. She laces her fingers into my hair and balls her fist, clutching my head tightly to her chest. Another switch flips on inside me, the machinery of my need for her crackling and shivering in the dark like vacuum tubes in Frankenstein's lab.

I pull away and fumble with the button on my shorts. "Hmm.

Someone's a little eager," Natalie says, propping her elbows on her knees and her chin on her knuckles. "What are you in such a hurry for, little girl? What is it you want so badly?" I drop my shorts on the floor and lean back with one knee bent slightly inward to hide my clit, which has stiffened without my consent as usual.

"You," I whisper. "I want you inside me, I want you to fuck me, I want you to fuck my ass, I want to come 'til I'm crying..." She's still sitting there watching me, smiling just a little but not saying anything. She's waiting for me to say something specific. I know what it is. "I want your cock," I say, almost too quiet to hear over the noise outside.

"Sorry? I didn't quite hear that."

"Your cock," I say, a little louder but not so loud that someone in the next room would hear. "I want your cock."

"Shout it," she says, tugging down her zipper. "Shout it and you can have it."

"I can't—" I start to say, glancing back at the open windows behind us, but she begins to pull her zipper up and the words burst out of my mouth, "Cock! I want your cock! Please, please, fuck me, I want you inside me, please!" I crane my neck around to look out the window behind me and can see the reporters glancing at our building. The old man's son is looking too, and he turns to answer a question the old man just asked. This is probably not going to help the "sex freak" rumors, but right now I don't care too much. Later I'll care, but right now all that really matters is Natalie, her lips and hair and breasts and her beautiful cock. She pulls open her jeans and it pops out, she isn't wearing underpants. I jump up and crane my neck toward it, but she puts a hand on my shoulder to stop me.

"Condom," she says, and I panic. Do we have any left? We used the last one in the bedroom before we left, where could we have had more? Is there one under the couch, is there one in my purse, is there one in a drawer in the kitchen? Nothing seems likely. I look at her and she's grinning. "Relax," she says, "you look like you're going to pop." She pulls one out of the pocket of her jeans. "I always have a spare in my wallet. I might not have been a boy, but I was a Boy Scout. 'Be prepared.'" She taps the knee of her jeans. "Take care of these for me while I put this thing on, pretty girl."

I grab her pants and tug, slowly revealing her long, gorgeous legs; the sparse layer of wiry black hair, dry knees, the little ridge of scar on her calf where she sliced herself on broken glass as a child swimming in the creek that everyone's parents told them to stay out of.

I drop her jeans into the shadows, and I'm about to lean up to put my head between her thighs, but instead she drops to the couch between my legs and lowers herself onto me, her lips on my lips, her breasts on my breasts, her cock on my clit. She kisses down the side of my neck and then back up to my ear and whispers, "Admit it: you like telling the world what a slut you are." I press my body against hers and don't say anything, but she's not wrong. "Maybe they already knew. Maybe I told them. You don't speak Spanish, you don't know what I say to the people next door." She presses herself down onto me. "Maybe you're too beautiful not to talk about."

She reaches down into my panties and slides the flat of her palm over my clit, covering it completely, one finger gently stroking the closed space between my thighs. I gasp and squirm and above me, shadowing the light, she's watching me approvingly. She cups her other hand around my left breast, pinching my nipple until it crosses the line between sexy and sore, then easing up just enough to cross back, then slides her hand slowly across the curve of my belly. A thunderstorm is sliding into place inside me, her hands drawing cloud-shadows across my skin. The air tastes electric, the darkness is vibrating at the edges as the candle flickers and exhales a string of smoke at the ceiling.

Shivering, I reach down for the lube, pop the cap and squeeze a cold dollop into my hand. I'm sweating, my face is soaked and the makeup that hides my facial hair is probably ruined, but it doesn't matter. It doesn't matter here.

Sliding my cold hand back and forth across her warm cock, I raise myself up and kiss her neck. "I love you so much," I moan, "you don't even know." She sighs and finally lets herself go, lets out a murmur of pleasure.

"Turn over," she says, and I yank my panties off as fast as I can and obey. She squirts some lube into her palm and gently grasps my clit, lining up her cock with her other hand. In the flickering light I can see us reflected in the screen of the television across the room.

A stranger looking at us now would call us "MTFs" instead of women, would name us by our genitalia—"pre-op," "non-op"—would call us trans before they called us anything else, if they did call us anything else. A stranger would call our bodies gender ambiguous: her cock about to enter me, my clit poking out of her fist, her tiny breasts on her large rib cage and the shadow across my cheeks and chin. A stranger would say that, and that stranger would be wrong: our bodies aren't ambiguous at all, only the meanings people misapply to them. She's a woman and her beautiful body is a woman's body; I am a woman and seeing how beautiful her body is makes me think my body might be beautiful too.

She begins to press into me, creeping in by agonizing millimeters. I want to push back, push her all the way in, but I let her control the pace. She slides a fingernail down my spine and rubs the palm of her hand over the head of my clit. Her hips meet my ass and she reaches around with her free hand to hold my breasts as I clutch the arm of the couch, whimpering with joy.

I want to come while the media people still have their microphones on, to scream Natalie's name on the six o'clock news. I want to show the world that I'm not afraid, that I'm exactly what they say I am and also that I'm not, and if they can only see one of those two that's their problem. Natalie is kissing the back of my neck and her cock is deep inside me. Manic birds are chattering to one another in the trees outside, announcing a thunderstorm coming to break the heat. The partiers next door are drunkenly singing; their children have been called inside. Reporters are taking reactions from the neighbors, cameras rolling. Out of the soup of language, two words keep rising from the street: *fire, electricity, fire, electricity.*

Natalie pulls me in close, presses herself all the way inside me, and together we build a better world.

SOMEBODY'S WATCHING ME

Alicia E. Goranson

Amanda is out watching the sun set between the two ramshackle houses across the street, waiting for Naoto to come over. Then her cell phone chimes. It's Derrick, her ex-boyfriend from three states ago. The one she left at midnight after he had fallen asleep. He had been a real prize: a straight boy, proud he didn't have a fag bone in his body. Amanda opens it because that's what you're supposed to do when you get a call.

Derrick shouldn't have her number. He asks her how she is doing. "Fine," she says. He tells her he has someone watching her right now. That her brown roots are showing through her strawberry pink hair. That her favorite floral dress is getting splotches and she is resting her left elbow against the mailbox. Amanda focuses on the setting sun, while the corners of her eyes search for movement.

It's an old Georgia suburb with porches covered in sand pails, beer bottles and boxes slumping from the humidity. There's wind in the street and televisions flickering behind every window. Of course there's movement everywhere.

Amanda breathes slow and doesn't move. She waits for Derrick to get bored. He says she should behave herself or he's coming over. He has friends in town. They're recording her right now. He'll put it up on Viddler or blip.tv if she makes him.

Amanda lives on display, especially when she leaves the house. She tries not to think about anything that isn't ten feet around her. It's easy for her to numb herself and dress in bright colors when she's already a target. Derrick isn't doing anything special.

Eventually he relents. "You be good or I'll know," he says and hangs up.

Amanda grabs the mail and wanders into the house she rents with a half-dozen other queers. It would be nice if the house could fly, as long as the garage comes with it. That's where she keeps her bike.

Later in the evening, Naoto parks his uncle's hand-me-down VW Rabbit nearby. He calls it "The Zombie" after the ring of rust that has eaten the underside of the car's chassis. He has a bike too, but it's not safe to bike at night from this house in this neighborhood.

The odds were against him ever meeting Amanda. His uncle runs a pawnshop in the next town, where Naoto lives since his mom kicked him out. One evening, a kid came over with a half-dozen laptops to sell. Naoto's uncle had him keep the kid still while phoning the cops. Amanda came over the next day to reclaim the laptops. The kid had been one of her roommates. Naoto complimented her on the raccoon-girls and badger-girls she had drawn over her own laptop. Amanda said they could always use another player for game night.

Of course, he needed a warm place to stay after game night ended, since he'd biked over that first time. Her pointed elbows bruised him and she left bites deep enough to last into the next month. It was the best night he'd had in a long time.

Naoto lets himself in the house and waves to the bodies on the couch. He knocks on Amanda's door but she doesn't respond. He calls her on her cell phone. She realizes where he is after she takes off her headphones.

"Hey," she says between heavy breaths as she pounces on his lips. She squeezes his butt to flatter him and drag him out of view from her roommates. She slams her door shut. They kiss until it's silly.

"Just a second," she interrupts. She darts to her laptop to save the story she was working on and close her chat windows.

Naoto strips off his clothes and flops naked on her bed. He doesn't have the option of going naked all the time but he wouldn't decline it. The fan on her nightstand cools his hair.

"How was your day?" he says.

"Derrick called me," she says.

He sits up. "Really?"

"It's no big deal," she says. "He doesn't have the bus fare to come all the way down here."

"Well, hon, you should at least file a report. If anything happens to you, they'll know who to look for."

She isn't looking at him. "No, I'll tell them anyways if it comes to that."

"You're sure?"

"Yeah," she says and presents her laptop to him. "I wrote this today for Telianna. Tell me what you think."

He lets it go. She thinks ten feet around her and that's the only way she'll survive.

While he glances at the laptop screen, she slips her dress over her head the way water nymphs shed their modesty before diving into a lake. She is proud of her hairless skin, ten years younger than it was before she started estrogen. Naoto would have her body if he could. His own skin is peppered with dark Italian hair, which regrows faster than a hydra's heads. It's better to ignore. He admires her instead and closes her laptop.

"Do you mind, hon? I'm not really in the mood to read this," he says. "Someone brought in a box of porn DVDs and my uncle spent all day watching them to make sure they worked."

"Anything good?"

"Did I bring any of them with me?" he says. "Argh, most of them were these bad transfers from VHS with eighties floof hair and sitcom sets."

Amanda wraps one leg across his hips and sits on him. Her smooth shaved ass straddles his cock. She leans over to rub his shoulders; not too deep though, with his muscles as tight as they are.

Her own cock flops on his belly as a curious prehensile tail installed on the wrong side.

"So, did he have his pants down all day?" she says. "You should have pulled the fire alarm on him."

Naoto looks up to her predatory smile, creepy as a wolf that hasn't decided whether to kill him yet. "No, that was the freakiest part," he says. "He had his pants on the whole time. He only got up to turn down the volume during the gang rape scenes."

"Ooo," she says and hunches over him. Her nipples graze him while his cock bounces against her. "You know what? I should burn a bunch of DVDs of the dyke porn I have on my hard drive. Then you can swap them with your uncle's collection. So someone will buy one from him, thinking they're getting gang rape but instead it's a bunch of lovely lovely dykes fucking the body paint off each other."

Naoto glowers at her. Her nose is within reach and he bites it. She squeals.

"It'th tempting," he says while he squeezes his teeth against her cartilage. "But I like having a job."

She wriggles on his hips. He grabs her hands so she can't squirm free. "You're being mean," she says.

"You're being delicious," he says. He licks her through his teeth.

She struggles and forces one of her hands into his long-curled hippy hair. She pulls hard, balling it in her fist. He shakes as he keeps her other hand from going for his head as well. After one good pinch on her side, she collapses on his chest. Their entwined arms smack the fan on her nightstand, which knocks the lamp on the floor. The bulb fizzles out, leaving them in darkness.

"Fuck," she says. "We let go of each other together. Ready?"

"Why?" he says, still gripping her nose.

She rocks back and forth, trying to wriggle her nose free. He can feel her grimacing every time she sways her hips. "If you're trying to keep your nose, this isn't the way to do it," he says.

She releases his hair and goes limp. "I surrender," she says. "You may do with me as you will."

He strokes her back, drawing curlicues down her spine. "Okay," he says, "Tabby and Maybelle are having a fight again about a journal entry Tabby made that outed Maybelle. Terrillip's cranky about having to live with his mom for three years now. Califlora is mad because she didn't have any ecstasy when Ballyhoo came to town so they didn't hit it off. I'm tired of giving them all advice. You do it."

Amanda licks his chin with a viper's flick. He softens and releases her sore nose so he can bite her tongue and suck it into his mouth. It's rough on the edges where she chews it. His lips stroke hers and he passes his own tongue to her. Her teeth are sharp. They never came in right. They bite so much nicer than his.

She rests her forehead against his, stroking down his neck. "I thought Maybelle was already out," she says.

"Not in that community," he says. "For crying out loud, it's why I like you, hon. You never ask me for relationship advice."

She purrs and kisses him slow, down his cheek and neck while mixing little nibbles in between. His firm, tired hands reach under her to knead her breasts. He rolls his fingers to hear her gasp.

"Though you know," he says, "there are times when I wish you would ask me."

The salt of his skin has a lovely taste and his cock is pressing happily into her. If only he could keep his thoughts to himself.

"Look, I know what I'm doing," she says. "Derrick got his jollies off by calling me. As long as I don't block his number or anything, I'll be okay."

"Okay. I just worry."

"I know."

Amanda is getting better at making him unintelligible. She extends her tongue as a record needle and plays his chest hair all the way down to his cock. She nuzzles around the base so slowly, stoking its heat with her breath. She licks small strokes, lapping his workday sweat and musk. He's dirty, broken, like her. She maps the rigid veins that collapse under a little pressure and the smooth top of his cock, soft as sealskin. She bats the tip with her nose before diving over it, sucking it as if it was the sweetest sourball ever.

Her box of gloves and lube tubes fell between the bed and the wall months ago, and remained there due to convenience. Her lips and tongue slide up and down his shaft while her hand grasps for a glove and bottle. She lifts herself up long enough to slip on the glove and slather it with the room-temperature lube. Two of her fingers wake the fleshy tips of his anus, which relax and part for her. He purrs and pants as she plunges onto his cock again. But she's going too slow. The edges of his anus, pressed together for too long, are open, free, radiating pleasure the more she strokes them like a bow on a violin. He lifts his hips up to speed the touch his ass craves. She gets the message. She speeds her rhythm until he begins to lose control of his legs.

Naoto grasps at his own nipples, wishing his chest were as prominent and sensitive as Amanda's. If only his body were as accessible and pliable as hers in public, so that desirable strangers would want to touch him as they wanted her. His body shakes as some reptile thing inside him is stirred. His cock is him. His anus is him. But his hips, his belly and the absence on his chest are not him. If only he could move the pleasure welling up his shaft to deep inside him. Then the pleasure would spill all around his legs and chest instead of emptying into the air inside Amanda's mouth.

He grasps the mattress as his body convulses. "Stop hon," he says. "Please, not yet."

She withdraws her fingers and sits up in an instant. He thinks about his uncle in front of the DVDs and holds himself together until the urge to cum subsides.

"Too much?" she says.

"No, perfect."

She ties her glove inside out and tosses it in the approximate direction of the trash can. She listens to the moans of a job well done. Then she remembers.

"I still need you to read that story I wrote for Telianna sometime," she says. "I got the check from the last story I wrote him today. One more like that and I can get that latex catsuit from Canada."

He reaches up to cup her hips in his hands. "You suck," he says.

She smiles. "Very well. I picked up a long coat from Goodwill last week. I was thinking I could wear my catsuit outside under it."

He strokes her softly, which tickles her. "You would wear a hundreds of dollars catsuit outside in this weather with the sort of neighbors you have?"

"Uh-huh."

He pinches her until she squeals at the pitch he's listening for. "Darlin', I'm not questioning your intelligence. Just your sanity."

"Ow. My what?" she says.

"Exactly."

He waits while she basks in her own silliness, repeating the conversation in her head. While she is distracted, he thrusts himself up, grabs her and pulls her on top of him.

She bats at his face. "Eeep! Let me go."

He drops his arms and lies still. "Okay."

She snorts. "Fine, you can ravage me."

"Really?"

"Well," she draws out. "Unless you would prefer Miss Cobra to ravage you."

Miss Cobra is a green snake dildo who lives on a shelf over Amanda's bed. Miss Cobra has her own supply of condoms that come in all the colors of a free clinic grab bag. There is only one fluorescent pink left but Amanda is willing to risk using it for the chance to wield Miss Cobra.

"I wouldn't mind a visit from her," Naoto says.

Amanda strokes his cheeks and rubs her face over his. "Miss Cobra will expect you to be extra good," she says. "Miss Cobra will expect you to cum extra hard."

He runs his fingers over the rim where her hair meets her scalp, following it back down her spine. "I don't care what Miss

Cobra wants," he says. "As long as she gives the Nebula-winning performance she always does."

They kiss again. "I'll see what I can do," she says.

She rises over him using only her calf muscles and sways in the warm Southern air. She rattles the harness off her shelf so he can hear it jingle. She imagines this will instill some Pavlovian response in him eventually, if they don't break up first.

"I'd like you on your knees," she says.

"Not tonight. They've been acting up."

She rubs the leather straps against each other as she loops and tightens them around her leg. "Well, I can pretend," she says.

"That's fine," he says. "I appreciate whatever she wants to do to me."

Another snap and Miss Cobra is ready for her close-up. In the darkness over Naoto, a condom pouch rips and a new bottle of lube has its cherry popped.

Amanda shakes her hips to make sure that Miss Cobra is well secured to her.

"Miss Cobra will make you especially beautiful tonight," she says. "But to be a good little toy for Miss Cobra, you must only speak words that contain the letter *s*. Do you understand?"

"Yes, Miss Snake," he says. He raises his hips off the bed, ready for the pillow that will hold them up.

She bops him on the chest with her pillow, teasing. "Good toy," she says, and hisses as she slides the pillow under him. "Miss Cobra thinks she deserves a kiss before she starts."

She slides up his chest and lets him taste the condom before it enters him. He wraps his lips around the serpent's head in gratitude.

The moment always begins with a kiss to Miss Cobra. Touch, taste and fellatio can only bring Amanda and Naoto so far. The hot scented skin of a lover reveals scars, moles, coarse hair and fat when examined too closely. Amanda needs a room of her own to seal away the rational world and create a joyful realm where she rules with a tender hand. Only then can she guide Miss Cobra into him. She can be the diva she was always meant to be. Naoto squeezes Miss Cobra in his mouth with the tenderness that only a very docile fleshbot can provide. When the tip comes in, his tongue must fall. When it strokes the back of his mouth, his throat must open. His cheeks suck in and he lifts himself back with care. He only has three simple things to do. Forget the world. Forget his uncle. Forget everything but the worship at hand.

Naoto's tongue ripples around Miss Cobra and Amanda feels the aftershocks in her own mouth. If she could capture this moment, turn off all desire in Naoto except to fellate Miss Cobra, she'd use it to ride the beat of Miss Cobra against her crotch throughout the night.

Instead, she waits for him to slow before he strains his neck.

"Shh," she says and slides away from his lips.

Naoto pets her arms as she anoints Miss Cobra with the sacred lube. He wants to feel every glob fall. He can live without its processed smell but...oh, god. When that finger strokes between the cracks around his prickly anus. The ring spills pleasure as her fingers orbit it. Fuck bodies and their shapes. Nothing trumps the moment and.... Oh. My God.

Miss Cobra slips her head in him while Amanda holds his wrists down. "Miss Cobra will let you touch your breasts," she says. "Provided that you squeeze mine when I tell you to."

He surrenders to the smile that spreads over his face. "Yes, Miss Snake."

Amanda leans her hips deeper between his legs and frees his arms. She pushes Miss Cobra one twist deeper, in and out.

His anus nubs and the hollow within him beg for more touch. Amanda takes her sweet time and keeps to her own rhythm.

If only the world could see her now, rocking her hips like an Olympic gymnast. The magic of sex shrinks the universe to bubble size. Everything there is, was or will be shakes on this bed and hungers like Amanda's skin. She knows all the people who have ever lived wish they could lie between Naoto's legs as she is now. Each thrust from her washes through the generations. The faceless, exotic people in her mind worship her, stay jealous of her, and urge her onward. Oh, god, for this short moment, they love her. This phantom horny mob turns her on so goddamned much. If only they could stay around to fuck her and Naoto afterward.

She pushes Miss Cobra deeper as his warm hole widens to plead for her.

"Now," she says. The hands that paw and pinch her breast are mere puppets, jerked about by the audience. Her toes clench. Her toenails leave marks on Naoto's thighs.

In his mind, Naoto is metamorphosing into something very smooth and full of light. He floats in a wire-frame wonderland and his tongue can't stop licking the inside of his mouth. He pushes himself into Miss Cobra lest the world fall apart if he stops. The rings of flesh that seal him from the universe melt away. He softens as Miss Cobra shakes his cock and balls with every thrust. The nubs around his anus demand and receive all the attention they can ask for. His nipples cry for pressure but he cannot release Amanda's. He grips hers as hard as he wants to grip his own. Amanda's rhythm would make stones dance and the dead rise. He drives her down, shaking her chest as a rider whips the horses. He gasps as Miss Cobra completely enters him, in and out. Intensity above; greed, hunger and wide mouths below. Oh, god, his cock is radiating enough light to consume the sun.

"Please, please," he says.

"Do it!" she says.

He takes ahold of his crying, aching cock, as large as the moon. It shrieks at his touch. His crotch wells up in electric pleasure. He is bringing joy to the galaxy. All the unloved and the denied are given unconditional joy and rapture. He can have everything he's ever wanted. Just a little pressure and a few deep, fast caresses.

He rockets Amanda out of him as he orgasms. She giggles.

Miss Cobra is held aloft by Amanda's own excitement. Amanda smears his semen on her belly as a war trophy, and bends down to kiss his cock once. He shudders.

"Too sensitive," he says. Story of her life.

Miss Cobra is released and replaced on her perch, and her condom is hurled somewhere near the trash can. Amanda nestles in beside her happy boygirlfriend and lets his gentle breaths graze her face. Naoto wraps his arm around her waist and lets his forehead fall into hers.

Then the phone rings. It's muted—under something. They both shake. Naoto isn't sure where it's coming from. Maybe they'll need light to find it. He waits for her to speak. He keeps waiting as it rings again.

"Oh," she says. "That's my roommate's phone."

Naoto takes his arm from her waist and gently slaps the back of her head.

"You're just going to let this go," he says. She doesn't move. She just breathes.

He blows his sigh on her nose. "Okay, hon," he says. "If you're going to be self-indulgent, I'm going to be too. I'd hate, more than anything, to have someone come in here, tie me up and do whatever they're going to do to you in front of me. Not that it wouldn't be horrific and unforgivable to you, and that

that bastard wouldn't deserve anything that came to him. But this is me I'm talking about now. And what this would mean about me. I would rather be there on the bed, getting beaten or raped beside you. I could take that. We'd get through it. But I couldn't take being treated like some guy like my uncle, who needs to be tied up and have his girlfriend abused in front of him to make a point. I don't want to be put in that position. I don't think I could take it. I don't know if I could come back to you after that. That's not me. I'm fucking queer. I couldn't take being made a guy like that, you know?"

If the lights were on, he would see her staring at the pillow under her face, not at him. This life would be very empty without him. But she's been there before and she'll be there again someday. It isn't as if they stare at her any less when she's in his company. She stays quiet longer than she should.

He drapes his arm over her. "Come here," he says. She nestles into his chest and holds him close. She never had the chance to be a little girl. It's nice sometimes. But not right now.

"Fuck him," she says.

"What?"

"Fuck Derrick. Come on."

She steps over him out of the bed and takes his wet sloppy hands in hers. "Stand up," she says.

The bed is very comfortable and the dark floor is dangerous to sensitive feet. But he drags himself up anyway. "Okay," he says.

A few misplaced steps and a near fall on the glove, and Amanda has brought him to the window. She presses her back against his naked body and kisses his hand. She reaches for the shade and tugs it quick. It rolls up, flopping on its spindle.

The streetlight in front of her house burned out a while ago. The houses across the street have some lights on but none in the front. The night wind has carried most of the clouds away. The stars twinkle through the atmosphere.

"He has someone watching me out there," she says. "Get me off, please?"

Naoto kisses her ear. "Sure."

He smiles and reaches around her. One hand takes her breasts and the other takes her cock. She is pretty excited already. It isn't long before she shudders, face out to the neighborhood. It doesn't matter that her room is as dark as the street outside.

Derrick sees all.

PUNCHING BAG

Rachel Kramer Bussel

Kyle still wasn't sure, two years in, if he liked punching or being punched better, in or out of the ring. All he knew was that boxing made him feel alive, lit up, excited, manly...and had even when he was a woman. He'd started lurking around the gym when he'd been Kim, binding his breasts, mostly using the inert punching bags. He was afraid of hitting another woman, but he wouldn't be afraid of hitting the block of muscle in a man's chest. He didn't even need anyone else, at first, to get that special high, one he'd never gotten from running or swimming or tennis.

There's an energy to a boxing ring that he had never experienced in any other sport, not even wrestling. This was pure, raw aggression, tempered only by the rules of the game and sometimes not even that. It made grown men and women drop all pretense and simply get down to the business at hand, and he liked the way it sliced away every false veneer society put on his shoulders until it was just his mind and his fists, working in concert.

Transitioning from female to male had made the process mostly easier, though he'd had to switch gyms. With his red hair, freckles and still a bit of a baby face, no matter how flat and firm his chest, how bulked up his shoulders, he couldn't risk someone saying something and outing him before he was ready. He knew that if he'd been born a guy, he'd have gotten picked on, no question. He was only five feet six: decent for a woman but short, scrawny even, for a guy.

So he switched to an all-male gym, where the level of aggression, testosterone and drive suited him perfectly. For the past year or so, ever since his surgery, he'd been trying to figure out so much about himself that dating had fallen by the wayside. People were easier when consumed on his computer screen, in flirtatious notes or all-out dirty chat sessions, where he could say things like, "Punch me. Pummel me. Use me," and go there, completely, in his head. He'd never wanted to get punched like that before—not for real.

He'd assumed that since he'd been mostly a dyke as a woman, going more for the athletic types than the overly made-up ones, that he'd continue to want those kind of women, but something had changed somewhere along the way. He'd always assumed that he wanted to be the tough, brawny, roaring hulk he'd watched countless times in the ring and fought against once or twice. That was the kind of fantasy that, at twenty-eight, he knew was never going to quite come true; there wasn't a surgery he could endure to make himself taller, to make himself a completely different person. All he could do was make himself into the strongest, healthiest person he could be. Thankfully, he had savings he'd grown with some good investments in school, ones that had supported him ever since. He was finally ready to look for a job in computer science but hadn't wanted to go through a public transition on the job, with all the explaining.

He was too private for that. For the moment, he could take his time looking for work, as he worked on himself. He got top surgery and he was taking T, and while he felt different, he was still sorting out exactly what that meant, and what that made him.

His heart, though, if it belonged anywhere, was in the gym. The energy there rippled in waves, flowing through him like a computer's motherboard. His first waking thought was no longer about his unruly body or his first cup of coffee, but for his gloves, the new black and red ones he'd had custom made. When he put them on, he felt invincible.

He woke up and stood staring at himself in the mirror, indulging a few minutes' vanity before showering, closing his eyes and smiling at the muscles that seemed to have sprouted all over. They seemed to be telling him, on a daily basis, "You made the right choice. Here is your reward."

He didn't let himself admit, except in rare moments, how much he did miss the little intimacies he'd forgone in the last year, the kisses on the back of his neck, the spooning with his usually taller girlfriends, the flirtatious banter of a first date, the holding hands, the making a girl come with his hands. That, he thought as the hot spray blasted his face, was second to the sublime thrill of cutting the perfect right hook. And then he felt it, what would've been an extreme hard-on in what he was sure, if he'd been born with the right parts, would have been at least a nine-inch cock. He stepped back and let the luxurious spray blast his flat chest, now sprinkled with hair and bursting with muscles. He reached down and touched himself, shocked at how close he was to orgasm. When he came, he didn't think about getting his ass or what had been his pussy pounded. He thought about someone pounding his chest, slapping his face, using him as a personal punching bag. Kyle had to force himself to turn off the shower, step out clutching the sink, then drop, dripping wet, onto the toilet seat, lest he collapse with the sheer joy that image had brought him.

He went back to bed for a few minutes, lying damp and naked between the smooth sheets, mentally reviewing the guys he knew at the gym, considering which ones might be worth pursuing to live out this fantasy—because this wasn't the kind of fantasy he was willing to wait for. His mind flitted from one to another until he finally roused himself again. Maybe this wasn't his decision to make.

He went to the gym after everyone else's workday had ended, lurking, observing, but sticking to himself. There was still a sense that he didn't quite belong, not because of gender, but personality. Maybe he needed to be gruff and demanding, but that wasn't really Kyle's style. Hanging around proved useful, because eventually there were only four guys left. He'd seen the owner give James, a huge, hot, hulking white guy with a buzz cut, stubble and a killer body, the keys. "Wanna spar?" James had asked. Kyle looked around and realized he was talking to him.

"Sure," he said, shrugging casually, like it was no big deal. And, in a way, it wasn't. He took a few minutes in the locker room to suit up and put on his gloves and mouth guard and psych himself up. He didn't have time to think too much about the man who was almost twice his size, or he might chicken out.

Kyle was totally into the match when he first sparred off against James. His new gray tank top clung to his muscular body, loose red shorts hung to his knees. He was fired up, ready to dart and strike, to unleash not fury but energy and passion. When the first blow landed against his chest, he liked it a little too much, liked it in ways that weren't fit for a boxing ring, that had no way of translating into the ancient sport they were engaging in.

No, the way he liked it was all about another ancient sport, that of men sparring with men...in the bedroom or in his dreams. Only they were in public, and for perhaps the first time ever, Kyle was glad he didn't have a dick, because if he did, there'd be no way he could've hidden his erection. There was barely a way to hide the sensations now as his two urges battled, one to win, and one to chance another beautiful blow. Boxing was an eat-or-be-eaten world, and suddenly Kyle wanted to be beaten, slapped, choked. The sensation almost overtook him, but he hopped back, shook his head, tried to get a glimpse of James's eyes to see if he was the only one feeling this way. He hoped not.

They went on for a few minutes, but Kyle realized he'd have to throw the match if they were ever going to move on to the real thing, the best part. He didn't think, just then, about the fact that this was his true test of manhood: to be able to give up the mantle of macho, to abandon being in charge, to revel in the thrill he'd never dare try as a girl of going over the edge, giving himself to someone. He'd spent so long building himself up, pumping iron, pumping hormones, priming himself to be someone mighty and powerful, that he'd never let himself truly savor the possibilities.

He poised his body to take a blow, then fell, using the few acting classes he'd taken in school to make it look as realistic as possible. There were only two friends of James's watching, ones who were all too happy to call it for their pal. James leaned over him and tapped his face, sending another jolt through Kyle. "Hey man, you okay?" Kyle looked up into James's pale, piercing blue eyes, hoping what he saw looking back was a reflection of his own desire. He wasn't sure, but he nodded and stood. After James got pounds from his friends, the two men went into the locker room, where James quickly pressed Kyle up against the lockers.

"What the hell was that?" he asked. His voice wasn't angry so much as serious, wanting a real answer. Kyle wanted to ask, "What?" but didn't.

"I don't know. I mean, I do; I just don't know if I should tell you." James didn't answer, just stood hovering over Kyle, like he had all day to wait, but his eyes were patient, not menacing. Kyle flushed, looking down momentarily before looking back up into James's gaze. "I liked it, okay? There was a moment right after you slammed me in the chest that I liked it, the whole thing, the pain, the rush of the blow, the power behind it, the way it almost knocked me down. I liked the sensation and I wanted more. I want more. Now. From you."

The smile slowly crept across James's face, tilting first the corners of his lips, then moving up his cheeks to those mesmerizing eyes. "You mean you're a masochist, is that what you're saying?" Their gloves were off, but Kyle suddenly longed for something to shield his face with. He was new to actually engaging in BDSM; new, even, to truly fantasizing about it in such a deep way, so he didn't yet know that wishing for it to end while secretly wanting to prolong it was one of the best parts of being a bottom.

"Yes," he said, as his voice trembled. "I think so, anyway. This is new to me." He paused, not sure whether to keep going and reveal the even-bigger secret.

James stepped closer until one sweaty body was pressed against the other. "I know," was all he said, so much meaning imbued in five little letters. And with that, Kyle sank back against the lockers, yielding his body, his mind, all the ways he held himself together, to James.

"Get in the shower," James said, then turned his back on

Kyle. *Here? Now?* he thought, but he knew this was his first test. He never showered at the gym, but no one else was around; James had a key to lock up and his friends had gone off to some bar, so they were completely alone. Kyle had absolute freedom, at least, in this way; freedom from discovery and prying eyes. Some men might have been afraid to do their first scene with no one around at all to hear if something went awry, but not Kyle. The fact that they had the gym to themselves was a luxury he couldn't take for granted.

Still, he moved into the deepest recesses of the locker room and took off first his sweaty tank, then the shorts, then the briefs. He felt it again, that phantom hard-on, only not so phantom this time. He was excited, aroused, and it was centered between his legs, the area he didn't know what to call, the area he'd tried to ignore for as long as possible but no longer could. He looked up and saw James and his eyes immediately went to James's cock, one so big it almost made Kyle swoon. He hadn't known he was a size queen, but he couldn't deny that the mighty weapon made him long to get on his knees.

"Get going, boy," James said. "Boy." He'd learned it in one context in school, a negative, racist word full of hatred, but now, Kyle heard it differently, maybe because he'd never been one. He'd rushed to become a man and now had a few moments to regress, to be a boy full of the wonder of hormones, of sheer exploration, of going with his instincts. James seemed to be able to read him like a book because he slammed Kyle up against the tiles of the musty shower stall and grabbed him by the throat. "Your safeword is *girl,*" he said, the irony nowhere in his gruff command.

The tears that sprang to Kyle's eyes came unbidden, and he didn't bother blinking them away. James raised a knee between Kyle's legs and he didn't protest. "Okay, boy?" the man asked, that word again making him shudder, and he suddenly didn't care what James's knee found there. James managed to keep his hold on Kyle while turning on the shower spray, blasting them both with water hotter than Kyle usually used. He liked it, or maybe he didn't, but he wanted it, because James wanted it. This was his chance to prove himself, as a boy, a man, a sub—as himself.

James's hand stroked Kyle's cheek once, sweetly, softly, before he raised it and slapped him hard, the wet handprint lost to the next one that followed. Kyle didn't try to stop the tears, couldn't have, releasing all the emotions he'd thought he'd been getting out in the ring. James was mostly silent, save for a few grunts, the sound of the spray loud in their ears as he pummeled Kyle with his bare hands, slapping his cheeks and nipples, punching him hard in the chest, then turning him around to thrash at his back. Kyle trembled, the pain secondary to the tenderness he could feel coming through with each slap. James knew what he was doing, Kyle could tell, and finally he had to do something he could never have predicted: without asking, Kyle reached down between his legs and touched himself. In many ways, what he felt was the same as it had been, but he knew he was different. He knew this wasn't his pussy, but something else.

James gave his back a few more hard, wet slaps, then let his fingers join Kyle's, making him turn around and stare right at him as his fingers invaded. James could've gone for his ass, Kyle thought, but he didn't, he went there, and when Kyle came, the climax roared through his body, making him dig his nails into the grooves between the tiles for purchase. He'd been so focused on the pleasure of giving in, going over, he'd almost forgotten about James's cock, and when he looked down, he saw it standing straight up, as if to say, "Yes, this is for you."

Kyle shut his eyes and reached for James's hand to remove

it. He was done, at least, with that, but not with James. With the water still pounding them, he got on his knees, putting his hands behind his back. It was the ultimate submissive, servile posture, yet it made Kyle feel, like almost nothing else had, like a man. Not the kind of man he saw on TV or was ever taught about in school or even saw in the muscle-baring ads plastered around the gym, but the kind of man he was, the kind of man he wanted to be, one who could claim every inch of his manhood by owning himself. He knew the moment his mouth met James's cock, one so big he had to stretch his lips and even then could barely get it inside. James helped, grabbing him by the neck and pressing himself slowly into the recesses of Kyle's throat, and this time he made noise.

Kyle found he couldn't look up and see James's face, but he could picture it as he sucked, as his aching body screamed not with pain, but belonging. He knew they couldn't stay there all night, but they didn't need to. Kyle had found everything he'd come to the ring to find. He swallowed what James's cock gifted him, taking pride not only in being the bigger man's personal punching bag, but in knowing he was now, finally, his own man, the kind he was meant to be, one with a solid chest, a pounding heart and a smile on his face.

YOU DON'T KNOW JACK

Michael Hernandez

Jack was trying oh so hard not to tap his fingers on the counter. "Good," by Supreme Beings of Leisure, was blasting from the speakers. He'd been waiting quite a while for the overpriced shot of vodka that the barkeep was utterly bound to screw up. He'd quickly discovered that unless the place had an Eastern European clientele, inevitably, the vodka would be chilled on the fly. As a result, it would reach room temperature far too soon and the unpleasant "gasoline fume" experience would occur. Why didn't bartenders understand that for a shot of vodka to be enjoyed at its perfection it should be so cold as to be viscous? Nonetheless, Jack had hope against hope that since this establishment proffered a house-blend raspberry-infused vodka sold by the six-ounce carafe, there was a slight chance that it would in fact be properly served.

Jack didn't do bars anymore. He'd lost his tolerance for sloppy drunks long ago and yet he'd been lured from the comfort of his den by an event that greatly resembled the Smoke & Ink gatherings that took place at IML in days of yore. He missed "the good old days" and given the smoke-free mood that prevailed he just couldn't pass up the chance to enjoy a good cigar with a bunch of hairy tattooed guys, which was what he'd be doing if his fucking drink would finally arrive.

As cranky as he was, the wait was not sooo terrible that walking posed a temptation. There'd been a good turnout for the event, and the joint was teaming with eye candy and music that revved the old engine. "I'll be good / I'll be good tomorrow / I'll be good another day": lyrics he could live by. He quickly squeezed his dick through the black 501s that he was wearing before moving his hand north through the thicket of salt-and-pepper fur on his stomach and chest. His nipples were pierced and had ten-gauge circular barbells. His beard was hard to tame no matter how much he conditioned or trimmed. The hair was wiry, wavy, and had more salt than pepper. His eyebrows were jet black and he'd been accused on more than one occasion of having dyed them. Damned fools! Thinking that he'd bother to dye his eyebrows, but nothing else. He wasn't that vain. He'd earned every damned white hair on his body and he wasn't about to do a thing to change that.

As he stepped down memory lane, an array of aromas increased his visual pleasure. The testosterone-laden muskiness blended perfectly with the earthiness of blue cigar smoke wafting above them. He could detect the unmistakable scent of leather mingled with a hint of something very familiar that he just couldn't place. In a Pavlovian response his dick twitched.

He was surrounded by men of all shapes and sizes. Nary a one was clean-shaven, although some had perfectly groomed beards or moustaches and one or two were even manscaped. That handful of guys wouldn't even rate a first glance, let alone a second one. This was a private event and there was clearly a dress code, which was perfectly fine with his dick. Yeah, there were plenty of guys who were into younger, well-groomed men, but he wasn't one of them. He liked his men to look like men—mature. Leave the baby-faces for others to admire. They had plenty of admirers and in several years would catch his eye. He wouldn't rule people out because of their age, so long as they had reached the age of consent, but it didn't happen to be what caught his eye. Jack wanted someone who looked like and had actually been around the block a few times.

Where the fuck is my drink? he thought. As if on cue the bartender arrived with a carafe on ice. Jack's left eyebrow rose along with his irritation. Before he could growl his displeasure, the bartender apologized. "I'm so sorry, Sir." You could hear the capital in the word *sir*. "We've been having issues with the refrigeration and I wanted to make sure that the vodka was properly chilled. I know that you only ordered a shot, but the carafe is on the house." Jack started to reach for his wallet. "Oh, and the shot was paid for by the bearded tattooed guy in the corner." *WTF? There are 350 tattooed guys with beards in this place.* Clearly, this evening's crowd was not the regular crowd. Before he could say anything the bartender disappeared to assuage the next customer before he started grumbling.

Jack poured himself a shot. Normally, he'd hold it up to the light to check out the hue, but it was too dim to do so. He could smell the cranberry when he held the glass up to his nose. He took a sip and was pleasantly surprised by the flavour. The raspberries were the perfect combination of tart and sweet. Jack took a deep breath, swallowed what remained of the two-ounce shot and exhaled. It was smooth with very little burn and no fumes to speak of. Not long after, he could feel the heat spread from his belly, into his chest, up his throat, onto his cheeks and to the tip-tops of his ears. "Divine," he murmured.

He continued to cruise the crowd. As the DJ started a mix of "Trouble" by Bitter:Sweet, he pulled out and clipped an Arturo Fuente Curly Head and rolled it once counterclockwise then ran it in and out of his mouth to coat the end with spit. That's the way he always prepped his cigars and...well...anything that remotely resembled oral sex was bound to get attention. Jack was in quite the mood. He was long overdue for some good head, but lately cruising felt like too much work. More often than not an Internet hook-up would fail to appear or the guys didn't bother to read the damned ads. It didn't help that he didn't like to host. That required a bit of driving on his part. Sure some things were easier, but the chemistry was sorely lacking. If he had a nickel for every chat that started with "woof," he'd have a full-time fluffer on staff. It was easier to hunt in public. He was assured that he'd have the undivided attention of the object of his affections.

Jack stopped swirling the cigar around in his mouth. He pulled out a matchbox and lit a wooden match. Cupping his left hand near the end of the cigar, he sucked several times, watching the flame rise and fall. When he got a good cherry going he flicked his wrist and put the match out. Out of the corner of his eye he spied a bear sporting an earsplitting grin. Jack made eye contact then gave a quick nod. It had taken him some time to graduate from the two-by-four school of "dating." He was substantially better at picking up cues while they were happening rather than half an hour after the fact. As he puffed on his cigar, "Piggy," by Nine Inch Nails, began to play.

And here he comes. As if on cue, the bear ambled over, allowing Jack to get a good glance at him during the approach. The guy appeared to be tall, but then just about everyone was tall when you stood at five and a half feet. The prick had a full head of auburn hair with a wee bit of gray. The maturing *M* hairline was starting to become slightly pronounced. His hair was short and neatly trimmed in comparison to his beard, which was full and busy. He was heavily inked over both his pecs and delts, but they were difficult to make out between the lighting and the jungle of fur covering his chest and arms. He had a bit of a belly and overall could be regarded as smooth and undefined, but it appeared that there was a slab or two of muscle under the insulation. His legs were like tree trunks and what was swinging between them was represented by a decent bulge.

"Evening," he rumbled, sounding a little like Sam Elliott.

"Good evening," Jack responded.

He extended his hand. "The name's Gus. I couldn't help but notice the red hankie in your left pocket."

"Yeah, well, leopard and tan were a given, but I've never been quite fond of leopard. The tattoos speak for themselves. Tan seemed a bit redundant in this crowd."

Jack stepped back slightly as he poured himself another shot. Gus caught the bartender's attention in record time and ordered a Blue Loon, the local microbrew. Jack took a sip of vodka as an excuse to sneak a peek at Gus's back pocket. He was flagging yellow on the right.

"I hope you don't mind that I took the liberty of buying you a drink."

"That all depends," Jack responded slyly. "Liberties have a price, and I don't see you wearing a single stitch of red. "

"Nope, always wanted to try though. I've got a bit of a tight ass," Gus said, matter-of-factly.

There was something to be said for handball. If you had the ability to collapse your hand down to the width of your wrist, nothing more than a handshake and a candid smile were required to get the ball rolling so to speak. Anyone who watched Jack maneuver his hand into another man's ass, oblivious to any possible audience, hazel eyes locked intently, trying to gauge physical reactions, anticipate mental ones, and managing to fuck the cum out of 90 percent of his partners without so much as breathing on their dicks would quickly be waiting in line. Jack had a knack that made him very, very popular. If everything was just perfect—sights, sounds, tunes, breath, eyes and aromas—Jack could shoot a load without touching himself either. Handball was about asses and hands. Dicks were peripheral and rarely hard even when the bottom was shooting dust after cumming so many times.

Jack felt the all-too-familiar tightness of a hard-on starting and became slightly annoyed. *And now we are going to have to have that fucking chat.* Jack had done this so many times that he knew every possible reaction to The Conversation. The outcomes were varied and had torpedoed his plans more than once. Anyone who has had The Conversation can attest to the fact that things that were going rather well before the talking began could suddenly go off the rails. Sometimes what should have been a short conversation led to a much longer discussion followed by either sex, a raincheck, or ranging forms of rejection. It was the price that Jack paid for having pursued his deepest, darkest desires.

Months or years later that guy who rejected him came back around. He never held it against anyone. Whether they fucked depended on the connection and the attitude. Jack enjoyed a good fuck as much as the next guy, but he hated the assumption that the guy on the receiving end was a bottom pretending to be a top. He knew plenty of tops who loved being fucked and had no hesitation telling you exactly what to do and how to do it.

Jack looked directly into Gus's eyes. He took a deep breath. *Here goes nothing.* Before he could get the words out, Gus said, "I know, and I'm okay with it."

That stopped Jack cold. He frowned. "Okay with what?"

"You know." Jack could hear the twinkle in Gus's voice.

"Really, and just what would that be?" *Could it be? The Conversation is actually going to be amusing?*

"Well, I know that you are into fisting, but as you know my ass isn't that talented. I also saw you sneak a peek at my hanky, so you're either not into piss or are piss shy. Frankly, I don't care that you are HIV positive because I always play safe. You're hot. None of it matters to me."

Jack sighed. *And here I thought—wow, a cherry!* Jack looked down and saw the outline of Gus's cock. *"Always play safe" my ass. When some cock comes along you aren't going to bother with the rubber, so long as the unspoken rule* "don't come in my mouth" *is followed.* A dime-sized circle of moisture was forming at the tip and beginning to spread. *A good sign if there was any.* Jack reached down and brushed the front of Gus's jeans with the back of his left hand. He started tapping out a pattern. *Thwack, thwack, thwack.*

Gus gasped and pulled away before leaning into Jack's rhythmic taps. He put his hands behind his back in parade rest position and spread his legs slightly. Jack shoved his right hand down the front of Gus's jeans while continuing to thwack with his left. He grabbed Gus's cock, smearing precum across the head and used his left hand to grab his ass. Jack lowered his mouth, maneuvered around the chest hair and took a nipple between his teeth before flicking his tongue. Gus sucked in his breath. Surprised at the sensitivity, Jack flicked out a pattern of quarter notes before speeding up to eighth notes. Having played a brass instrument in high school had its benefits. Jack felt the cock jump in his hands, stopped the tongue action and started sucking.

"Please stop or I'll shoot."

Jack pulled back but continued to circle the head of Gus's cock. He removed his hand and traced Gus's lips with the pad of his thumb. Gus immediately slurped Jack's thumb into his mouth. Jack grabbed Gus's crotch and started a slow downward pull, maneuvering Gus so that he was standing between him and the bar. Gus gracefully slid to his knees and looked up before beginning to nuzzle the front of Jack's jeans. Jack resumed puffing on his cigar, back to the other patrons, his crotch trapping Gus under the bar.

Gus was intent on getting Jack hard. He rubbed his face and mouth all over the front of Jack's cock. His efforts were not rewarded with the tumescence that he was used to. Jack was enjoying Gus's struggle to please him. The DJ seemed to have a thing for Supreme Beings of Leisure. "Give Up" was playing.

Gus looked up, concerned that he was doing something wrong.

Jack smiled wickedly, enjoyed his second shot of vodka, then slapped Gus. He leaned down and said, "You bad, bad boy. I was trying to tell you something, but no. You had your own agenda, Mr. Know-It-All. It's time to give up. Open your mouth." Jack undid and removed his belt, yanked open the buttons of his 501s, and pulled his jockstrap out of the way. He looped the belt over Gus's neck and held him in place before shoving forward.

Gus got a glimpse of a thick, fat, thumb-sized dick before it was rammed into his mouth and his head bounced against the bar, stunning him momentarily.

"Suck," growled Jack as he used the belt to pull Gus farther onto his cock and prevent him from bouncing his head off the bar. Jack rammed into Gus's face several times. Gus, panicked that he would gag, instinctively tried to pull away from the onslaught, but found himself trapped by the belt.

"Relax dipshit." Jack pulled back slowly until a quarter of

his dick was still in Gus's mouth, then gyrated his hips forward, burying his cock again. It took a few strokes for Gus to realize that he didn't have to worry about his gag reflex unless Jack slammed into him up to the balls. Gus was rock hard and drooling precum through the front of his jeans. He started to move his hand and suddenly found himself gagging on a throat full of cock.

"Don't you dare touch yourself!" admonished Jack as he pulled back slightly. "This is about my pleasure, my needs, my desires. Right here, right now, in this moment, your mouth is mine." Jack punctuated his next words with hard vicious strokes: "You-are-just-a-fuckhole-who-needs-to-be-filled."

"In the Waiting Line," by Zero 7, started to play. With the cigar clenched firmly between his teeth, Jack abruptly slowed his motions and moved his hips back in time to the music until just the head of his dick was in Gus's mouth, before sliding forward and ordering Gus to suck harder. Legs shaking, sweat dripping down his spine, Jack threw his head back and around, grunting and moaning his pleasure. Gus had a purty mouth and sure as hell knew how to use it. Jack was torn between face-fucking him into unconsciousness or edging himself into cumming so hard that Gus's face and chest would be dripping from his orgasm.

Jack managed to edge for just a bit. He believed in the adage that a bottom should be left wanting more. As Thrill Kill Cult's "Hit and Run Holiday" hit its last refrain, he pulled back and shot all over Gus. Gus was shocked as the slick stream of fluid hit him on the jaw, dripping down his beard. A second and third shot caught him on the chest. Jack grabbed and squeezed his dick, shaking it twice before putting it back in his pants and buttoning up his jeans.

Gus wiped his hand up his chest, scooping up some of the

fluid and bringing it to his nose. It smelled musky and faintly of piss. He stuck out his tongue. It tasted a little pisslike, but clearly wasn't piss. For one, it was thicker. But it wasn't semen.

Jack finished putting his belt on and swigged one last shot of vodka before leaning down to a perplexed Gus. Jack slowly approached Gus's lips, getting as close as he could get, teasing him with his breath. He finally kissed Gus's lips and flicked his tongue inside Gus's mouth, tasting himself on Gus's tongue before kissing him in earnest. Just like he had claimed Gus's mouth with his cock, he now claimed it with his tongue. When he ended the kiss they were both breathless.

Jack placed his mouth near Gus's ear and sucked the earlobe in. He rumbled in a voice slightly higher than a whisper, "You don't know Jack, Mr. Know It All, but ya could if you continue to play your cards right. If you wanna know Jack, keep your hands off your dick and drop me a line tomorrow morning." With that he stood up, dropped a trick card in between Gus's knees, and turned on his heel. He left the bar without ever looking back.

The end of his cigar was chomped to bits, but he'd enjoy the last of it on his ride home. He was looking forward to a little edging and milking session tomorrow. Oh, they still needed to have The Conversation, because Jack wanted so much more from Gus.

CANADIAN SLIM

Shawna Virago

I moved to San Francisco with just a backpack and my guitar. As soon as I landed, I caught a cab in from the airport. I moved here to find myself, not love, but I wasn't in the cab more than two minutes when the driver looked at me in his rearview and said, "My wife is a Jehovah's Witness. She hasn't given me a blow job since our honeymoon! We just celebrated our twenty-fifth wedding anniversary. I'm a man! I have needs! Sir? Ma'am? Sir-ma'am? You look good to me. We could work something out." I was speechless. I was tempted to demand free cab fare and have him carry my bags up the three flights of stairs to my flat. Instead, I started singing in my best *basso profundo* the old gospel standard, "Jesus Gonna Hunt You Down," which deflated his profane desires instantly. He got the message and didn't speak to me again the rest of the ride, his tail curled flaccidly between his legs.

Arriving in San Francisco and coming out as trans, I was afraid that being transgender would be a liability when it came to finding dates, but boy (or boi) was I wrong! Instead of being a liability, it made me the most popular girl at the dance. Literally. I remember going to a line-dancing event put on by the Tranny Chasing Society of North America, and I was on my feet all night, Texas two-stepping with a room full of lonely men. I was like honey attracting bees. I'd finish with one man and then immediately be scooped up by another. Still, even with all the attention I found it unsatisfying.

By day I worked under the table at a downtown hot-dog cart where I watched hordes of European tourists crowding into department stores to buy sweatshop clothes they could buy back home. By night I was getting dolled up, finding out that fishnets are a girl's best friend and hooking up with guys who were very interested in transgender ladies. I'd meet them at bars or through personal ads for passable T-girls. I met a lot of nice guys who oddly had names like Thomas Jefferson, Jimi Hendrix, Captain Tennille and Friedrich Nietzsche. I realized quickly that guys using pseudonyms weren't interested in calling me back the next morning. I was both a source of desire and shame, and it didn't feel good.

These dates were always after dark, very covert, in the shadows, in hotel rooms. It was all about quick sex, especially me fucking them up the ass. Sometimes I used my Colt ten-inch dildo when I couldn't get it up. With some guys my arm got tired from all the anal ring toss they wanted to play. Some guys just wanted to sit around and jerk off to dull she-male porn. Initially I found it amusing that so many guys wanted to do nothing but lick my boots or have me breastfeed them, but there was no give and take, just a lot of giving on my part. It got to be boring. Sometimes I just wanted to go out to dinner. Sometimes I just wanted to lie on my back and be fucked.

Sometimes, of course, a guy would venture out in public

with me and guys like these would get a big turn-on from taking me out to dinner because nobody else knew he was out with a transgender woman. "Isn't this exciting! No one knows you're a tranny," I remember one guy telling me, with clam sauce around his chin, my hand covertly jacking him off under the table of a posh restaurant. The next time this guy took me out to dinner, the restaurant was packed. We had to wait for a table, so I gave the hostess our name for the wait list. A few minutes later the hostess called out, "Transsexual party of two, your table is ready. Transsexuals, your table is ready." My date bounded out the door like he was escaping a house on fire. I applied some lip gloss and told myself I was done with those kind of guys. I craved more pampering.

Around the same time, I would also meet women, and I found my escapades with queer women more satisfying. These encounters usually happened after I played a show with my band and there would be dyke stage-door johnnies wanting to hook up. They usually gave their real names—but this being San Francisco, real names meant Tiger and Wind Chime. There was a lot less ass play and sometimes we even ventured forth in daylight hours or took road trips. I remember fondly the butch lesbian who took me to Portland and pumped me full of crystal meth and beer and asked me to go-go dance for hours to her Ferron cassette. Eventually the crystal wore off and we cuddled the remainder of the weekend.

The other demographic I'd have hook-ups with would be straight swinger couples. I found myself in a lot of Pacific Heights homes, where usually the wives thought it would be fun if I fucked their husbands up the ass. As I got behind these guys' backsides, they would shriek things like, "I'm a bitch! I'm a bitch! I'm a bitch!" As I pumped away, I found myself distracted, wondering to myself, *How on Earth did heterosexuals take over the world?* These encounters were so boring I did very few of them. I'd usually leave with cab fare and a very expensive bottle of wine.

I finally got tired of the fetishized objectifying. It wasn't gratifying. I wanted a legitimate relationship with someone who had clean hygiene and would treat me right. I realized I wanted a real relationship but felt a sense of futility that I'd ever find one. I took a couple years off from dating anyone, to sort out my head. One thing I knew for sure: I was done with cisgendered men and women.

There were two pivotal events in the formation of my adult self. As a child my family moved around a lot and I had to change schools frequently. No matter which part of the country I ended up in, I found myself perceived to be the class faggot by my classmates. When I lived in a small town in North Carolina, one boy in particular bullied me nonstop. His name was Armitage Rufus Peppington. Armitage devoted his days at our school to making my life unpleasant, filling me with fear and terror. To make matters worse, come summertime, my parents forced me to go to Jesus Camp and I had to share a tent with this lout! After three days of torment I'd had enough and devised a plan. After Armitage fell asleep, I pulled some Nair out of my backpack (I never traveled without it) and very carefully applied it to his eyebrows. Hours later, when he woke up looking like a surprised extraterrestrial and cried like a baby, I realized I loved to dominate boys.

As a teenager growing up in my Christian household, I knew I was trans, but the feelings were very uncomfortable. I had a lot of shame. I thought if I got a girlfriend, maybe I'd be cured of these sinful feelings. I prayed to Jesus to give me a girlfriend, to make me "normal." My prayers were answered shortly afterward, in tenth grade, with the appearance of Blaine in my life. Blaine was on the high school softball and soccer teams. We got along great.

After dating about a month, I was invited to meet her mother. I was shocked when both of them said I would make a better girl. That was confusing, and I wondered if Blaine would keep dating me. But then we began having lots of sex at motels, where we'd register under names like Mrs. Abraham Lincoln and Blaine insisted on dressing me up in girls' clothes and putting makeup on me. "You're real pretty," she'd say, then fuck my brains out. So much for Jesus making me normal. Or maybe Jesus was answering my prayers. At school the next day I didn't know if I felt like a dirty schoolboy or a dirty schoolgirl. But it had to be secret. I was a secret.

These were the two formative conditions of my burgeoning self. I was discovering I was a naughty girl who liked to dress up and teach boys good manners. If only I could find someone who didn't only want to do this clandestinely.

When I met Canadian Slim that all changed. I was at Café Du Nord, a nightclub in San Francisco. I had played a show earlier and now was at the bar. I saw him come out of the night and down the steps into the bar, illuminated in light. He was a tall handsome trans-guy who I later learned was from Vancouver. He saw me and kinda blushed, which I found very cute. We began talking and an hour later I was in his room pulling his cock out of his denim.

I began to work his cock with spit, tugging and then sucking him. He came right away, shuddering a little. Then he grabbed me hard by my hair and pulled me up. He pulled me to him and unzipped my dress and pulled it off me. He took off my bra and pushed me on his bed, my stiletto heels still on. He then did what no one had done for years—pleasured me. He fondled, sucked, licked my girly stick until I shot my wad, breathless. He was very beautiful. He began to fuck me, our bodies sweaty. Later as we lay on the sheets, and discussed the misogyny of Godard films and our mutual love of 1930s erotica, I considered I might be capable of a real relationship.

The next night (our first proper date) he took me to a restaurant at the very top of a hotel. In the elevator the sexual tension was so strong, I couldn't help myself and took my panties off, which was easy because I was wearing a miniskirt. He began touching me down there just about the time the elevator made it to our final stop. We pushed the DOWN button, forgot about dinner and went back to his place.

After we were together about three months, Canadian Slim and I were invited to take care of a friend's house in rural Northern California. We spent the first day hiking and exploring through beautiful grasses and countryside. The next day we woke up early: the ranchers down the valley were dynamiting holes and rocks, whooping it up. Canadian Slim and I had no choice but to get out of bed, pull the curtain back and let in the morning light and open the floor to ceiling glass doors. Canadian Slim exclaimed, "What a beautiful morning," pointing out the different trees on the ridgeline and breathing in the clean air. I brought out some coffee and gave him a kiss. "This is the life," he said, pulling me close, and I smiled in agreement. Over the top of the hills we saw a plane off to the south and then a feral cat hushed on by, just past the stairs. I threw a piece of sausage in the grass just in front of the cat, because I always liked cats and I was wondering if she might eat it. The cat stopped, sniffed the sausage and looked back at us before taking a big bite. Slim came up behind me and began softly kissing my neck. I prayed this relationship would work out.

Last night was our ninth anniversary. We had dinner in the Castro and were walking by one of the boy bars, when a drunk older gentleman yelled at Canadian Slim, "Lose the fish, honey," referring to me. We both laughed at his obnoxiousness, and also at the fact that he didn't know he was looking at a transgender couple. I felt some satisfaction, I admit, at having my gender affirmed by this clown, and so did Slim.

When we got back home I slipped into the bedroom and put on a red satin corset, matching G-string and red silk stockings with garters, with my fuck-me pumps. I invited Slim into the room. "I think I'm going to get lucky," he said. "You're psychic," I replied and took off his shirt and caressed his masculine chest and his beautiful chest scars. "You've been very bad," I told him and pushed him onto the bed. I got his pants off and flipped Slim on his stomach and begin to lightly spank his taut ass. I got his underwear off and lubed my fingers and began to work his ass very gently. I pulled out my Colt ten-inch dildo and fucked him in the ass and I reached underneath and stroked his tranny boy cock. I worked that dildo and touched his cock until he finally moaned, and his body shuddered with coming.

THE HITCHHIKER

Sinclair Sexsmith

"Get in," the driver said, after flipping the dial on the stereo of the small blue pickup truck, quieting Big Black's "He's a Whore."

Alice leaned her elbows on the window, made her legs into an A-frame, tipped her ass to one side and flipped her wheat-colored hair over her shoulder. She could spot one when she saw one: someone else with an insatiable appetite, someone who would take her for a ride, someone who would play dirty and queer and like they do in the bad films.

She took a long look at the driver: the blond fauxhawk, messy overalls, lean defined arms in a life-partner beater, dark tribal tattoos peeking out from the collarbone. A dark, worn cowboy hat sat on the passenger's seat. The driver flashed a nice smile: simple, a little mischievous.

Until now she didn't know it, but this was who she had been waiting for, and this was exactly why she'd hitched all the way to the good beach by herself today.

The scent of grass and sod wafted from the back of the truck. Alice spied power tools, a lawnmower, some rakes and shovels secured to the racks in the back. She gripped the handle, opened the door and slid onto the vinyl bench seat, taking the cowboy hat into one hand and easily sliding it over the crown of her head.

"My friends call me Jack."

"I'm Alice." She slid her eyes sideways to watch Jack maneuver the stick shift as the pickup pulled back onto the Pacific Coast Highway.

"Where you heading?" Alice asked.

Jack watched as she adjusted her long legs and ran one ankle against the opposite calf. "Wherever." Good answer. South on the PCH was good enough for now. Alice wanted to end up in the city somewhere, it didn't matter where. Cliffs and beach rolled by their windows. This was as good a direction as any.

The cab smelled like grass, too; grass and dirt, but in a clean, organic earthy kind of way. "You been working in the sun all day?" Alice asked, tossing the hat onto the dash, then flipping her hair again and strategically placing her elbow over the back of the bench seat between them. Her fingers were dangerously close to the overall buckles. The skin beneath was tan, a little pinkish.

"Yep."

"It was nice today. Not too hot for August."

"Yeah."

"So you're a gardener?"

Jack downshifted through a tight curve and held the clutch in a moment too long. "Landscape architect." Pressure on the engine. She watched Jack's mouth move and wanted to taste it already. Wanted to feel its suck and bite.

"Of course. You enjoy that?"

"Yeah, I do."

Alice let her fingers drift onto the muscles of Jack's upper arm; soft skin. "You look like you're good at it." She let herself picture Jack shoveling, digging; big bags of fertilizer slung over these broad shoulders; squinting in the sun.

Jack didn't answer, just smiled softly, looking out at the road. Concentrating. Waiting. Already playing the game. The quiet was comfortable. Alice lifted her small satchel bag from her shoulder. "Do you smoke?" she asked.

"No."

"Mind if I do?"

"Go right ahead." Such a gentleman. She rolled the window down a crack, lit an unfiltered Lucky Strike from a soft pack. Only a few more left. The small cylinder felt good between her fingers, on her lips. She slipped her slender tan feet out of her white beach sandals and brought them up onto the seat, exposing her creamy caramel inner thighs. They rode in silence as Alice smoked, Big Black still soft on the stereo. Jack watched her from a sideways glance, one hand on the stick shift, palm starting to sweat, not making a move, not yet. Alice's tank top exposed her toned navel and hip bones peeking out from the top of her tiny jean shorts. She brought the cigarette to her lips deliberately.

Jack took a breath, still not looking at her. "I like the way you do that."

"Yeah?" Alice leaned against the door, moved one leg farther up onto the seat between them. "I like the way you drive."

The corners of Jack's mouth curled. "Thanks, darlin'." Her toes shuffled toward the exposed side of the overalls, the thin, thin fabric of the undershirt. Jack shifted in place, muscles tightening and releasing quickly, expertly.

Alice watched, considering Jack's hard body, the sweet smell of sweat and physicality. She flicked her cigarette out the truck window and rolled the window back up, pulled her knees up underneath her, leaned in close to Jack's ear.

Now.

"Any interest in a fuck?"

"Uh," Jack's eyes flashed. Alice already had her hand on the bulge in the crotch of Jack's overalls.

"I'd like to see what you've got under there." Jack unsnapped the shoulder buckles, pushed them out of the way. Alice pulled a thick, marble-blue-colored strap-on from soft gray Calvin Klein briefs. It was bigger around than her hand would fit. She milked it with her fingers, real as anything. Her mouth watered for it. Jack's eyes never left the road, but were increasingly glossy with lust.

"Looks good," said Alice. "Big and hard already."

"Gave me quite the boner, you on side of the road like that."

That's right. Play with me. "Oh yeah? Little ol' me?"

"Soon as I saw those legs, I wanted them wrapped around me." Alice bobbed her hand in Jack's lap, dipping her face nearer to the cock, small murmurings of *mmm* coming from her mouth. Jack left one hand on the wheel and didn't slow down, hugging the curves of the road with precision. Her lips grazed the head, licked it like an ice-cream cone with her long tongue, sucked it into her mouth while she left her hand pushing into the base of the silicone.

Jack groaned. "Damn, you're good at that."

Alice smiled and sucked; swirled her tongue; worked the head against the ridge at the back of her mouth; applied pressure.

Jack moaned again, deep, from the gut, hips thrusting a little, heavy foot on the gas pedal, not slowing, eyes on the road. Jack took a blind curve around a cliff, suddenly swerved into the dirt pull-off overlooking the beach and cut the engine. Alice didn't stop, head bobbing on the delicious blue cock. Jack leaned back, feet on the floor, hips lifting, hands gripping the steering wheel and then the ceiling of the cab, pressing against the truck at every angle to get the cock farther down Alice's throat.

"Fuck." Jack shuddered, bringing a hand to Alice's long hair and pulling her off of the cock. She wiped saliva off her mouth with the back of her hand, lips swollen, eyes wide. Waiting. She had made it real; now it was Jack's turn to make her real. To fill up her desires without apology, without Madonna or whore complexes, without any stereotype of her girlyness, but with only the raw instinct of their animal-brain hunger. She wanted to feel that insatiable appetite coursing between them, body against body, mouth to skin, silicone sliding inside. That's the way she liked to open.

What's next, Jack?

"Come with me." Jack threw open the door to the cab and half guided, half dragged Alice out of the driver's side door. The sun hit them both, insistent and thick on its fall into the ocean. Jack pulled the tailgate down and hopped into the back of the truck with one quick leap, then leaned and offered a hand to Alice. Barefoot, she climbed in.

There was not much room with all the tools. The lawnmower was covered in flecks of grass and a dark petroleum lubricant for its rusty engine, and it sat next to a red gas can, both with a strong, pungent smell. Dirt stuck to Alice's bare feet. She made her way up to the cab of the truck and pressed her stomach to it, lifted one leg at the knee and stared out into the beach and setting sun, at waves lapping. It was pretty much deserted this far out of the city. A sporty two-door car zipped past, then it was quiet again.

From behind her, Jack let go of the overalls and they fell, exposing skin and muscle and curling tattoos, and seemed to gather the courage to stay that way. Alice had her thumbs in the waist of her shorts, a promise, a reward, and twisted around to face Jack. She barely glanced down, knowing the tenderness of overexposure, of gazes too thick on your misaligned places, of scars on chests now chiseled like David. She stepped close enough for them to feel each other's breath and whispered, "You're gonna fuck me with that big thing of yours, aren't you?"

Jack's mouth watered. "Yes."

"Do it then." She bent over the cab of the truck, slithered the shorts down over her ass and left them at her knees, creamy tan beach skin exposed, cunt exposed, neck twisted to watch Jack approaching.

Jack slid the cock into her in a swift gasp, stretching her taut. Alice lifted onto her tiptoes to tilt her pelvis, curve her back. Jack took hold of her hips and thrust, hard, and again, and again, thick inside her.

"Tight little pussy," Jack murmured, one hand on her ass, spreading her cheeks. "Feels so good to open you with my big cock."

Jack thrust harder, grunting. "Aw, yeah; aw, god, yeah." Alice gasped with each hard thrust, impaled, in a bit of pain but also exquisite sensation, hips pressing apart, back arching deeper, mouth open and gasping. She lifted one foot up onto the three piled bags of garden dirt in the corner of the truck and spread her legs for Jack.

"You like that, don't you? Dirty girl. You've been waiting for someone like me to come along and fuck you right, haven't you? Haven't you?" Jack thrust harder, slower, then sharp.

"Yes, oh, god, Jack, fuck me, just like that," Alice moaned. *That's it, that's exactly it.* Jack slid one arm around her waist and twisted, pulled out and shoved her onto the bags of fertilizer, dropping her on her ass harshly, and she reached down to catch herself with her hands, her legs slightly tangled in the fabric of her tiny shorts.

Alice reached up and gripped the bar of the lawnmower next to her, lifting her feet off the ground, legs together, balancing on her ass. Jack slid the shorts down her tanned, slender legs and stepped between them, squatting, pushing her knees back against her chest, their faces inches apart.

Her big blue eyes were wide open.

Jack slid the cock inside her eager cunt again and tried to keep looking at Alice, tried not to miss a minute of this, sun and surf behind Alice's head, California traffic zooming by on the PCH, Alice's face flushed, neck arched, hands gripping, pulling, steadying. The lawnmower shook as Jack thrust and thrust, harder, gaining speed, getting faster.

"Your pussy feels so good," Jack mumbled. "So tight around my cock. Squeeze me, oh, god, yeah, just like that, feels so good, feels so fucken good."

"Oh yeah, fuck me," Alice breathed. "Come inside me, oh, yeah, you can do that, can't you, big boy? Fuck me hard until you come inside. I'll pump that come from your cock with my tight pussy. You like that? You can feel that, can't you, Jack?"

Jack bucked against Alice, tight and hard, shoving into her over and over until Jack came, swearing, and softened, slowed. Alice caressed the back of Jack's head, the short-short hairs and longer 'hawk in the middle, *just a little, just for a minute,* until Jack's eyes, gleaming, met hers.

"Strip."

Alice's eyes narrowed. "What?"

"We're going in." Jack nodded toward the beach and stood, lifting the A-shirt up and off, revealing toned chest muscles, those thin red strips of scar, the swirls of dark tribal tattoos, California-brown skin. Hopping out of the truck, nearly naked and completely unselfconscious, Jack jogged toward the cliff's edge and found a path down, through the beach grass and lines of rocks against the road. Another car zipped past, an old sedan, then the sound faded around the corner of the PCH.

Alice followed, watching as Jack awkwardly stripped off the CK briefs while attempting to run in the sand toward the water, body exposed to the elements, shivering for a second. Alice thought she sensed a moment of reverence as Jack's hands ran along opposite upper arms, shoulders, pecs, head dipped slightly forward. *Finally at home in this body.* Jack opened up, arms stretched like wings, wide as the horizon. Alice felt giddy, high with delight. She let her body pick up speed while gravity pulled her down the path of the cliff's edge and broke into a run when she hit the sand. Her shorts were still in the back of the pickup somewhere, her legs bare, feet bare, only her cut-off tank top remained, and she pulled it over her head, dropped it near an obvious large boulder.

Jack splashed into the water, tossed the words back at her: "Come on!"

Alice hovered near the edge of the surf, ankle deep in lolling waves and wet sand, kicking at the water. She watched Jack immerse and surface, strapped blue cock and leather harness wet and becoming looser around Jack's hips, hands running through the wet 'hawk falling in both eyes, and Alice dove into the surf, slid through the water, cool and soothing against the heat of the day. She surfaced and couldn't see Jack, then let her body float, weightless, on the rolling waves, until something abruptly pulled her under.

She opened her mouth with a startled "Oh!" and then it was full of salt water. Her arms and legs flailed as she struggled back to the surface, gasping at the air.

Jack was smiling, stifling laughter, next to her.

"Oh, you think that's funny, do you?"

Jack's laughter stopped suddenly and changed to a falsely serious playful face. Alice closed the distance between them quickly and, smirking, grabbed for the strap-on, pulled hard, forced Jack under the water, both of them struggling, Jack grabbing onto Alice for support as they were both pulled deeper under the water.

They untangled, emerged, gasping and laughing. Jack lunged for Alice in a tail dive, took hold of her waist, lifted her legs. She leaned back into the water as Jack found her clit, slid fingers inside, held her hips up.

"Ohh, that's good," she crooned. "Oh, god. Damn. That's perfect...oh fuck, your fingers inside me feels so good. I can't—I want—" She had no leverage. She could feel the sandy ocean floor with her toes, but wanted her ankles up on Jack's broad shoulders.

Jack pulled-pushed her farther toward shore, half walking, half swimming, bodies touching everywhere, Alice being pushed backward as Jack walked along the sand, both of them holding each other's eyes and bodies up in the water, Jack's cock bobbing against her leg. She bit her lip to keep from sucking her tongue in her mouth, remembering how that blue cock tasted and felt.

The ocean rocked around them, then she hit sand with her butt first, soft sandy ground, then Alice was laid out as the wave receded, kissing, nude, Jack's hands between her legs, greedy, pushing her thighs apart, thick fingers entering her and she gasped.

"I think it's time you came for me," Jack whispered gruffly, mouth rough on her cheek, pressing Alice against the sand, pushing her legs apart. "Come on, open up that cunt for me, squeeze my fingers. You feel me deep inside you?"

Alice gasped, body balanced on every sensation, heels in the air, thighs pressed back against the wet sand. Jack worked her clit with expert precision, making slow circles, a slick thrumming, and then another wave broke at their feet.

"I'm gonna make you come so hard," Jack breathed into her neck, fingers moving harder, faster, between her legs, pulsing over her clit. "You're going to come just for me, just for me, pretty girl. Feel my fingers workin' your pussy? You're gonna do it for me, aren't you? Let go, just let it all go and come for me, come on girl, fuck, yeah, do it."

Alice, gasping, toes curling, swollen cunt pressed hard against Jack's hand, felt her muscles tighten and vibrate, swell and then explode, thick and fast and deep, Jack's fingers thrusting, pressing hard against her hard clit, as her stomach contracted and body shook. She screamed a string of profanities and gripped Jack's wrists, clawed at the muscles of Jack's shoulders. She moaned and yelled, eyes open and suddenly aware of the darkening sky, the bright stars beginning to be visible outside of the city, twilight fading fast to blackness.

Jack touched her thighs and stomach for a minute as her body calmed. Alice became suddenly aware of her wet feet, bare body, the breeze coming from over the ocean, the sound of the water, waves still tickling her calves and knees, cooler than the air and soothing.

"I, uh," Jack stammered, suddenly quiet again. "Guess we should get back on the road."

Alice nodded. She wanted another Lucky Strike, was beginning to feel chilled. And she wanted to blow Jack behind the wheel again.

Jack offered her a hand up and they both brushed sand from their bare skin. Alice took in the toned chest and arm muscles, the dark curly tattoos, and Jack let her look, glancing at her face and stripping off the wet leather harness.

Her eyes sparkled.

Walking through the sand, gripping the cock and letting the harness dangle, Jack headed toward the truck. Alice stood for a moment, watching the shimmering reflection of the rising new moon in the surface of the water, listening to the crash and rush and whoosh of the waves. She turned away from the water and watched Jack's ass and thighs moving along the path ahead of her, wondering how many miles until they'd reach the city, how long before their insatiable appetites would flare up, and how long until she would get fucked again by this beautiful man.

OUT ON LOAN

Arden Hill

The sweet boy I'm borrowing looks younger than ze is, though that might be rude to mention—especially now that ze's changed out of those baggy black pants and into one of the smart little sailor suits that I keep in the spare room closet. I haven't told hir about the dungeon yet. I like the element of surprise, blindfolding submissives and shuffling them down the hallway into a space they had no idea existed. The elevator was installed in 1987 by the woman who owned the house before me, and it shakes so much that it's impossible to tell which direction the elevator is traveling. I use this to my advantage, riding up to the attic and proclaiming, when the door opens, "Not this level, people might still hear the screams." The door shuts and the submissives shudder as we descend into the basement. When I lead them out, they think they've been traveling for miles. There is a sign in the dungeon right near the elevator. The submissives don't see it but the Dominants I bring down here do and get quite a kick out of it. The sign reads HALFWAY TO HELL. Really it's only a few feet away, behind a red velvet curtain.

The boy has been polishing my gear for about an hour now. Ze rubs the cleaning cloth in small circles and looks up at me every now and then. If I hadn't talked to the boy's owner I'd think ze was perfectly submissive, but Rose says the boy can quickly turn cheeky. I'll be ready when ze does. I've been studying hir, starting with the expression on hir face when ze entered the small room and saw only a few whips and modest restraints decorating the four corners of the bed. I could practically hear hir disappointed sigh. I do respect that ze tried to hide those feelings from me, even mustering a "Thank you, Mistress, for inviting me over."

Cleaning allows the boy to informally tour my collection of erotic items. I've seen hir eyes widen at a few pieces. This lets me know what to bring with me on the next step of our playdate. Ze's traveling down into the space well. "Boy," I ask hir, "What do you think of my collection?"

"It's beautiful," ze whispers.

"And how does it compare to your owner's?" I ask sweetly.

Ze almost grins knowing that this is a trick question, believing that ze can show both the proper respect to me and to hir Mistress, whom ze knows I am quite close with. "I've never seen so many kinds of floggers," ze begins. "Each one looks as though it has its own purpose."

"They do," I say.

"My Mistress only has a few floggers; she favors canes," ze adds.

"I'm sure her cane collection is quite impressive," I purr.

"Yes," ze agrees, "it is."

"And is there evidence on your back?" I ask.

"Yes," ze says shyly, "bruises from a third of the collection."

I smile and tell hir ze'll be showing me later. The boy goes back to polishing my gear. There is a row of boots in the closet that I'll set hir on next time. Today I'm eager to work on hir flesh and have hir provide the other services I need.

As the boy cleans, I walk past hir to a small picture of a curvy girl in a corset. It's a black-and-white, very well done and taken by an ex-lover of mine. At least when they leave, they leave something to remember them by. I bring my hand to my left nipple and feel the barbell. It had been fun training that New York submissive to pierce me. I practiced on her flesh for months, showing her how it was done, and enjoying myself in the meantime. By the time New York and I parted ways, she knew how to play pierce me as well. She never got a smug attitude, never got confused as to her role in servicing me. I hear she's switching now, back in the city. Maybe she'll like it. Me, once I started topping, I didn't go back. I get my variety by co-topping and triple teaming. Sometimes the feminist leather daddies lend me their boys to cure any squeamishness they might have about girls. I start those fags off with a little bit of glitter strap-on girl cock and have them finish by licking my pussy and working their way back. Everybody has an ass, right? And nipples.

I graze my piercing again before flipping the black-and-white photograph over to reveal a metal ring set into the wall. The boy looks up open mouthed. "Careful dropping your jaw like that," I tease. "I might just fill it up. You didn't really think I had no tricks up my sleeve did you?

"No, Ma'am," ze confesses.

"Come now boy," I scold, "you know my reputation." Ze nods. "Don't you think I earned it?" Ze nods again. "And do you think I could have earned it with just four restraints on a double bed?"

"No, Ma'am," ze replies.

I move over and slap hir lightly across the face. "Doubting my skills," I hiss, "wrong answer." Ze whimpers a bit. I'm keeping hir where I want hir. When ze's finished cleaning, I'll put the blindfold on and have some fun.

"Finished, Ma'am," ze says, gently putting the last curved piece of stainless steal back into its case.

"We're just starting," I tell hir. I slip the handcuffs over hir wrists and lock them. Ze whispers as I push hir roughly to the wall and fasten the cuffs to the metal ring with one of the padlocks ze's just cleaned. "I expect there will be quite a bit to clean once I've finished with you," I say.

My favorite blindfold is black leather with a padded inside. I slip it around hir head now and tie it tight. "I'm going to take you down into the dungeon now," I tell hir as I unlock the handcuffs from the wall. Hir mouth shows hir surprise though I'm sure hir eyes are wide, too, if they are open under the blindfold. "Walk forward," I say when I've got hir by the chains. I guide hir slightly by pushing on hir shoulders. "Turn left. The elevator is down the back hall. I guess Mistress Rose wanted you to have a surprise," I tell hir.

We reach the elevator and I press the button. Ze hears the elevator creaking before the doors open. "Oh, good," I say. "It wasn't too far down." I shove hir in and ze slams against the wall. I stick my foot under hir and ze hits the floor. "Careful boy," I warn. "Stand on up." The elevator lurches and ze struggles to stand. By the time ze's regained hir feet, the elevator has reached the attic. I let the door open. "Hmm," I muse, "Perhaps another time. I think today we'll use a different level." I smile at the boy, though ze can't see me. Soon we're stepping into the basement dungeon. Ze's still wearing the slit pants. I grab hir roughly and jerk the pants down. "You can keep those boxers on, for now," I tell hir. Hir skin is goose bumped, a combination of anticipation and the basement's slightly cooler climate. I cup hir crotch and am not surprised to find hir hard. "Big boy," I say. "Like a ripe mulberry and you're just as juicy. I'll wear gloves so you don't stain my fingers."

"Thank you," ze says.

"Now tell me," I say, "are you nervous?"

"Yes," ze replies.

"And," I ask, "are you worried you won't be able to take it?"

"Yes," ze says.

I smile, enjoying the power I've coaxed hir into giving me. Ze's mine for the evening. I won hir from hirself in the little bedroom upstairs and while ze may be a sore loser, it will only be in hir tender flesh. Rose told me how much ze wants to play. I flick hir dick and slip a finger into hir before ze can pull away. I don't doubt that desire and I'm as wet as ze is. I pull my finger out of hir and whisper, "My turn."

With the blindfold on, the boy is hesitant to move. I tug on hir hair and yank hir collar to urge hir closer to the table in the middle of the dungeon. Once I have hir leaned against the front, I shove hir chest hard. Ze falls back and I fix one of hir wrists into the restraints. Ze's squirming but ze's moaning so loudly I know ze doesn't want to get away. "Time for those briefs to come off," I tell hir. "Be a good boy and lift your ass." Ze complies, slowly raising hir cheeks off of the wood. Because of how ze landed, hir ass is not over the table's adjustable section. Ze'll find out soon enough how special my table is. "I flick open a knife. Ze instantly stills. "You know that sound?" I ask.

"Yes, Ma'am," ze replies.

"Do you think I will cut your clothes or cut your skin for disobeying?" I ask.

No clever little grin on this boy now. Ze has no idea what the right answer is. I've decided that the right answer is going to be whichever answer ze does not give.

"My skin?" ze guesses.

I don't answer but I bring my hands down on hir flesh. Ze jerks as though ze's been shocked. "I don't want to dirty my knife right now," I tell hir as I slice through the sides of hir boxers. Ze's dripping and hir ass is clenching and unclenching like an eager little mouth. I lick my lips and position hir free wrist and legs into the restraints. I unhook hir binder and ze gasps a little. "Back in a minute," I tell hir. I've got just the toy. I move silently around the table and reach into the side container which holds the butt plugs that work with the mechanisms I have rigged under the table. I pick a medium-sized plug that looks like a purple snowman. Under the last ball the neck is wide and short. I turn a crank and a circle of wood lowers from under the boy's ass. Ze flinches and struggles. That reaction isn't just from the cold air. When the circle is low enough I screw the dildo into place and pour some lube over it. I watch it drip down like sauce over ice cream.

"Your ass is just going to eat this up, boy," I say as I put lube on my finger and reach up. The boy's ass is smooth. Latex makes it difficult to tell if ze's shaved hirself or if, sans testosterone, ze's naturally hairless. Ze squirms when I enter hir and tries to lift hir body off of the table. "Oh, I have a way to keep you still," I warn. Ze whispers and I pull out of hir slowly. I just used one finger but I could tell from how ze opened that ze's taken a lot more than that. If I know Rose's love of toys, it hasn't all been fingers.

With the boy lubed up, I turn the crank and raise the butt plug closer to hir ass. I turn it slowly and tell hir what I am doing, "I'm going to lock you into place as Rose says you have a habit of forgetting it."

"I'm sorry," the boy offers.

"Sweet thing," I say, "I really hope for your sake you're not going to do anything you need to apologize for."

"I'll be good," ze promises.

"I'm sure you will," I say as the tip of the plug makes contact with hir asscheeks. "I just need to make some adjustments. Relax."

The boy follows orders and is not rigid as I slide the plug over so it is aligned with hir slick hole. Ze's dripping so much from hir front hole that I probably didn't need to use any lube on hir ass. The boy tightens up when I start to crank the plug up into hir but loosens hir muscles without being told. When the first ball has slid in, I play with hir nipples just a bit. Ze shivers and pushes down on the plug. I ease the second ball in. It's just slightly larger than the first. The real jump is between this ball and the last. I grab a cock and a harness and strap it onto the boy while hir legs are still decently maneuverable. It's a beautiful leather harness and it's holding my favorite cock: a thick, ribbed one with a sharp curve and a bulbous head.

I make sure to adjust all the harness buckles. Once the butt plug's third ball is in the boy, ze'll be locked to the table by hir ass. "You might want to take a deep breath," I tell the boy. Ze gulps air. "Now let it out nice and slowly," I tell hir while I turn the crank and push the last ball into hir ass. This one doesn't go in as quickly as the other two. Ze takes another quick breath and by the time ze's let that one out, hir ass has allowed the plug in. I run my finger around the ring of hir ass surrounding the plug's neck. "Nice and tight," I say and reach for hir nipples again. Now when ze flinches the plug tugs on hir ass, keeping hir securely in place.

I climb on top of hir and squeeze hir cheeks together so that hir lips pout out. "If you can put that clever tongue to some good use," I tell hir, "you can avoid my meanest ball gag." Ze nods hir head and I put my pointer finger into hir mouth. It easily slides down so I add one then two more. "Rose has you suck her cock fairly often doesn't she?" I ask. I feel hir lips tighten and know ze is nodding yes. "This feels nice," I tell hir and when ze smiles I take advantage of the opening and pop in my pinky finger and thumb. I can stroke hir throat. Ze doesn't choke. "Good job," I whisper. "No ball gag for you, but let's see how well you do with nipples." Ze waits patiently as I unlace my corset, only flinching at the surprise of the material falling off of me and hitting hir stomach.

The boy has a truly sweet mouth. I push my left nipple in and ze latches on like ze's found mommy. Hir tongue pulls my nipple toward the back of hir throat while hir teeth are light against my areola. I moan a little and shove my breast over hir face till ze can't breathe. Ze keeps working the nipple, not panicked, trusting that I'll let hir come up for air again, and I do, eventually. I pull away and when ze gasps for air, I touch the nipple of my right breast against hir lips. Ze's not interested in breathing anymore, just in swallowing my nipple. I put my palms over hir unbound chest and dig my nails in. Ze flinches as much as the butt plug will allow, but doesn't lose focus on giving me pleasure. If ze were not blindfolded ze could see my look of building enjoyment.

"Can you feel me dripping on you?" I ask.

Ze nods hir head vigorously, shaking my breasts.

"I want you to keep doing that while I fuck your cock," I say.

Ze nods again.

"Oh," I say, "and I want you to feel good down there too, so I'll just get something from my bag."

My nipple pops from hir mouth with a wet sound as I

dismount the boy. The nipple clamps are easy to find and I bring them back to the table. I loosen the harness buckles just enough to slip my hand in and attach one clip to each of hir labia.

"Oh, fuck!" ze cries out.

"I know it's hard to take," I whisper, "but I want it to be hard and I want you to take it."

"Okay," ze whimpers. "Thank you."

The boy trembles as I climb onto the table and kneel above hir. I'm eager for this, but I tease myself slowly over the head of hir cock. The pressure is light enough that I'm sure ze can feel only the anticipation of the clamps pressing harder into hir tender bits. When my cunt is halfway over hir cock, ze whimpers in earnest.

"Feel it, don't you?" I ask.

"Yes, Ma'am," ze moans.

"Do you like it?" I ask.

"Yes," ze says, "so much."

When I force my weight onto hir, ze screams out.

"Still like it?" I ask, rocking my hips back and forth like I am riding out a slow canter.

It's harder for hir to speak but ze eventually murmurs, "Yes."

I take advantage of hir open mouth and slip one of my nipples in. Ze suckles with a singular intent, focusing hir body's awareness to hir mouth and away from hir sore genitals. The strategy isn't completely successful, which turns me on as I like the submissives I fuck to hurt, especially boys who beg for it by rocking their bodies up. If the butt plug weren't holding the boy down, ze'd probably be lifting me into the air and damaging hir flesh with hir desperate pumping. I do enjoy taking care of boys; naughty girls too, though I have a habit of slicing off their pigtails.

The boy circles my nipple with hir tongue and I lean my

weight onto my right hand so I can reach for my clit with my left. I flick the tip of it, feeling the blood fill me and make me hard. I'm as hard as this boy's dick straining up against the leather of the harness. I push a finger into myself feeling it slide along the cyber-skin veins of the boy's cock. I pull out to rub my clit again. The boy is moaning and trembling but I'm focused on getting off. Ze comes and I clench my thighs together forcing my clit to stick out farther. I let my fingers make wider circles around my clit as my thighs tighten up. The boy sobs as I push myself down and come hard.

"Oh, fuck," ze says, releasing my nipple from hir mouth. "Oh, fuck."

Grinning, I quietly exhale. When I finish coming I reach under the harness and remove the nipple clamps from the boy's labia. Ze yelps and almost clears the third ball of the butt plug.

"Steady boy," I tell hir as I lift myself off of hir cock. My wetness slides onto hir stomach and ze, realizing how equally turned on I've been, smiles from the corner of hir mouth.

"Thank you," ze says in a tone that makes it unclear what ze's thanking me for.

"Watch yourself," I say, laughing. "You're not too old to spank." Before ze can smirk I finish the sentence, "With one of the spiked paddles I keep down here."

"Yes, Ma'am," ze says, shy again.

I take the harness off of the boy and examine hir. Ze's ejaculated all over hirself and hir labia show small purple bruises where the clamps were. I turn the table crank and the butt plug begins to emerge from hir ass. Ze moans. *They always put up more of a fuss when it comes out then when it goes in,* I remark to myself. When ze clears the final ball, hir ass winks shut. If I hadn't been the one putting the plug in hir I never would have guessed ze'd been fucked there. Rose must stick her clit in hir ass as often as she sticks it in hir mouth. I'll ask her about that later. Right now I have a boy to tend to. I undo the restraints.

"When you think you can walk," I tell hir, "I'll lead you to the elevator. There's only a cold water shower down here and you've been too good for that." I lead the boy naked into the elevator. Ze leans against me, nuzzling hir shoulder into my neck as we make the ascent.

When we step out of the elevator I can see it's night. Rose has let herself in and is sitting on the love seat drinking a cup of tea.

"I'm glad you ran late," she says in her sultry voice.

God that woman is sexy. How people mistook her for a man, I'll never comprehend.

"How was Mitchell?" Rose asks.

"Ze's having a bath, not a shower," I reply, "if that gives you a clue."

"I'd hoped so," Rose says smiling. "I actually took the liberty of drawing hir one a few minutes ago. It should still be warm."

"I wonder where your boy gets hir cockiness from?" I tease. "Want to wash hir up yourself?" Rose nods.

"Hey, baby," she says, lifting up hir blindfold.

"Hello," the boy replies, looking like ze's just been born.

Rose takes Mitchell by the hand and leads hir to the bathroom. She's familiar enough with my house to know where the soap and washrags are, so I settle into her seat. I sip from her cup and wait for them to return.

FROM FUCKTOY TO FOOTSTOOL

Zev

You had me on my belly, knees bent, feet in the air, ankles trussed to my left wrist. This was uncommon—you know I hate being tied up.

"You're my good boy," you said. "My favorite fucktoy," you told me, as you reached for the rope. "And I'm taking your legs away tonight."

You draped the rough twine around my legs and pulled tight, making me wince from the burn. All the BDSM safety manuals say to use polyester rope, or well-seasoned hemp, but an idea had struck you as we were heading back to our hotel room after a long day of work—you reading from your book and teaching a workshop on how to talk about and around our bodies and genders, and me holding your Blackberry and name cards and trying to be useful. And now that you were finally done, you'd be darned if you needed anything more than what the big 7-Eleven around the corner could provide to unleash your evil twisted imagination upon my body.

I looked up at you and, hungry for your touch, I squirmed and wrapped my still-free right arm around your comfortingly bigger-than-me frame, snuggling closer.

"I love you, Daddy," I said, softly.

"Aw, shucks," you said, just a trace of meanness on the edges of your rich, warm voice. You reached over for a pair of your old boxers from the laundry pile and held the waistband open.

"Wriggle your head into these," you ordered. "For once, I'm not interested in your mouth tonight."

I hoped you knew how grateful I felt that you were using your underwear for this purpose and not mine. When we are apart for long periods of time, you leave me a T-shirt soaked in your sweat, and your heady scent becomes my drug: poppers and Rescue Remedy all in one. Happily, I sniffed my way into the stripy cotton, using my free hand to settle the waistband neatly against my throat, making sure there were no wrinkles in the fabric resting against my face. You laughed at my fastidiousness.

"My little faggot," you said, fondly, walking around me, patting my flanks in that way you have, not quite a caress and not quite a blow, just hard enough to make me nervous.

Now I couldn't see what you were doing. Cocking my head like an attentive pup, I tried to listen for your movements, but you grabbed me by the throat and slipped something around my neck. I drew fast, deep breaths, and you jerked my head higher, forcing me to arch my back, tightening something sharp and clamplike onto my nipples, making me gasp even harder.

"You won't need your tits for this," you said, and you did the same with the lower half of my body, telling me you were putting my hungry little boycock away, but not before giving it a couple of hard smacks, which made me whimper and squirm. Much as I mourn my lack of testicles and a bigger cock for you to torture, you seem to have no trouble inflicting pain on what I've got.

My thoughts were interrupted, as something smooth slid against my only free limb. You cursed as you struggled to get the glove on my right hand.

"Should have done this before the first knot was tied," you mutter. "Oh, well. This is all you are tonight, boyo," you said, smoothing the nitrile over my wrist. "Your hand and your devotion. That's all you've got to make your Daddy feel good tonight."

I choked as you yanked me into place by the noose around my neck. As it tightened, I felt something cold and unyielding against my skin, probably a buckle. It must have been your belt wrapped tightly around my throat, cutting brutally into my flesh. Or maybe it was mine—you loved to subject me to that indignity. I'd have marks the next day, and I wondered what the BDSM safety manuals would say about that, too.

"Get to work, good boy," you said, and squeezed something cold into my right hand.

Lubricant! For the last few years, I'd fantasized silently about playing a role in your orgasm. I knew I was pleasing to you, and not just because I'd gone back to school, gotten a real job and learned how to deal with my family of origin. You fucked me as often as you could, what with the miles separating us, but your body had long been kept away from me, you preferring to slam me up against a wall and explore my holes roughly with your hand. I couldn't complain, of course, but I was hungry for your skin, a desire I kept firmly under wraps, except for occasionally asking you if we could please snuggle without any pesky clothes getting in the way of your warmth and your scent.

In other circumstances, I would have gone "squee!," bounced on the bed, and looked up at you with big puppy-dog eyes, saying, "Really, Daddy?"

Perhaps this was why you'd placed me in such a state, helpless, tits and cock in pain. Perhaps it wasn't your dreamy-eyed boy you wanted tonight. You wanted your fucktoy and his conveniently shaped hand, short fingers and wide palm.

I couldn't so much as inch myself closer, but you helped me with that, looping my leash against your wrist, forcefully bringing me closer. Using the reference point of my head against your thigh, my hand went to work.

I couldn't see your face, but you were kind enough to send certain signals my way, your groans coinciding with a tightening noose around my neck. I abandoned all thoughts of rubbing my fuzzy head all over your crotch, marking myself with your sweat and precome. The more difficult it became for me to breathe, the more frantically I sought your pleasure and not mine, hoping that your favor would grant me mercy.

"That's right, boy," you growled. "Give up your air for me, make your Daddy feel good."

I angled upward, slamming into the space that engulfed me, and I kept going until panic set in. I flailed about, urgently needing to breathe, barely noticing the fresh wave of pain when my struggling dislodged the clamps from my tits. You just laughed at me and my attempts at protest confined to the movement of one hand, which you must have found pleasing because you let out a long, low note of satisfaction, and mercifully adjusted your grip on my leash, loosening the noose a bit.

I redoubled my efforts, putting my heart into every stroke, living for those happy noises you were making up above me. My sore tits and tortured cock forgotten, I was my hand, all of my strength, spirit, love and devotion surrounded by your warmth and your scent, each spasm of yours, each clench a reminder that you were wrapped around me, protecting me even as I served you.

"Ohhh, your Daddy's going to come, boyo," you said, and though I'd been silent to this point, muffled as I was by your underwear, I begged you to please come; please, Daddy; please, Sir; pleasepleaseplease, oh, please, Daddy, please. I was desperate for your pleasure, and you kindly obliged, unleashing a roar, seizing my wrist in your thick paw, first holding me still and then letting me out when you were done.

I nuzzled my head against your thigh through your boxers, soaked from your sweat and mine. You laughed indulgently and dehooded me.

I slumped against your leg, too fucked out to even hump you. My tits had come unclamped, but my cock was still imprisoned. I winced as I shifted my weight, but you just laughed merrily and ruffled my hair, reaching for your computer to check your email as you shifted me into place with your feet, resting your legs on my bound body as you turned me effortlessly from fucktoy to footstool.

"My good boy," you said, as you ran your toes through my hair.

SELF-REFLECTION

Tobi Hill-Meyer

The resemblance is uncanny. At first I don't notice anything because her short blonde hair standing in spikes is so different from my own dark curls working their way to my hips. Yet something about the way she holds herself draws me in. She clearly doesn't mind standing out in the crowd. She's wearing baggy pants with a tight-fitting tank top and a leather jacket with the word DYKE embroidered on the back. In this moderately conservative town, her outfit clearly screams "Fuck you!" at the straight world. At the same time it enticingly coos "Fuck me!" to the queer world.

I stop and can't help but stare as everyone else walks by. As she gets closer, I begin to notice little things. Her face is fairly distinct from mine, but there are definite similarities. Then when I catch her eye she flashes a particular smile at me: a crooked half smile that I've never seen on anyone but me before.

"That looks like my smile," I say with a touch of amazement in my voice.

"It *is* your smile," she replies.

I stare at her dumbfounded for a moment, not sure what she means by that. Then the other pieces begin to fall together: The same arc of her eyebrows. The same look she's giving me right now. The same skin tone. The same double-Venus symbol tattoo just below the left side of her collarbone. The same smart-ass tone of voice she's using with me. She is even wearing a handmade TRANS PRIDE button I designed.

"You're me," I say, "Aren't you?" She sits down on a bench next to me and takes her jacket off. I notice the embroidery again. It's a technique I've been learning, but it's far tighter and more orderly than my skill can produce. I look at her eyes and see small laugh lines beginning to develop. "...But older."

"You're a smart study, I never doubted that," she says, smiling.

"Does that mean you're from the future? How does that work? Can you tell me about what happens? Why are you here?"

She laughs for a moment. It's odd to hear my own laugh. It sounds different when it isn't coming from my own head. "I'm not really supposed to tell you those kinds of things. I'm not really sure how it all works myself." She leans over and in a hushed tone says, "But you might want to transfer your inheritance money out of the stock market before the end of 2007."

"It's 2009."

"Oh, well, you'll be fine. You'll get by without the money anyway." She gets up and pulls me into a more secluded space. The crowds disappear.

"So if you're not here to give me a message or a warning, what are you here for then?"

"I need a reason to visit now?" The joke seems more odd

than funny. "The truth is that I'm here for a while before I can move on, and I don't really know anyone else here. I figured I might as well look you up. You'd understand better than anyone else we know. In 2012, I visited Mom and she almost had a heart attack."

I don't know why, but it kinda makes sense to me. I look back at her. She glances at the ground, and for a moment her face looks very tired and somewhat sad. I don't understand anything that's happening, but I realize that I don't need to. I put my arm around her shoulder. She looks back at me and smiles again, then embraces me in a long, comforting hug.

"Somehow I knew you'd understand." She looks at me a moment longer. "You said it was 2009. Does that mean you're dating Saphira right now?"

"For a year and a half."

"And you don't know Cayne yet?"

I think for a moment, then nod.

"And you're still poly, right?"

"Yep." I cock my head to the side. I can't really imagine a future where I'm not poly.

"Good, I just had to make sure. You can't always assume that all the details are still the same." She pauses then shoots me a smoldering look. "Anyway, if that's all true, then unless I'm mistaken, you haven't seen a trans cunt up close yet."

I perk up. "No, but I've been curious."

"That's another reason I wanted to stop by," she says, looking me up and down. "How would you like me to give you the opportunity?"

"No way," I say in disbelief, "But I'm non-op."

"You might be, but I'm not."

I've thought off and on about how I'd like to check out a trans cunt up close, but I didn't feel like it would be appropriate to just go ask someone. Having my future self here creates a valuable new opportunity. Before I know it we are back at my place, in my bedroom.

She gets on the bed and starts to take her pants off. A pulse of excitement runs through my body. Everything feels surreal. Like I'm not even sure if it's happening or not.

"Before we begin, we should check in about things. Part of why I haven't had the chance to do this yet," I explain, "is because as much as I want to know what it can look like and what it can feel like, the more significant part to me is that I really want to explore the sensation of it, how it feels to you."

"Oh, I'm well aware of that, Sweetie. Why do you think I came? I might get some details wrong now and then, but I know you inside and out. I came here because what you want is what I want. Besides," she adds, "you're a hottie and I've been envisioning this scenario for a while."

I smile at her. Suddenly I realize, regardless of the trippy context, I've got a strong and brazen beauty in my bed who knows every one of my desires and wants to play through them with me. This is hot.

She finishes taking off her pants. I glance down. Her legs have a different shape to them, probably due to a few extra years on hormones. That's not all I notice.

"Where did you get those scars on your legs?"

"The big one on the outside of my thigh was from a fight—don't worry, I messed him up even more. The smaller ones are from cutting." She watches me closely. I think she's looking for a reaction, but I'm not sure how I'm feeling. "You don't need to do that, by the way, if you can find a better alternative."

I decide that a minimal reaction is best. "I'll keep that in mind."

She must see my awkwardness with the topic and redirects us. "Come and get a closer look."

I move forward to look at her. The pattern of pubic hair is somewhat sparse, and I can see her labia underneath it fairly well. I glance up and notice her staring at me. I can feel myself blushing.

"It really is okay to touch it," she tells me.

I don't know why I'm being so hesitant. I pull her labia to the side and take a closer look. Her clit is actually pretty cute. Her bits really look like any other cunt I've seen, as unique as any other. "What made you decide to do it?" I ask.

"I realized that I had always been interested. I had just thought that if I had a spare twenty grand hanging around that I might have better use to put it to. But there are some real benefits to it. I don't have any problems in clothing optional space anymore, and I can go stealth in locker rooms, with Michigan festies, or even with one-night stands."

"You're stealth now?"

"Only for a few hours at a time." She flashes me my crooked smile again. "But I suppose the main two factors that pushed me over the edge were that my healthcare plan covered it—actually Saphira's health plan—but most health plans cover it now. And that I didn't want the risk of getting placed in a men's prison again."

It takes a moment for me to catch the significance of *again*. I should be disturbed by it, but for some reason I'm simply concerned. I look up at her questioningly, hoping for more explanation.

"Oh shit, that was insensitive of me. I didn't mean to tell you like that. But don't worry, I already took precautions to prevent it from happening to you."

"How did it happen to you?"

"It's a long story I'd rather not talk about. Let's just say it had to do with an abusive partner and survival crime. Life sucked for a while, but I got through it and I'm stronger now than I was then."

I can see the pain again. She's been hurt a lot. I wonder if, despite her mysterious precautions, that will happen to me.

"Hey, mind if we get back to the fun stuff? I know you'd love to see me get off, and I've actually been wanting to try this for a while."

I smile back at her and let her change the subject. "I'll grab the gloves."

"Hmm, that brings up an interesting question. I wonder if it's possible for me to give you anything? That seems like it would be a bit of a paradox."

I think about it a moment. "There's enough paradoxes floating around already. Besides, it's a part of my agreement with Saphira."

"Oh, certainly. Of course. I just get curious. Those kinds of things are hard to figure out."

I move closer to her and run my hand up her leg.

"Before you start..." She beckons me over. I come to her side and she pulls my head toward her and kisses me on the forehead. "Have fun, darling."

A little more relaxed, I cup my hand over her cunt and hold still a moment. Then I back off slightly and give her some light and teasing touches. She responds positively, with a slight shudder and a sigh. A smile comes to my face. I'm getting really turned on. I run my tongue over her thigh. Then I turn my focus to mapping her vulva with the tips of my fingers, enjoying every tactile sensation.

Once I'm satisfied I slip on a glove and douse my hand in lube.

I move my hand between her legs and find her opening. After rubbing the lube around a bit, I slide a finger in. Her eyes flutter as she takes a breath. It went in easily.

I feel around a bit, drinking in every sensation I can. I'm in up to my last knuckle. She's moaning softly. I back out to insert another finger. This time she gasps. I do a come-hither motion and she arches her back.

"There, oh fuck, yeah," she says between breaths, which are coming faster and harder. "Please, right there."

"You're a lot of fun to play with." With my other hand I squeeze her clit between her labia and rub it. She lets out a series of staccato breaths. Encouraged, I increase my pace. She writhes under me.

A moment later I slow to add another finger. I push all three in as deep as I can. She starts lifting up to me and I can feel how much her cunt wants me.

"Oh, yes," she cries. "That's what I need, fill me more."

I use a fourth finger as well. There's more resistance and I slow, then drizzle more lube over her cunt. It takes some time, then I can feel her cunt opening up, begging to swallow my fist.

"Try your whole hand."

Doing as she says, I tuck my thumb under my other fingers and press in. I'm in awe and not sure if it will work, but I keep the pressure on. As her moans and movement build, my hand slips into her. She's gasping. I'm filled with a sense of amazement. Her pulse beats around me.

She reaches down to stimulate her own clit. Her whole body is tensing and pulsing. I can feel it as her cunt clenches around my fist. I hold her hip tightly as her body rocks. Then she's spasming. I feel her cunt quiver around me. Her abs tense and she almost sits up. Then her body slumps back and goes slack.

I take the cue to slowly remove my fist. When I finally am out she lets out a long breath. I lie down on the bed next to her and she puts her arms around me.

"A thousand throngs of thundering thespians, goddamn, I needed that!" She gives me a peck on the cheek. "It's been a while."

"Of course. I should be thanking you."

"You really are an adorable sweetie. I kinda miss that part of me." She brushes the hair out of my eyes. "So, what do you think?"

"That was incredible. When did you get it?"

"In 2015. As soon as I could after I got out."

"You know, I don't think you lost it," I say, "the sweet caring part of yourself, I mean." I lean over and give her a kiss. She's somewhat surprised at first, then kisses me back with a gentle tenderness that makes my heart swoon. I run my hand through her hair and kiss her harder.

I roll over her and run my hand down her side. Her hand moves up under my shirt and scratches my back. The sharp sensation intensifies the arousal I'm feeling. Her fingers find and undo the snap of my bra.

She gets my shirt off and cups one of my breasts in her hand. She pinches my nipple between her middle and ring finger. I moan. She twists. I gasp and pull back slightly. I'm disoriented for a moment, then she pushes me onto my back and is sitting on top of me and holding a royal blue dildo.

"The Empress! You still have her after all these years?"

"Of course. When you form a psychological connection with one of these babies, it doesn't go away easily." She leans over me. "You did such a nice job with me just now, how would you like it if I returned the favor?"

"Please."

She gets off the bed and walks around by my feet. She's

wearing a strap-on harness, but I don't remember her putting it on. I grab the lube and spread some on myself. Kneeling at the foot of the bed, she lifts my legs into the air and leans over me.

She kisses my ankle and guides the Empress to my ass. I'm hungry and ready for her. She pushes the tip into me. I moan. She holds still for a moment while I adjust. Minute by minute, inch by inch, my ass swallows her. When she knows I've had enough time, she pulls almost all the way out, only to sink deep into me in one fluid motion.

I arch myself into her and she alternates between a few slow thrusts and several faster ones. I let out a slow groan. She reaches down with one hand to play with my breasts. As I get more into things she shifts her position so she's lying on top of me and kisses my neck. She's panting.

"How much can you get out of using that?"

"Quite a bit, actually." She moans into my ear while making several quick thrusts in succession as if to demonstrate. She grips my hair and grinds her hips into me. Her head lifts up and leans back. She's a lot louder. Her energy is intensifying, then suddenly she downshifts and returns to her previous patter.

She smiles at me. "A little more of that, and I could have come."

After a while I roll us over so that I'm on top. I've got room to touch my bits now. She's still thrusting up into me. Everything feels so good. She's staring straight into my eyes with such intensity and focus. The sensation is arcing. Waves of pleasure crash over my body. I collapse onto her. A tingling sensation is still making its way back and forth over my spine. I wrap my arms under her back and clutch her to me.

After it subsides I lift myself up and pull the dildo out. I snuggle up to her side. "Damn, I love you," I say.

"I love you, too." She laughs. "But seriously, I'm really

glad you still think I'm worthy of your love."

"I don't think you've changed as much as you think you have. At least not in the important ways."

"Keep that in mind," she says. "You and I, we're resilient. I've been through a lot. A lot that I hope you don't have to deal with. But even with all that, you can still love the self that I've become. I hope you never stop loving the self that you are."

It's a rather beautiful sentiment. "Is that the message you came here to give me?"

"Maybe." She grins and looks to the side. "Hey, you wanna try something really weird?" She pounces back onto me and changes the subject, a habit I hadn't noticed about myself before. It's also interesting to realize how much bubbly energy she has, and I wonder if I'm like that too. She interrupts my thoughts and holds up a condom. "I'm creaming all over at the thought of you fucking me with your bits—if you feel comfortable with it."

I smiled. "I like how you think."

We keep going like that for who knows how long. We try everything we can think of. I'm getting to know her body really well, and she already knows mine. Occasionally we take breaks and she tells me more about her life. Time slips by. It's hard to keep one moment distinct from the next. I don't remember it becoming night, but suddenly it's morning. I must have fallen asleep.

I feel arms around me. I turn around to kiss my future self, but she's not there. Instead, it's Saphira. She's awake and kisses me.

"Saphira, when did you get here?"

"I got back really late last night and you had already fallen asleep. You looked so happy I didn't want to wake you."

Now that I'm more awake, I think I realize what happened. *Oh well,* I say to myself. *I guess I can never deny being vain again.*

“I had a thought last night, darling.” It would be nice to keep my options open. “What would it take for me to be on your health plan?”

FACE PACK

Penelope Mansfield

Rory says bukkake sounds like an Asian martial art, Jane says, "Are you sure you still want to go through with this?" We're standing outside the warehouse Rory has rented. Rory practices a high kick against the door.

I say that I'm sure, I've waited long enough for this, and where would we send all those guys? Inside, though, I feel jittery, knowing soon unless I back out I'm going to be the center of attention.

"This is where you'll kneel," says Rory. "You get tired of kneeling you can sit for a while, or writhe or whatever. Just make it look hot." Rory's the skinhead in charge of videotaping the event, and it's making him all directorial.

Janey hugs me and says she'll be there if I need anything. She's happy to help, just don't call her a fluffer. Rory's busy reciting stats about the airborne velocity of jizz while Janey holds the hug.

I run my hands over my face, checking by touch that yes,

I'm ready, it's fine. No hairs at all—plus no shaving nicks, no tiny abrasions. "Four hundred hours," I murmur, "thousands of dollars." This is the reward I promised myself.

For years, every week, Rosa has stood over me and jabbed at my face with steel needles, one spike per pore it seemed like, until the electrolysis machine chimed victory in its attack on the follicle and she could rip another hair from deep inside my face. The anesthetic cream didn't help, her conversation about television shows and sports didn't help, her Dolly Parton CD on infinite repeat definitely didn't help.

The only thing that helped at the time was imagining me on my knees, a hard-on everywhere I looked, even straight up, all of them in the shivers of pre-ejaculation, aimed and ready... While I squirmed as the bug zapper went into my face, I imagined squirming under a completely different barrage. I couldn't turn pain into fun like some girls could, I just had to make my own distraction out of fantasy.

Rory reminds me it's time to do my makeup, which needs to be perfect even though it'll be ruined soon. Already a couple of guys straggle into the back of the room, chubby and plain in jeans and T-shirts. They size me up in my sweats and sneakers, so I duck into the bathroom to change and primp.

I smooth on tons of foundation, though there's nothing to cover up. I remember when the first hairs appeared around my mouth, how I cheered for them because they made me normal. Now years later, they're gone again and I'm amazed to realize there's something I'm still a virgin at.

I slide lingerie up my smooth legs and strap on my fuck-yeah pumps. I imagine dozens of men—did Rory say thirty-three or thirty-seven?—jacking off to this, and hundreds more getting off on the video later. I touch my sensitive girlcock, then stop and save it for later. It would suck if I lost this thrill of desire now.

Whenever I would get used to the electric current going into my face, Rosa would ask if I could take a little more. She'd turn it a bit higher, cranking up the AC or the DC, just to make sure the fucking follicles would up and die already, die and not come back, for a change. My beard had a will to live almost as fierce as my determination to be my truest, most beautiful self. I would stagger out of Rosa's back room at the beauty salon, red-faced, blistered and so exhausted from gritting my teeth, I could barely stand up. The endorphins were a long time coming during my sessions, and they only made me feel more tired afterward.

I draw another mouth over my mouth with lipliner, then fill it in with lipstick. Blush takes my inner tremors and projects them onto my cheeks, as if I don't know how such an innocent girl came to be in such a fix. I'm still telling stories about my eyes with brushes and pencils when Janey knocks and asks how I'm getting on. I invite her in.

"There are so many out there," she says, "I think some guys brought friends and there's no game today."

I breathe heavy. She hugs me again, offers to get me off a different way if I need to back out of this. I shake my head, finish my makeup. Not that I'm not tempted. Janey can do things with her fingers a million dicks could never learn. "Please, soon, yes," I say, "just not today."

"I understand," Janey says, "you're just too much slut to keep under wraps, you're for public consumption." The heel of her hand runs from my knee up to my pelvis bone, over and over. I purr and then whimper.

"All those men will look down at you, literally and figuratively, they'll baptise you and chastise you, you dirty little cream tart," Janey says. I moan, I can't believe such a hot dyke wants to be my lover, that by itself was my great fantasy for years, now it's come true and I'm greedy for a bigger, weirder fantasy.

"Shameless," Janey says, as I back my ass up against her thumb, "shameless girl." I can't tell if she thinks today's plan is sexy for its own sake or just because it's sexy for me.

"Okay," I say, wishing I could stay in here longer, "time to go face my public."

I lose count of them at thirty. They stand in a huddle near the door. Nobody's smiling or talking much and they scare me a little. Then when I'm halfway into the room, they turn and take me in: fake diamond earrings and necklace, satin bustier and thong, thigh-high stockings and dangerous heels. They just stare and I force myself to smile and wave at the wall of workaday guys.

Just when I'm about to flee back into my dressing room, one of them claps, then a few, then all. They throw in cheers and, yes, wolf whistles. I curtsey and promenade to my place at the center of the tarp.

I used to fantasize about just going to sleep for a week, being sedated or whatever, so someone could exterminate every hair on my chin and my body, once and for all, while I slept. I used to shave twice a day and put on heavy foundation to try and get rid of my beard shadow, and on the days when I had to grow out my beard so Rosa could yank it out, I wanted to hide from the world. I would wear my heaviest overcoat walking to Rosa's place, and afterward, I had to cover my red, blistery face, still with some hairs that we didn't get to.

Rory is barking instructions at the pack of men. "When you cum, leave the front of the circle and go to the back if you think you're going to cum a second time. If you're close, shout, 'Here!' so Clari can turn her face to catch your spunk. Do not touch Clari. She may touch you, she may not—it's up to her."

I hadn't planned to touch any of them, but now I know I will, as many of them as possible. "Whenever you're ready," Rory says, and I nod and get on my knees.

I keep my Miss America smile in place as the first guys move into position around me. They look as nervous as I feel, for some reason. None of them is exactly my type, but several of them are very conventionally handsome. A few of them return my smile.

And then the first line of guys unzip their pants and pull out their cocks. I notice Rory aiming his camera as closely as possible to capture just their dicks and my face. I turn slowly on my knees, taking it in.

The shadow over my face lifted slowly, almost like black snow melting, and then one day I looked in the mirror—and I saw skin. My features looked totally different without a dark cloud obscuring them: I looked delicate, pretty. That week, when I went to see Rosa, she noticed it too.

"We're making good progress," she said. "Still plenty hairs on your neck though."

And then I lay down, and she slid the needle into the skin just below my jawline, like a red-hot poker going into my throat.

Everywhere I turn, inches from my face, there's a rising cock. It doesn't matter anymore if the guys are handsome, if they like me, if they vote Democrat or not, all that matters is the ring of pricks in every direction. I try to guess which one will pop first and can't. They just stroke and stroke, nobody talks.

I start telling them how sexy they all are, how much I want their cum. I hesitate, then reach out and touch one of them. Its owner lets go and I take it in two fingers, kneading and caressing. The guy rotates his hips. I work my fingers up and down on the shaft.

I have a free hand, so I reach for another one. I lubricate my fingers with spit and start the same rhythm on both cocks. Both guys grind at me.

I'm looking straight at another cock right in front of me. Of course, unprotected oral sex isn't completely safe, and I don't have time to put condoms on the circle guys, so I wasn't planning on sucking any of them. I didn't exactly promise Janey I wouldn't, but I heard her concerns. But now it's happening and that cock is so close to my face...*Four hundred hours*, I think.

I open my mouth and the cock tastes so good, like an oyster only not so slippery. It presses against my tongue just the right way, and the guy puts one hand on my head to guide it. I know this is the right thing, I'm only going to do this once, after all. I taste precum and lick it off the shaft without slowing down. I make my little cock-hungry noise, between a moan and a gulp.

"Here," a guy says behind me, one of the guys I haven't been pleasuring. I swivel to face him and nothing happens. He blushes, jerks harder. I take his cock in both hands and make a steeple around it, roof rising toward me again and again. Then he grunts and shoots and it's going right on my face.

I wasn't prepared for the heat. You always hear about hot cum, but I never realized before how hot it really is. It makes sense, it comes out of your body and all. It feels almost scalding for a second and then it's just there on my face like an extra layer of stuff.

"Here," a second guy says and shoots a moment later. It's pack mentality: half a dozen of them cum within seconds of each other. I have to remind myself each time to close my eyes and mouth. Some of it will get in no matter what I do, I just have to keep it to a minimum. Now my face feels itchy with the stuff and it's all I can do to keep from wiping.

More guys push forward to replace the ones who have cum. I fill my hands and mouth, playfully this time, no rush about this. I try to smile with a cock in my mouth. I feel like a lion tamer surrounded by lions, but in a good way.

I taste a salty rush and for a moment I think the cock in my mouth has cum, but it's just a lot of precum. I let it go and lick another man's balls, so his cock slaps my face again and again until it sprays. The cock I was sucking before that splashes my face a second later.

"Here." I turn 180 degrees to see a large Asian man holding his quivering prick in both hands. I give a come-hither smile, wink and tilt my head. I close my eyes just as the rain comes down.

"Here," a guy to my right calls out and I press my lips against the base of his cock, nibbling and tonguing until he groans and explodes. "Here." An uncircumcised guy nearby pulls back his foreskin and spurts. "Here." A man with creamy brown skin adds to the mess on my face.

If only Rosa could see me now, I think and it makes me giggle. She provided the clean slate, the canvas I'm letting these men paint on. All those hours of her eyestrain and my gasps as the needles went in and stayed in, the tweezers slowly pulling the hairs out.

I'm starting to relax into it. At the start, I was as stiff as the men on all sides of me. Now I'm more at ease, flirting and giggling and daring the men to go ahead, mark me, I'm your bitch. The men all blur together after the first few facials, but I feel like I'm getting more warmth back from them as well, like they're responding to my playfulness in kind.

I realize I'm still fully, if scantily, clothed. And my clit is making a bit of a dent in the front of my panties, along with its own smear of precum. I wipe my hands on my bustier and then undo the hooks one at a time, swiveling my hips and winking at the men in front of me. One of them cums on my chest as soon as it's bare.

Normally I'm self-conscious about my teeny breasts, but

right now I don't care. It seems they're nice enough to cum on. My hairless torso gleams with sweat and semen.

I put my hands on either side of my crotch and thrust. I pout at the next man to get him to hit me right between the eyes. The scent of so much sperm excites me even as it makes me sick, it's getting overwhelming.

I take another man in my mouth, both hands still toying with my stretched thong. I deep-throat him at top speed, head to root in half a second over and over again, then I let him go and move on to the next guy. For once I don't have to feel guilty about interrupting a blow job—it's almost my duty to taste as many of them as possible.

Part of my mind is still thinking about how to put on the best show for everyone, but mostly I'm just losing myself in the moment. I pull my clit out of my panties and touch it, just enough to confirm my own excitement but not enough to get off yet. Another man cums on my face, then another one. My eyelids are coated in the stuff, I have to wipe my eyes before I open them and even then I can only squint.

Here, here, here. I lose track of how many guys have used me as their cumrag, and whether any of the guys are coming for a second time. I notice that I'm panting and moaning, not fake porno moans but the real kind, the kind I usually make only for Janey. I can't see her, so I don't know if she's jealous or turned on.

I stop jacking off, I can't risk coming now. Instead I go back to sucking one guy while playing with two others. I roll over on my back and that way I can kick my shoes off and use my feet to get off a fourth guy. The crowd is roaring over the music, which sounds like Prince or Madonna.

The fourth guy cums on my stocking feet while the guy in my mouth pulls out just in time to cover my nose. I try the same thing, only this time on my stomach with my legs kicked up and stroking a cock.

Now I'm getting as many guys off with my hands, feet and mouth as I possibly can. I have to fight the urge to take a guy in my ass, it would be hard to get lubed up enough, let alone make sure he wore a condom, and Janey would kill me. Instead, I just toy with as many guys as possible with all my extremities.

My face could be covered with shaving cream, the stuff I hope I'll never use again. This feels like a rite of passage, a unique way to prove I've arrived as a girl and all the pain has led somewhere, though I know deep down that you never really arrive, it's always going to be an uphill hike in high heels.

My hair, the soles of my feet, my ass, the nape of my neck, all feel sticky. My mouth and hands get tired but I can't feel any sensations but endorphins and lust. My excitement is more pleasurable than any physical sensation could be, it's like the pure joy that physical pleasure aims to copy.

For the first time I can see past the circle of open-fly guys. The group is thinning out. Many of the guys have retreated to the wall to watch. Janey stands nearby with a huge grin on her face, which relieves me because I was worried she'd be upset by how many cocks I've licked today.

I'll get tested soon, I silently promise her, *I'll be really good after this.* Then I go to work on the last ten men with renewed energy. I'm naked except for my stockings, soaked and ruined with sperm. I wiggle my butt and pull on every man in turn. They catch my face from three different angles at once.

I lie on my back and spread my legs as wide as they'll go, rubbing my calves against two different men. I manage to get two cocks in my mouth, something I've always wanted to try. My reward lands on my thighs and my tits.

Finally the last guy adds his contribution on my chin and I

look around, no one urging, "Here," for the first time in ages. Rory walks up, asks if I mind. I shake my head with a grin and he unzips. I've never sucked him before, but it's still not just another cock today. I bob my head like it's my first.

I feel Janey stroking my hair in spite of all the stuff in it, her touch feels gentle and reassuring. It brings me back to my real life, the one where I'm her lover and not a gangsuck cumshot facial whore. I purr, Rory's cock still in my mouth. Janey reaches down with her other hand and touches my clit.

Rory pulls out and taps the bridge of my nose. *Tap, tap, tap.* Janey thumbs my sensitive spot in time with Rory's drumming. He adds one last load to the dried-out mass on my face.

Then a second later I wail at the top of my lungs. Tons of cum pours out of my clit, some of it flying almost as high as my nose. I cry out some more, twitch and gasp and release my own reservoir onto my saturated body. My eyes go starry like during a sugar rush and it's almost too much for me, it feels like it'll go on forever.

Janey keeps stroking until she's sure I'm done. Then she wipes her dirty hand on my hair, not as if it'll make a difference. She brings a towel and wraps it around me, then hugs me. The men around us are applauding and I'm blissed out, almost too tired to move. "You did it, baby," Janey whispers. "You were amazing," and I laugh and let her lead me to a long, hot shower.

THE BOY THE BEAST WANTS

Skian McGuire

I want a boy to beat on. If I say it often enough, write about it, describe him to myself, imagine what I will do to him in loving detail, maybe the Goddess will let me have him.

I bow my head in apology to my already-underserved lovers. There's the sweet boy I sometimes play with, my butch partner who is the love of my life, a fuckbuddy whom I never get enough of as it is—all the masculine creatures I could want to extract my pleasure from. Aren't they enough? They ought to be. But the problem is, I care about them. I could never bring myself to do to them any of the things I see myself doing in my mind's eye to the boy that my Beast has invented.

He's not very young, as some boys go, but not quite as old as thirty—not a grown-up. I know he will be mine for only a short time, then move on. I imagine him following the progression that leathermen did in the old days, earning what he wears by the trials I impose on him, growing into the topman he will become. Not that he won't long for the release of masochism and submission, when that day arrives—but who could follow me? Oh, ego! This is my fantasy, and I want to be the top that boy can never find again and so has to become, instead. Maybe someday, when he is tired and jaded and longs for release more than he longs for his next breath, maybe then he'll find another Master, or Mistress even, and the old dog in him will learn new tricks. Why not? It happens. But first, I want to be the one he remembers for a long, long time.

I picture him—a skinny, scrawny, surly thing, all bones and cowlicks and wary eyes. I see him looking at me, his chin lowered, no smile, no light, just heat. He is wearing the uniform of the novice: jeans and a white T-shirt, no leather, not even a belt; tan construction boots. His arms are at his sides, fists clenched. His feet are flat on the floor, squared. I see him across the big room of a dungeon we all go to, and even though the place is crowded, no one is playing yet. We might as well be the only ones in the room.

His eyes burn into mine for a moment, then drop. When he looks up again, I look at a spot in front of my feet and call him to it with my gaze. He comes.

Now he stands before me, eyes down, nervous. I can see his chest rise and fall, too quickly. He knows better than to speak before he is spoken to. I walk around him, inspecting carefully. His shoulder blades are pathetic, bony little wings. His breasts are bound. His ass is nonexistent, but his arms are wiry. The muscles in the back of his neck twitch under my gaze.

"Boy."

He holds his breath. I come back around to face him.

In real life, I might ask him his name now, and he would answer, looking up at me with those wary, animal eyes, adding the "sir" only after a long pause. And I would allow myself to be amused, if only slightly, and never enough to show. After a pause long enough to make him glance nervously away, like animal prey looking for escape, I answer, repeating his name, and then:

"You want somebody to beat the shit out of you, don't you, punk?"

His mouth is dry; he has to work up spit and swallow hard before he answers, his voice hardly more than a whisper.

"Yes, sir."

In real life, I would grip his shoulder and push him ahead, guiding him through the labyrinth of rooms until we could find a quiet place to talk, negotiate; Get To Know Each Other. I would inquire about his limits; his safeword; his state of health. He would find out what he can do to please me. I would find out what he needs to learn. But this is not real life: this is my fantasy.

I grab a handful of the T-shirt at the back of his neck to propel him to the place we will play, jerking him around corners, shoving him into the space ahead when we reach it. Before he has time to recover his balance I grab his shirt again and deliberately trip him, sending him onto the rug on his hands and knees.

The names I will call him won't be nice ones, but he won't be surprised. This boy knows what I am. When I call him a *shit-ass little motherfucker, scumbag, filthy little asswipe, pussy, fuck-hole, punk faggot sissyboy, you little shit, you dirty snot-nose little freak,* in that low voice, that crazy voice that says I am a hair's breadth away from losing it, the blood will run cold in his veins. He will wonder exactly what he has gotten himself into. He will know it is exactly what he wants. When the side of my boot lands hard on his ass, and again, and again, driving him down, and my instep slams into his crotch, and my toe taps his spine and his kidney and his ever-so-tender ribs just hard enough to remind him of his body's fragility, when the steel-capped toe of my boot pounds into his ass and thighs again and again, until he curls up in a fetal position that I have to haul him out of, drag him to his knees by main force so I can grab his hair and slap him until he looks at me, *Look at me, you little fairy, you cunt, look at me!* he won't be crying. Not yet.

I will throw him over the hassock that is ever so handy and I will whip my black leather belt out of my belt loops with a hiss that he will hear in nightmares, and I will lay into his ass with a sound like cracking thunder, furiously, setting fire through his clothes to the meat of his ass and his shoulders, until he covers his head with his arms in that gesture of involuntary self-protection that only invites the Beast's rage. The strap of my belt will land again and again, my free hand will punch and slap and grab, until I come around in front, panting, sweating, to lift his head by the hair and demand to know, *Have you had enough, boy?*

His eyes before they focus on my face will be wild and full of pain and fear, but in an instant the look in them will harden. It will be a look of hate, hating what I do to him but still needing more and hating that, too. It will always be like that. He will say, "No, sir." He will say, "Fuck you, sir."

So I will reach under his scrawny belly to unbutton his jeans and yank them down, and this time I will lay angry stripes across his naked ass. I will lay welts of pain that blossom into purple bruises and blood blisters where the edge of the leather has bitten his flesh, and I will not stop until there is no unmarked skin to hit, until he breaks down, face wet with tears, and begs me to stop.

This is a boy I will not daddy. I will be his Master, and he will be a thing I possess. I will not comfort him. He will hate what I do, and I will take all that I want. What the Beast wants.

I'll unbutton my own jeans—next time I'll make him gnaw

on my denim crotch for the privilege and unbutton my jeans with his teeth—and haul out my hard cock for him to suck, gagging and hitching, snot running down his face. He'll kneel before me with his pants at his knees and swallow my cock to the hilt, so help me God he will, and I'll fuck his face until he knows exactly what that hole is for.

And the boy wants it. I know he wants it, and so does the Beast, and I know what I'll find when I've had enough of my cock down his throat and I turn him around, belly down on the hassock. My cock will open him up easily, slipping into him like a key in a well-oiled lock, because this is the thing he wants most of all, whether he knows it or not. His most shameful, unwanted part will betray him, and he will be grateful. His wet cunt will need no lube at all; I'll pound him until the Beast is finished with both of us, slamming against his ravaged ass until my own need for orgasm reminds me of mercy, and I reach around to jerk him off, my cock buried in him, my breath hot on his neck, my weight on his back.

In the end, I'll make him lick my boots to thank me, letting the Beast in me doze and dream of next time.

I'm sorry, I tell my lovers, silently. *I'm sorry it's not you I imagine.* And I know what you would say, each of you: "That's not so bad. I could give you that. I have given you that, or nearly, or would have, if you'd only let me." But it's only the beginning, don't you see? The Beast wants so much more than that. The Beast wants blood, and the cane that puts down pain like napalm, and doesn't care if it turns you on or not. The Beast wants to hear you scream. The Beast wants you to be so afraid you will thank your God when it's over that I am not really insane, that I did not actually spill your guts out on the bed of a cheap motel or crack open your skull on the dungeon's cinder block wall. The Beast wants to call you things you do not want to be called. The Beast wants to hit and kick and gouge and tear, the Beast wants to become a whirlwind of pain and fear, abandoning all control, abandoning love and conscience and hope for the future. The Beast—my Beast—is a beast of rage.

A woman I know, another switch, tells me that her inner sadist has several forms of expression, one of which she calls the Vampire, and he reminds me of my own Beast—amoral, hungry for pain and fear, satisfaction of his own desires his only care. There are other ways her top self can express itself; in me it seems that there is only one Beast, and every other way in which I might play top, even Daddy, is only a pale shadow of it. In my musings, considering what his nature is, I thought at first that there might actually be two Beasts—one that wanted a victim's fear and another that wanted to explode in physical violence. It made sense that there should be two, because I know where they come from, just as I know who my imaginary boy really is.

My mother's powerlessness. My father's burden of control and responsibility. She had no one but me on whom to let loose her fear of being a helpless cripple, her resentment of the trap she came to by circumstance and poor judgment. He did everything he was supposed to do, and God help anyone who got in his way when his leash finally broke. I am the child of both my parents. My Beast is their child, too. There is only one of us.

Do you see why it can't be you I imagine, my lovers to whom I owe much more than I've given? It has to be the boy who lives only in my mind; the sullen, angry, injured boy who hates the things I do to him, hates me, and still comes back for more. He is as tough as he is fragile. He needs pain like the rest of us need air and water, shelter and love. He needs to die so he can be born again, and maybe this time, someone will want him. I can hurt him because I don't love him like I love you. I can hurt him and scare him and even hate him. After all, he's only me.

If I say it often enough, write about it, describe him to myself, imagine what I will do to him in loving detail, maybe the Goddess will let me have him.

THE MAN WITH THE PHOENIX TATTOO

Laura Antoniou

"Of course I will; why wouldn't I want to see you writhing in pain while a big, burly, bearded guy hurts you?"

She accepted the request lightly, with good cheer, and left the obvious corollary unsaid. Because it had been a while since the last time she'd seen such a thing.

She picked him up in Brooklyn and they kissed in the front seat of the car. It was early evening, chilly and damp; their kiss was brief and functional. Through the open car door came the scent of fireplaces and layers of wet leaves still piled in the tiny squares in front of brownstones, trapped in the narrow spaces between stoops. Yellow and flickering blue light filtered from barred front windows when he closed the car door, putting them both in comfortable darkness.

"I'm sorry I didn't call sooner," he said quietly.

"You're such an asshole, Parker," she said, turning the wheel.

"I've missed you, too."

The studio was two flights over a pizzeria in Jersey City. The sign on the steel door was faded, and Rachel hit the buzzer several times before they heard the click of the lock releasing.

"Let's see the patch," the artist and proprietor said in way of greeting. Chris hung his motorcycle jacket up by the door and pulled his shirt up, turning to show the small area just over his waist, a spot of color on his skin.

Wolf nodded as he examined it. Bald as an egg, he wore a tapered black-and-iron-gray beard; his skull was etched with a ring of black barbed wire and his earlobes elongated by 00-gauge plugs. "Yep, looks good! Let's get you under the lights and make sure you're properly crazy."

"No doubt about that," Rachel muttered. But she hung her own coat up, and followed them over to the table under the spotlights. Ink, needles, wipes and gloves were all in place, and different prints of the final design were pinned up for reference.

"You should talk," Wolf said cheerfully. "How's your cat tat doing?"

She grinned at him. "Still biting me, but not much lately."

Chris heard the message and stripped without comment, down to the waist and then peeling his jeans back down his hips.

"I still like that rose," Wolf said admiringly as Chris prepared to get on the table.

"Thank you," Chris said. Rachel turned away to examine one of the drawings, and Wolf picked up the stencil and started the transfer. When he was done, he nodded briskly as he stripped off his gloves. "Okay, take another good long look and make sure it's what you want."

Obediently, Chris got up to use the mirrors. The design was

huge, covering his ribs and the lower part of his chest. On his smoothly shaven skin, the transfer ink looked blurry, but the lines were right where they should be. Without the thin, dark hair that dusted his body, he looked pale; his eyebrows and the curly hair on his head seemed as dark as the transfer lines. He didn't touch the outline, but stretched and examined the way his new body looked, adorned only with scars and years of self-discipline.

"You look so hot," Rachel said from behind him. In her heels, she was two inches taller than he was, exactly. He smiled at her in the mirror.

"You always thought so," he said.

"Imagine that."

"You want music?" Wolf asked, as he started measuring ink into a disposable cup.

Chris shook his head and stretched out one more time before getting back on the table. "Feel free to put on whatever you like to work to," he offered.

"Hah! You don't know what you just got yourself into," Wolf warned. He used a remote to turn on the stereo and the sound of an older recording started coming from the speakers: heartaches.

ZZ Top would have been the obvious guess; heavy metal or something tribal and trendy might have been good follow-ups. Patsy Cline, though...

"Yeah," Wolf said cheerfully. "I am one *badass* motherfucker. Ready for the pain? Most people say this part is the worst."

"Hurt me now and get it over," Chris said. He reached out a hand; Rachel sighed and took it as the needle gun descended.

Rachel pulled off the road before they got to the Holland Tunnel and Chris looked up in surprise.

"You don't get to go back yet," she said.

"Ah."

On top of the cheap floral bedspread, she unbuttoned his shirt. The outlines were glistening under sheets of plastic bandaging, and she poked at one spot.

"Hey, now," Chris said.

"You asshole," she said softly. He reached up and ran his hands into her mass of thick, curly hair, pulled her down for a better kiss than that first one in the car. She pressed against him and the outline of the tattoo flared with tiny pains and itches. Their bodies shifted and he turned them onto their sides, pushing his knee between her legs and she moaned. "Yeah, that's it," she growled lightly, grinding her hips so she crushed herself against his leg. Her brief leather skirt rode up and she ran one stockinged leg across his, abrading her inner thigh along the rougher texture of his jeans.

He helped her, tugging the skirt up farther, around her waist. He ran his hand across her ass and made false disapproval sounds in her ear as he bit the lobe. "I didn't realize you'd want to fuck," he said in a low voice, not stopping as he worked her panties down her asscheeks. "I didn't..."

"Pack?" She arched an eyebrow at him in amusement. "Since when did you need anything but what you came with to fuck me silly?" Pulling back just slightly, she reached one arm between them, into her bra, and pulled out a small tangle that unfolded into two black latex gloves.

"If lube is a problem, it's your fault." She bit him back, on the lower lip, sharp enough to break the skin, and he grabbed her head again to force their mouths together so hard their teeth scraped. They laughed as they wrestled for position and clothing removal, and when he finally managed to sink his fingers through the tangle of her pubic hair, she stopped her faux struggle to work her hips and take more of him.

"I guess you forgive me then," he said, twisting his hand to turn his curled fingers up against her G-spot. He rocked his hand steadily, her slickness easing the way, the smell of her salty and spicy.

"Hell, no," Rachel gasped. "You make me…crazy."

Crazy for loving you, she didn't add. Instead, she arched and slammed her hips down over his hand, engulfing him to the wrist and then farther, getting that treasured exhalation of surprise and that brief look of ecstasy in his eyes before he closed them.

True love, she thought. *Or something close to it.*

Two weeks later, the coloring and shading began. Rachel made the drive from Long Island to Brooklyn and then to Jersey City. Wolf met them at the door, tobacco on his breath, the studio sparkling and ready and smelling of pepperoni. Chris once again let the man choose his sentimental old music.

"You know, k.d. lang had her start as a Patsy Cline tribute singer," Wolf said, as he put out the array of deep reds, oranges and blues. "Looks like you took good care of the outline. Let's get you colored in, shall we?"

Rachel watched as the claws were done first, Wolf expertly working the gun with one hand and wiping away pools of ink and dots of blood with the other. Chris ground his teeth as the needles worked on his lower abdomen.

"Aww, it doesn't hurt that much!" Rachel chided.

"Tickles," he responded between his teeth. She rolled her eyes.

"It'll hurt more when we get to your ribs," Wolf promised. "Not that much, though. You're real good about sitting still. Sometimes, I swear I want to take these young fuckers who come in to get the latest tribal fucking thing they saw on TV and strap 'em down to the table. Guess you have more experience with that, though." He chuckled as the claws began to take shape, reaching for the skin under the pubic bone.

"Are you kidding? Chris thinks bondage is insulting to his personal honor," Rachel said.

"At least he don't go all moaning and humping the table like some people I know."

Chris smiled and raised an eyebrow at Rachel. She shrugged and grinned back and for a while there was only the buzzing of the machine and the orchestral and choral accompaniment to a rich, bold contralto voice pining away for loves who would never return.

That time, he knew to be prepared for the exit before the tunnel. Much better prepared.

"You fucker, you fucker," Rachel cried, as she pulled against the rope anchoring her wrists to one leg of the sturdy old bed.

"Insulting to my personal honor?" he teased, sliding his cock very slowly into her body then easing it out again. The bandages crinkled across his lower body and he hissed through his teeth as he moved. "Feeling insulted yet, sweetheart?"

Snapping her eyes open, she lifted her legs to wrap around his waist, kicking him as she did. "Don't fuck around with me, Parker, do me right!"

He slammed all the way into her and stretched his body on top of hers, pressing his forearm across her collarbone to push her down. "I'll go one better and do you the way you need," he whispered. "But you'll have to ask nicely."

"Fuck you!" she growled, and tried to kick him some more. But he was stronger now, so much stronger than she was these days! He slapped her once to startle her and used the surprise to force one leg and then the other from around his body. Withdrawing from her soaking pussy, he rose from the bed for more rope and she cursed him. But there was a feral glee in her eyes, a kind of mysterious pleasure that only came when this one man treated her so badly—made her into someone she really wasn't, just as he had made himself into the man he really was.

It didn't matter that she had another lover who aroused her body and pleasured her mind; it didn't matter that she had occasional partners to delight her senses and provide variety. The parade of desperate-to-please slaves and would-be slaves were just so many sprinkles on her erotic sundae!

But they don't dominate *me*, she thought with a savage bolt of hunger as Chris tightened the ankle ropes. She pulled against them anyway, hating that hunger, loving it, cherishing it. *They don't dominate my mind and soul like you, God damn it.*

The few times she'd tried to turn those tables had been complete failures, culminating in that time she tried to get him in a skirt for her pleasure. It wasn't that long ago, but she couldn't ignore the fact that shortly after that disastrous vacation he'd left Long Island. Sure, it was because that woman summoned him, the woman he always obeyed.

But the timing was just so painful.

Almost as painful as his cock shoving into her ass, while his fingers tugged on the gold rings through her nipples. Jolts of pleasure mingled with the bright, fiery pain, and she groaned at the stretching heat in her ass.

And as usual, she swore to herself that she would not ask nicely.

As usual, she eventually did.

The wings of the phoenix took shape over his ribs and their flames flickered over the scars.

"The second surgery did the job," Wolf said with admiration. "The old scars would have been a bitch to cover. But you know, there's no telling how the ink will stay over the tissue. You might have to have them re-inked sooner than the rest of the tat if you want to keep the colors consistent."

Chris nodded, his eyes closed. "That's fine," he said.

"No one will ever be able to see them under all of this," Rachel said, watching the colors come up. "Not that you're such a fucking exhibitionist anyway."

"That's what the arm tattoos are for," he said to her. "I can show them off."

"Do you? Did you show 'em to that pretty boy you told me about?" Rachel didn't ask if he'd shown them to the woman whose call he'd answered, the woman who could draw him on some invisible leash.

Chris controlled a disdainful snort of derision so he could keep still. "Why would I do that? He's an ass. Clumsy, dim-witted, spoiled...I have no idea why he's even there." She was surprised to hear genuine annoyance and confusion in this little explosion and eyed him curiously.

"I think you like him!" she announced.

This time, he did snort, and Wolf pulled the gun back. "Hey, careful with the sharp movements, I want to get these feathers right."

"Sorry," Chris said, as he stilled himself. He glanced at Rachel and said, "No. I don't."

"Whatever," she sighed. *Tra le la le la*, she thought in rueful amusement. *Yeah, you do.*

That night, she rode him while he stretched out on his back, trying not to claw at his chest and nipples the way she usually did in that position. Instead, she caressed the growing portrait on his ribs and chest with the lightest of touches, avoiding the freshly inked areas. As she got close to orgasm, he reached for her hands and they twined fingers so tightly she felt her wrists aching with the strain.

She fell against his body, the thin plastic under his chest crinkling against her breasts. *I should hate you*, she thought, cuddling against him. *You come into my life and love me and fuck me and make me crazy and then you leave any time she crooks a finger and you don't answer calls and you fall in love with other people and I should hate you so much.*

But she fell asleep in his arms and had sweet dreams.

The final visit finished the piece with the most delicate shading and some detailing over areas previously inked. When Wolf put the gun down and massaged the hand holding it he grunted in satisfaction.

The phoenix covered his torso. Claws rose from a pile of glittering ashes that vanished into his black public hair; each taloned foot seemed to be either arching as the bird rose or reaching for his cock. Across his stomach and ribs, the body was outlined in powerful red flames; as the wings rose under his chest, the flames faded in size and intensified in color, with cores in blue. The eyes, centered on his chest, were black with red and gold pupils. Wolf had been very pleased with how they turned out; they were startling and angry, perhaps defiant.

The tops of the wings brushed and covered the scars defining the shape of his chest, and the very tips extended all the way under his arms. When he let his arms down naturally, the flames tattooed on each arm, from just above the wrists to his elbows, flanked the pyre of the torso tattoo neatly.

The years of running, push-ups, sit-ups, boxing and weight training had sculpted him. But this mural in his flesh turned him into something else. Rachel caught her breath at the sight of the whole thing and felt tears well in her eyes. She turned away fast and grabbed her purse. "Wait, don't bandage it up yet. I want to take a picture."

"It'll look neater after a few days," Wolf said.

"A picture? Really?" Chris frowned slightly as he got up from the table.

"Yes, a fucking picture. You can stand still for a minute, can't you?"

He heard the tone in her voice and kept silent as she came up with the small camera. His skin glistened with the fresh ink and the thin layer of antibiotic ointment, and he posed carefully for her, straightening his shoulders.

"You're the first to see it," he said gently, as Wolf taped down the fresh bandages. "Any of it. I swear."

She put the camera away, using the moment to wipe away the moisture around her eyes. *What'll I do about you?* she wondered. *Wait until the next time you need a ride? Wait until she lets you go out to play again? Or wait until you fall in love with the beautiful boy you don't know you like so much? Because there's always a new boy, or girl, or new...whatever. Like some restless wind picks you up just when I think I'm back in your arms again.*

She made him hurt her that night.

Perhaps he'd known she would, because he brought the knife and held it to her throat while he fucked her, fucked so hard and violently the bandages rubbed off. He used his fists against her back, thumping her into tears and cries of outrage, and then slithered his belt from the loops in his jeans.

She fought against that; fuck, she wasn't a slave, she was no naughty girl needing the feel of leather to set her right. But he wasn't interested in her fight; he took it out of her unfairly and quickly, driving the breath from her with rabbit punches. She cried then, as he pinned her and used the well-worn leather against her ass and hips and then up her back, bringing her own tattoos and their cut ridges up in a blaze of heat.

She cursed because that's what she always did, and he stayed silent under her torrent of abuse. Neither answering nor punishing or even responding in any way except to continue this merciless beating, he forced her curses to become shorter and finally deteriorate into cries of rage, fear and frustration.

And when he stopped and gathered her into his arms, she punched and kicked at him until she cried out how much she hated him and how much she loved him and all he could do was murmur and whisper to her, *shh, shh*.

Drained of energy and passion, she was quiet under him as he cut into her markings, refreshing the sharp teeth and claws of the cat on her upper arm and shoulder, the rays of the winged disk across her lower spine. For this, she was still; for the trickle of blood he wiped away as neatly as Wolf could, for the warmth of his breath across split, colored and beaten skin. Oh, how she wanted his tongue to lap it up, suck the blood from her wounds so she could be free to take his as well, the blood they used to share along with a banquet of other bodily fluids, a communion of flesh. The coppery smell was overwhelming and satisfying.

It hurt, the fucking, the beating, the fresh cuts, the love. *I want to hold you forever*, she thought. *I saw you first, I loved you first. I saw you right past that baseball cap and cigarette, those big shirts and that crappy old jacket you used to cover everything. I marked you the way you wanted first; I loved you when you cried and when you sneered and when you lost over and over again. When she sent you to schools and doctors and all over the fucking world, I knew the real you before any of them did. And I was first to see you now. Oh, it hurts me so.*

She put the picture up with thumbtacks on her wall. She didn't show it to her lover, any of her lovers. He called regularly now, the body art done, his life going on the path marked for him in Brooklyn while she stayed on Long Island. He didn't know if he'd ever be back, and she was a fool for expecting he might.

I've got your picture, she thought. *She's got you.* The cuts ached and itched on her shoulder and back and she stared at the photo, stretching out on her bed.

It took over a month to complete the tattoo, and she realized the words she'd heard each time were true.

Time only adds to the flame.

BIG GIFTS IN SMALL BOXES: A CHRISTMAS STORY

Patrick Califia

It was the second day of my visit home, and I was already regretting telling Pops that I would be there for Christmas. My parents seemed to be shrinking as they got older. It made me sad to see Pops, who had retired as a tool and die maker only ten years before, have trouble doing things that Mom just assumed he would handle. She was a frail old lady now, not the tall and fearsome woman who had dragged me to Mass every week until I turned sixteen and left home.

That was a bad day. I had foolishly left an empty beer can in the trash. Pops had chastised me and then convinced himself I wasn't showing enough respect. So he lost control. It was not the first time that had happened. But for the first time, I had punched him back. I didn't know how to handle my newfound strength and anger, so I left. He thought I wasn't a man. I knew that I was, but neither one of my parents could show me how to become a man who wanted to kiss and hold other men. A summer job had left enough money in my savings account to buy a bus ticket to Chicago. That city slapped me around harder than Pops had ever done, but you learn more from an ordeal that you've chosen. After I turned twenty-one, I kept moving west, until I ran out of land and could wade in the ocean. Since I was too lazy to learn Japanese, I stayed in California.

So here I was in my hometown, looking for a gay bar. I told myself that there had to be one. Twenty years had gone by, and it wasn't that small a place. Luckily, I had brought my laptop, and after some hassles locating an Internet café, I got online and Googled the gay geography of this place that I felt had rejected me for being gay. It was weird. But there was an address and phone number for Brothers, which apparently featured a piano.

And now here I was, feeling almost as out of place as I had in my parents' trailer, where I was too big and too loud. My folks were happy to see me but seemed almost exhausted by the effort of socializing, all of us wanting to be close but not knowing how. There was just too damn much they didn't want to know about me, too many years when we hadn't talked more than a few cursory words said over the phone at holidays.

I was used to living in such a gay city that we had diversified. The dykes had their own places, I guess. The sweater fags (divided into the twinks in their twenties and the "older men") didn't socialize with the leathermen, and the bears had their own hangout or two. Brothers seemed to be an old-fashioned kind of place, one that kept its doors open to anybody who didn't fit in sexually. There was a lesbian corner back by the pool table. A drag queen had been the first person to greet me, and we'd shared a drink. Most of the gay men were clean-shaven and in their twenties, with a sprinkling of older couples. The dress code seemed to involve a "nice" sweater, Dockers and some expensive athletic shoes or loafers. My large self, in engineer boots, jeans, a black T-shirt and a leather vest, did not exactly fit right in. I was sorry I had worn my black ball cap that said PITCHER. These are universally recognized back home as what you buy at the Folsom Street Fair if you forgot to bring a hat of your own and realized halfway through the event that you were going to burn the shit out of your carefully shaved head if you didn't cover up. The bartender's sniff hadn't exactly made me feel like the hot new top from out of town. After staring at all those clean-shaven mugs, I kinda felt like standing on my table and shouting, "Give me some goddamned HAIR!" And if I had one more beer, I might do just that.

So then I had a vision. I literally did a double take. What was that cute little cub doing in a twinkie bar like this? He was shorter than me, which I like, and the opposite of stylishly thin. Instead of a sweater, he had on a down vest, and his feet were shod in boots that were much more appropriate given the six inches of snow that had fallen yesterday on top of the eighteen inches that had already accumulated. So when this hefty vision of rural loveliness sailed by my table with a glass of beer, I looked right in his eyes and said, "Woof!"

He jumped. The brew spilled over the edge of his glass as he came to a sudden stop. Then he looked over his shoulder. There was nobody behind him. I had to laugh. Then I saw that he was blushing and pissed, and something else. Hurt? Jesus H. Cricket.

"I'm not makin' fun of you," I said, feeling as awkward as a newborn calf. "Sit down." One of my feet had moved of its own accord and shoved a chair toward him.

He sat, examining my face as if he'd never seen a man before. "Can I get you a new drink?" I asked, recalling my etiquette.

"Uh—no, I can, um, I can finish this one," he muttered. His voice was husky. Did he have a cold? I decided I didn't care.

"Is this your regular stomping ground?" I asked, indicating

our fellow imbibers with a sarcastic wave of my hand.

"I don't know, I guess so," he said, staring at the table, making rings on it with the wet bottom of his glass. Then there was a long, awkward pause. "I'm sorry," he said. "I've dreamed about this happening so many times. And now here you are, and I'm just messing everything up. I should probably go."

"You should probably stay right the hell where you are," I retorted. I put a paw on his shoulder and gently pushed him back into his seat. "I won't bite you. Much."

There it was again, that blush that took over his whole face. I'd bet if I could have examined the top of his head, it would be blushing too.

"Dude, how young are you?" I finally thought to ask.

"Old enough," he replied, finally finding a little grit. "I drive and vote and drink. Just look like jailbait. Wanna see my ID?"

Something was off, and I couldn't put my finger on it. Then I thought about how little sex I'd been able to scrape up in this place as a kid. It was twenty years later, but a young gay man who wasn't fashionably skinny might have a lot of trouble hooking up. Still, I didn't want to be anybody's first time. People got married young around here. There was no wedding ring and no shadow of one, but everybody's tan had faded by now. I just didn't like the idea of cheating, even if the person I was deceiving was somebody else's wife. A promise is a promise. "Well, good. Just so long as you know what you want. You've been with another man before, right?"

"Yeah," he said defensively. "Yes, I have. Well—sort of."

That was when a firm tap fell on my shoulder. I looked up to behold the bartender. "I have to talk to you," he said, casting a disapproving look upon us both. I thought there was something wrong with my credit card, so I got up and followed him to the cash register.

"Do you know who you are talking to?" he hissed indignantly, once he'd gotten four feet of polished wood between us again. He was scrubbing at a wet glass with a dry towel, sanding the shine off it. I was afraid he was going to break it.

I leaned forward, expecting him to out my potential trick for being poz. "Well, I was finding out, before you interrupted us," I said, none too politely.

"She's a girl," he said with complete contempt. We were no longer discussing a human being, his tone of voice indicated.

I looked back at my table. The cub gave me a hopeful wave. He also looked sick to his stomach.

"Come on," I said. "What are you trying to do, pull the wool over my eyes? Look at him. No way any girl grew a beard like that. He's cute as can be. What is your problem?"

The guy on my right swiveled to face me, and burped. "Georgie is right," he said. "That's no gentleman." He groped my ass. "Neither am I," he giggled. "Leon barged in on him when he was tryin' to use the stall. There's nothin' down there, dude."

I brushed his hand away and got ready to stomp off. Old gossips. They sure didn't know much about bears. Or about what it meant when you had your keys on the left, apparently.

I must have looked mad because my nameless trick had gotten up and was bolting for the door. Which wasn't that far away. I dug my neoprene heels into the cracked linoleum floor and ran after him. My body just seemed to make that decision for me. I didn't like the idea of anybody being run out of a gay bar—of all places—for what he looked like. Still, I am large enough that I lumber rather than sprint, so the kid was halfway down the block before I caught his arm and spun him around.

"They told you, didn't they?" he spat. He wasn't too far from tears. I knew if I let him weep, he'd always feel humiliated in front of me. Unmanned. So I grabbed his other arm, pulled him toward me (see why I like 'em on the small side?) and kissed him. Our beards mushed together, one of my favorite sensations, then our moustaches intersected with a brief tickle, and I could taste his mouth. The flavor of fear and excitement on his lips got me excited too. I tipped his head back and gave him my best tongue. A car drove by and tried to splash us with slush. "Faggots!" I heard somebody yell. I came up from the kiss long enough to yell, "Damn right!" and then went back to his mouth for a second kiss. This time, he let me know the attraction was mutual. There was enough desire and heat in that kiss to keep me hard all night long. Which I hoped to be.

"Look," I said, "let's get a six-pack and go someplace where we can talk. I'm visiting my folks, unfortunately. Do you have a place where we can be alone, or should I rent us a motel room?"

"Yeah, I got a place," he said, leaning back against the building. "But I didn't exactly plan on bringing anybody home when I left. So it's kind of a mess."

"Yeah? Well, let's see if we can mess it up some more." I threw my arm over his shoulder. "Did you bring your own car?"

"That's my truck, over there in the lot," he said, pointing to a restored Harvester. "Do you want to follow me home?"

"Can we ride together?" I asked, afraid he would talk himself out of taking me home. "If you don't mind dropping me back here. I don't really want to let you out of my sight."

"Afraid I'll vanish?" he teased, grabbing at my vest.

"Yes," I replied honestly.

"Well, I ain't going anywhere," he assured me, and got up on his tiptoes to bite my neck. Ouch! That was promising. Did he scratch, too?

"Then tell me your name," I replied, grabbing his jacket. I

kept him up on his toes and gave him a hickey.

"Owen!" he screeched. "Ouch, oh, damn it! What's your name, you big brute?"

"Glenn," I replied. I got us moving toward his truck. "Nice work," I commented. "What shop did you take her to?"

"Did it myself," he said shortly. "Always used to work on cars with my dad. Time hangs a little heavy on my hands. She's a hobby. Some guy offered me fifteen thousand for her at the county fair."

"You've put more money into her just in labor alone," I replied, pretending I knew something about it and watching the snowy streets go by. If I was to live here again, would time hang heavy on my hands? What would I do to keep myself from going stir crazy? Start building little birdhouses like my old man? Tie my own flies for trout fishing? Collect rodeo belt buckles? We drove past a lot of sad, unkempt houses, some with boarded-up windows. There were many small businesses, but only the grocery stores and the gas stations looked busy. Stained signs for produce and fishing worms for sale hadn't been taken down after summer's end. Layers of dirty snow, ice, mud, and a sky that was the mixed-up colors of all of these things, threatening more storms soon, was trying to put a damper on my mood.

I put my big mitt over Owen's hand as he shifted. He had calluses on his palms and long fingers. The air in the cab of the truck was cold enough to make my breath visible, but his hands still felt warm.

"So what did they tell you about me?" he demanded after a silence that I had thought was a comfortable one. Apparently not. He was still worried.

"Some bullshit about you not being a guy," I replied.

"What if I'm not?" he asked, giving me a sidelong glance. "Or not the kind that you're used to?"

"How do you know what I'm used to?" I asked. "I'm from San Francisco, remember? We, uh, we're used to just about... aw, hell, Owen, I'm a terrible liar. I don't know what I'm doing here. But I think you're handsome as all perdition, and I like you besides, so I figure that ought to be enough for us to figure out something we can do that's more fun than not."

"You think?" he said grimly.

I threw up my hands. "I can't keep on being cheerful if you are going to be Mr. Scrooge," I said. "Stop saying bah humbug. Let me be the Ghost of Christmas Present." We were at his house. I could see why he wanted a truck. The driveway up to his place was only partly paved, and there were some sharp curves, then a fairly steep climb up to the house. The old-fashioned house and a few outbuildings were set back into the trees so you couldn't hear the highway noises. But you could hear a dog, barking its head off.

"Don't get outta the truck yet," Owen said briefly. He went to greet the dog, a border collie, then opened my door and helped me out. He wrapped me in a big hug, briefly rekindling the heat I had felt at the bar, then asked me to crouch and let the dog smell my hand. "Friend," he said to the dog several times. "Friend, Sparky, friend."

The dog seemed to agree because he licked my hand and let me pet his head. I noticed that the dog was not young, and he had only one eye. "Rescue?" I asked. The dog sat down as soon as I quit petting him and gravely offered me his paw to shake. Then he went to investigate his owner's butt. I felt a little jealous.

"Yeah," Owen said, not inviting questions about the dog's unhappy life story. Then he took my hand and led me into the house. Black-and-white Sparky trotted behind us, happy that his fella was home. I really liked holding hands with this cub. His paw felt so right inside my own, a perfect fit.

Owen said, "I could make you some coffee if you want to wait for me while I do my chores."

"No way," I decided. "Let me come along. We can talk some more."

There was dog food and water to put down in the kitchen. Then he went outside to leave some dry chow and fruit salad for the raccoons. "Don't they forage?" I asked.

"Gets hard for them in winter," he replied.

There was also a homemade structure that looked like a couple of little huts on stilts. Those were for the feral cats, he explained. The openings were too small for the raccoons to bully their way in. They had little solar heaters on their roofs. "Running an extension cord out here for a heating pad got kinda dangerous when it rained," he explained. "There's one old tomcat, I think he has arthritis, he likes to lay up here and warm up. Last year I had some kittens born out of season." We had to hike several hundred feet to get to the limits of his fences. There was a lean-to that had a salt lick and an oil barrel with an open tap of water running into it, to keep it from freezing. "For the deer," he said, breaking open a new bale of hay. After we got back to his patio, he refilled the bird feeders. Then we went into the barn, where there was a horse. The stable had to be mucked out and the horse combed, then fed. Did I mention he also had a chicken coop? I got to look for the eggs—after I stepped on one and broke it. The baseball cap came in handy. Owen greeted each of the chickens by name. They preened and strutted for him and ran around like crazy to peck at the grit and feed he spread around. I decided chicken shit didn't smell that bad, but I was glad to get back out into the open. I had picked up Saint-fucking-Francis of Assisi.

"This is quite a little retreat," I said as we followed an icy path through the snow back toward his house.

"Yeah," he said. "I like animals. They have a kind of innocence that people lack. If they're violent it's usually for a reason. Territory. Food. Sex." He gave me a shy look to see if I understood. A stray sunbeam lit up his long, dirty-blond eyelashes and made his hazel eyes look green. How could anybody look at that face and not want to kiss him?

In his big kitchen, we sat for a while over diner mugs of hot coffee. I was glad to warm my hands up. I hadn't brought any gloves with me or a decent coat. I'd just planned to walk into the bar from my warm rental car, then walk back to the car and go home. I wondered whether I ought to phone home and finally decided I should. I left a vague message about running into some friends and going out for a while. My parents knew I didn't have any friends here, but they wouldn't question me. I just hoped my mom wouldn't wait up. Pops couldn't sleep if she didn't come to bed.

Owen asked me questions about them, and I found myself describing our troubled relationship and the family crisis that had persuaded me to come home. Pops needed debilitating cancer treatments. I was an only child, so there was nobody else to help Mom look after him. Owen was easy to talk to. I told him things I rarely think or speak about. But I didn't forget my main agenda. Eventually I got us out of the kitchen and onto the living room sofa, where I kept sliding closer to him or drawing him closer to me. Finally I got him leaning on me, with my arm draped over his shoulder. His dog was on the other side, leaning on Owen. We made a cute little tableau of domestic tranquility.

I can't remember who started kissing who. But it sure was nice. I was so happy to be enjoying masculine attention in a place where I'd never found it before. I wasn't sure if it was me kissing Owen or that sixteen-year-old gay boy who had so badly wanted to know if men fell in love with each other. In high school, I would have settled for a blow job, but underneath the adolescent hormones was a big fuckin' romantic. I wanted a boyfriend who would slow-dance with me and wake up in bed with me more than I wanted to come.

Back in the present, we had each other's shirts open, and I was playing with his nipples. I noticed that he kept wincing. "Don't put up with it if it doesn't feel good," I said.

"Scar tissue," he explained.

That made a finger of ice water run down my back. What the fuck? "Show me," I said quietly.

He stood up and took off his shirt, refusing to look at me. His arms were nice, muscles built up by hard work: a tattoo of his dog on one bicep, a barbed-wire cuff on the other. I realized I was avoiding looking at his chest. I studied the ant trail of hair that ran into his jeans, then let my eyes follow it up. It was...impressive? Scary? Different and new? He had two long cuts under each pec, and his nipples were an angry-looking red. But they were small and flat and in the right place. Looked like someday he would be so hairy chested that the scars wouldn't even show.

"How did they—do that? Where did you go? What exactly—Owen, tell me your story."

His chuckle was a little bitter. "How far back do you want me to go?" he asked. "These scars aren't the worst part of it. Can you understand that? The worst part of it was knowing, for years and years, that I was a man who wanted to be with other men. But no matter how many men I had sex with, it never worked, because they thought I was a girl. I thought I was a freak. There was nobody else like me in the whole world. And it was hopeless, there was nothing I could do to change it. But when I finally got up the nerve to correct this mistake, that was the happy part of my life. These scars prove how much I wanted to be a man. What I was willing to pay for the privilege. What I was willing to give up. Proof that there is no ambivalence, no turning back."

"Have you got, uh, anything else? Any more scars?"

He shook his head. "The rest of it is original equipment. Works good. Want the grand tour?"

"Yeah," I said. "I suppose I do."

"Scared?" he asked.

"Yes!" I replied. "Not of you, not exactly. But I've never done anything like this. I worry that I won't know what to do. Won't be able to please you."

"Won't be able to keep it up, you mean? I'll help," he promised. We went down a short hallway, past a bathroom, and there was his bedroom, across the back of the house. He had a four-poster bed with natural wood, the bark still on it, nodes where branches had been trimmed off. There were plaid flannel sheets and a thick down duvet that had a picture of (I am not kidding) a bear on it. Shelves in the headboard contained some books, a couple of bottles of different kinds of lube, and condoms. "I keep the toys down here," he said, gesturing toward a drawer on the side of the bed. "Not that I've had much call to use them on anybody except myself."

I thought about what I would do if Owen was the same kind of guy I was always bringing home. I decided I was going to follow that script as close as I could. "So get on the floor, boy," I said. "Down on your knees between my fucking boots."

When I think that I almost decided to stay home that night... what a mistake that would have been! Going out to a bar where people used to know you by a different name and a different gender is not a pleasant experience. I wasn't even sure why I bothered. Loneliness and boredom can drive you to hang out with people who will be mean to you, I guess. The dykes were all pissed off at me. If they talked to me, it was to loudly use my "girl name" and female pronouns. Before I transitioned, I was known as that weird woman who was way too butch and hated sex. The occasional high femme pressured me to take her home, but I didn't want them. I was staring at the guys, fantasizing about them. Now, none of the lesbians wanted to have sex with me. (Well, I did get the occasional drunk dial, but I wasn't *that* horny.)

I had a lot of fantasies about leaving, going some place more liberal, or at least a place where I could start over, without memories of my younger self always being thrown in my face. But I had inherited a house here, my auntie's old place, and my dad's business, and I didn't want to live in a city. I'm a small-town boy. I know that about myself. I like working on my truck in the driveway and the slowly changing seasons. And I'm stubborn. I guess I went back to Brothers for the same reason I kept my dad's auto body shop open and made the customers deal with me, the son he never knew he had. If I refused to go away, that unreasonable part of myself said, sooner or later I would wear down their resistance. They'd have to accept me because I wouldn't accept anything less. So I put on my flannel-lined jeans, my best pair of boots, a fisherman's sweater my mom had knit for me, and a down vest, then sailed in to confront their gender essentialist asses.

Darcy the drag queen is always nice to me, even though she can't quite understand why anybody would want to be a man. Her desire for change goes in the opposite direction. We sometimes have fun dancing together and making it look like we're going to go home. But of course she never takes me seriously as a potential trick. Darcy is a size queen.

Georgie the bartender completely hates me. That's because

he was a newcomer who hadn't heard the news about me when he got hired. On his first day of work, he was all over me like an octopus. We made out in between customers. The rest of the bar let it go on for a while. It was one big practical joke to them. I'm not sure who told him. But after he took a piss break, he barged out of the men's room mad as hell and actually took a swing at me. I grabbed a magazine off the top of the cigarette machine, rolled it up, and bopped him on the nose. He sat down with blood streaming from his nostrils and the wrath of a faggot who thinks he has been deceived. "How dare you!" he kept saying. "How dare you?"

Now he makes it a point to get in between me and anybody who shares my table.

So when that hunky newcomer started making eyes at me, I was nervous. Part of me wished he hadn't noticed me. I didn't want to let myself get turned on to him, get outed, then see his flirtatiousness turn into scorn. But there was something different about him. Self-confidence? Was he more secure in his homosexuality? That leather vest hinted at the fulfillment of certain fantasies I treasured. Whatever it was, it got past my defenses. So I let myself wink back at him, banter, and enjoy the rush the first time he squeezed my shoulders and drew me closer, so I could smell his sweat and sense the heat of his body. Everything I had between my legs was hard for him. But would that be enough?

George's loud revelation of my supposedly shameful secret hurt worse than it usually did. I guess that's why I ran for the door. The people in Brothers had never succeeded in ousting me before. I guess I ran out of nerve or lost all hope that they would change. Here was a man I really wanted, who wanted me, and they were going to ruin it. But it wasn't really their fault, was it? Because I could never be a real man, never have another man love me, and so the fault was in me. The problem was my fucked-up mind and body. I was never going to be good enough. Real gay men do not want FTMs. How could they?

When Glenn chased me down and started kissing me, I was beside myself. First of all, you just don't do that here. The gay activity is kept behind closed doors. I was afraid of getting beaten up, but when he acknowledged both of us as faggots to the heckler in the car, I was dizzy with happiness. How weird is that? I wanted to be a fag so much that I would have happily gotten my ass kicked for being one with him. He had spoken my identity out loud; nobody else had ever acknowledged my gayness.

I kept telling myself not to get attached, and he kept not going away. I couldn't remember the last time I'd been kissed; never with so much skill or passion. The boys I'd dated in high school, before I transitioned, were not allowed to have facial hair. I doubt they'd have wanted to let their beards grow even if the school dress code had allowed it. So the sensation of his beard and moustache was all new. I liked the way that felt, so much. It made my toes curl and my breath come fast. Those boys had always had something critical to say about the way that I responded to their attention. One of them said, "You aren't supposed to kiss me back like that. You're supposed to just relax and wait for me to kiss you. Just respond a little bit, don't get so aggressive!" It made me want to throw up because I knew what they were really saying was, "You aren't doing this right. You aren't being appropriate as a girl. I want a girl. So if you can't convince me you are one, I'm going to leave you." I couldn't, and they did.

Glenn's hands felt different on me. He was a gentle person, but he wasn't holding back. He wasn't monitoring himself to make sure he didn't overwhelm me. I'd never made love to a woman, but I knew how straight guys related to me—as somebody weaker and more sensitive. Glenn just did what he wanted to do and assumed I was strong enough to take it and respond in kind. It was good—affirming. I needed and wanted more of his hands, on me, inside of me.

I guess a part of me had thought that I was screwed up about sex. I thought that even if I took testosterone and changed my legal name, I would still be fucked up about the things people did to feel pleasure. I wasn't sure I could have that. Glenn's touch set me free because it was purely sexual—and I liked it. I was fully aroused, without any penalty. I wasn't nauseous, I didn't want to squirm away from him, I didn't have to put up with it or leave my body or count the minutes till it was over. I was just there with him, his scent in my face, his big warm body under my own hands, and I wanted to hear him groan the way that I secretly groaned when he moved his tongue in and out of my mouth.

Now we were here in my house. In the master bedroom, where I had so often jerked off and dreamed about gay boy sex, watched porn, fantasized, experimented with vibrators and dildos. I would go through a few days of sexual frenzy, when I couldn't keep my hands off my junk, then realize that masturbating was just making me feel more lonely. So I'd stop for a while; avoid anything sexual for as long as possible. But the need would build up, as it does when you are on male hormones, until I had to take care of it, even if coming sometimes made me curl up like a cooked shrimp and cry.

Glenn was sitting on the edge of the bed, and he wanted me to kneel in between his thighs. Was I going to do that? I looked at him sideways, from under my eyelashes, understanding that if I was going to have sex with him, he was going to take a dominant role. Did that mean he saw me as a girl? I didn't think so. He was being too macho, for one thing. I was so curious. What was it like to be a boy? Would I enjoy it? Would he take good care of me? If I sucked his cock, would that be as far as it would go? Well, if it was, so what? Sucking his cock was still more sex than I'd had since I transitioned. It would be something I could treasure, think about later, something more real than a picture in a DVD.

Could I flip him? (It took only a split second to have all of these thoughts.) I wondered if I could dominate him. Maybe, if I really wanted to, he would go under for me. But he would have to know me better first, I sensed. He would have to trust me more than he did tonight, on our first encounter. And if I did take control, would I get what I wanted? I wanted to know how another man would relate to my body. If I was on top, I could keep my clothes on, refuse to let him touch me, stay back from the experience. All of the sensation and all of the vulnerability would be his. So I let that idea slide, kept it for another time. And this was one of Glenn's gifts to me—the conviction that there would be another time.

Luckily, my boots just slid off my feet. I knelt, smoothly I hoped, between his knees. He gave me a quick squeeze with his thighs, and we shared a smile. "Do you like my boots?" he asked.

"Yes, Sir," I replied. His shoulders relaxed when he heard the word "Sir." Just three letters had communicated volumes about what I wanted from him and how far he could take me.

"Then give them some attention," he said. A shade of sternness crept into his voice, but he left it open-ended. I could deep-throat them or just try to see myself in the polished surfaces, I guessed. So I slid down onto my belly and took hold of his left boot. I gave it some kisses and licks, worried about marring the shine. "Other foot, too," he reminded me, so I changed directions and did the same thing over there. "How does that make you feel?" he asked, hooking a finger in my collar and bringing me up to his level.

"Safe," I replied. "I trust you." We looked into each other's eyes. His brown eyes were full of intelligence, curiosity and humor. "I hope I will deserve your trust," he said solemnly, then he kissed me.

Holy smokes! I wanted to touch myself so bad. I could feel his fingers on my buttons, opening my shirt, and was glad I had gotten rid of the sweater in the kitchen. He was exposing bare skin and sliding his hands over me, gently tracing my scars, tickling my stomach just a bit as he ruffled my newly sprouted fur. Instead of squeezing my nipples, he just sort of...noticed them. His fingertips wandered over them, he circled the base of each one, so I began to think that someday it might feel really good to have him pinch my nipples.

"It's getting kind of crowded in here," he said, undoing his belt buckle. I reached for the zipper, batting his hands away, and opened his fly. He put his hands on the bed and leaned back, watching me work. His face looked hungry. I gently squeezed the bundle I felt inside his shorts, then pulled the waistband of his briefs down and extracted what was inside. Getting his cock out was a bit of a wrestling match. It was just too hard. I had to sort of bend it to get it past the folds of his underwear and jeans. But then it was free, and that made it easier to scoop his balls out, too. He gave a little hiss when I wrapped one hand around the base of his sac and pulled his eggs down, so I continued to squeeze them. But I had another hand free, and that one was angling his cock toward my mouth.

Then he stopped me. "You don't know if I'm poz or not," he gasped.

"Oh." I was out of breath. Tossing my head once or twice didn't seem to clear it. I just wanted him in my mouth.

"I am negative," he told me. "I use condoms for fucking but I don't put one on for sucking unless the other guy wants it that way. What do you want?"

"I—uh, I don't know," I replied. "I never thought about it."

"Have you ever been tested?"

"For what? HIV? Yeah. I don't think I have anything to worry about."

"No hepatitis? No herpes?"

"No," I replied. "No."

"Do you know what to look for to make sure the other guy doesn't have syphilis?"

"No, not really," I told Glenn. "But can't you do sex ed later? I promise I'll listen to the whole lecture then. But for now—"

He laughed. "You like sucking dick, don't you?"

"Yes!" I replied. Then I got my mouth around the head of his cock, which wasn't hard anymore, and bathed it with my tongue. I was able to put his whole cock in my mouth because it had softened. For a few minutes, I just held it there, getting it warm, not making any demands. Glenn ran his fingertips through my hair. As his cock got a little harder, I let his balls slip out of my mouth, one by one. The shaft kept getting thicker, more firm. So I slipped it out too, but I also went back down on it, keeping constant friction and motion. He was cut, so I didn't have to worry about manipulating a foreskin, I could just put him down my throat and suck him until I desperately had to come up for air. Then it was as if his cock became something I needed as much as I needed air or food or water. I fed on him. But it was a never-ending feast, and the stream of his precome was thick enough to help his rod slide to the back of my throat. As he went deep, I inhaled and swallowed, kept my tongue busy on the underside of his shaft. When I unwillingly let him slide out, my hand was waiting to twist at the base of his cock, twist and pump.

Once in a while I would ignore his cock and put one or both of his balls in my mouth instead. He loved having his balls played with. I kept coming up with new ways to manipulate them. This sex thing required a lot of imagination and variety, but it seemed like it also generated a lot of new ideas as it kept unfolding. I just wanted him to know that I was no amateur. None of my high school boyfriends had complained about how I did *this*.

I was drooling, and I think my eyes were crossed. He was making my cock feel so good, I kept forgetting to pull on his hair and shove his head down. I just wanted to lie down and let him do me. I guess I've gotten more elegant blow jobs, but Owen wasn't trying to demonstrate his tantric proficiency. He just wanted me, with every molecule of his being, and he was doing a damn fine job of showing it. Whew!

"Get up here," I finally said, and took my cock out of that soft, sublime mouth. I got my hands around his waist and pulled his shirt out of the belt loops. Then I practically tossed him on the bed. He had already lost his boots, so I shucked mine, too. He rolled onto one side and looked at me, then unbuttoned my shirt and sucked on my nipples. He had sharp little teeth, and I could have let him torture my tits for another lifetime or two. But I had wanted something else when I got him up on the bed and horizontal.

The sun had gone down quite a while ago. I switched on a bedside lamp. There must have been central heating because the room was nice and warm. So I finished taking my shirt off and got out of my pants and briefs. I kept my socks on because my feet are always getting cold.

When I put my hands on him so I could undress him, he looked really scared. "Don't," he said. "I don't think I can—"

"But you promised me the guided tour, dude. I paid my moneys and now I wants my ride." I rubbed his shoulders, allowed him to turn over onto his belly, but I kept undressing him anyway. Two hands under his hips made short work of the zipper on his jeans, and I pulled them off a little at a time, teasing him until he began to giggle even though he was also scared and pissed off at me. I was happy to be having sex with somebody who was so genuine. The typical script was, "Look how hot I am. Oh, wow, I moved this way. Look how hot I am now. Oh, you're hot too. Wow. Look at us being hot together." Gag me.

"Hey," I said, whispering in his ear. He was wearing nothing but his underpants, and we were both covered by blankets. I was lying at his side, one arm over his shoulders, pressing our bodies together as much as I could, skin to skin. "Hey," I said again. "I really like you, Owen. You're a very handsome boy. I know that because my cock just doesn't get this hard for chicks. I've met a few women in my day who were so sexy that I wanted to do them. And I'm afraid I couldn't perform."

"Really?" he said, searching my face.

I nodded.

"I can't do it with girls either," he confessed. One of his hands made knots in the pillow. "I thought for a while that I was, you know, a lesbian, because I got called a dyke so often when I was growing up. But I just don't like, well, you know."

I nodded. "It's a different kind of sex and a different kind of relationship. But what we are doing is man-to-man sex. You are a different kind of guy, but men come in all shapes and sizes, Owen. I'm a bear. Bears believe that there is not a single standard for handsomeness. There's a wide range of cuteness in gay men. We also believe that there is more to being gay than just looking for sex. We want a community where we are honest with each other and treat each other with decency. You are a promising little cub, Owen. Cubs deserve to be loved and taken care of. Let me be good to you. Your body has been through so much. If you don't want me to look at you, just let me touch you."

I was gradually able to persuade him to let my hand wander down to the juncture of his thighs. There I found a small cock, about half the size of his own thumb, but it was rock-hard. So I scooped up a little bit of the lube that I found there and rubbed it on his cock. With my thumb and forefinger, I began to jerk him off. "I'd love to do this while you suck my dick," I suggested.

It took us a while to figure out a workable position. But when we got ourselves arranged on the bed, Owen was eager to resume his oral ministration. It was pretty difficult to remember to keep my hand moving while he was making me see stars. "Show me how you do it," I suggested, and he quickly put his hand between his legs and showed me where his boycock wanted to be stroked. I gently pushed his hand away and then found a moment of boldness. I said to myself, the hell with it, and put his cock in my mouth.

He jerked. He lost track of the rhythm that was bring me closer to shooting. I ordered him to keep on going, and he somehow found the concentration to start working me again. I barely moved my mouth and tongue. I just put pressure on his cock with my lips and tongue, and let him rub himself off in my mouth. Before long, we were both panting. "I'm not going to shoot until you get off," I told him, briefly letting go of his delicious piece so I could form words. "You have to get off really good, no faking, I want you to make me believe it, boy, and then I will feed you hot meat until your throat is raw."

He moaned and let himself go, pushing urgently at my mouth. Now I dared to gently suck and tongue him. The slightest gesture seemed to drive him completely crazy. I was guessing that nobody else had ever sucked his cock before. It wasn't long before he was making muffled shouts and banging my face. Within seconds,

I got what I had demanded—an authentic orgasm. His body was limp in my arms, covered with sweat, relaxed as a sleeping puppy. But there was no sleep for this little one. I rearranged our bodies so that I was sitting up, then I got him up on all fours and shoved his mouth onto my cock. This meant that his bits were pointed right at me, so I got another look at him. Two holes seemed intriguing. I drew a glove out of the box on the bedside table, pulled it onto my hand, and lubed my fingers up. Then I started stroking the outside of these orifices.

He spit out my right ball and said, "I don't know about this, Sir."

"Does it feel good?"

"Yes. But—"

"Then don't worry. The only thing you need to do is feel good. If something starts to feel bad, let me know. Otherwise, I want my cock down your throat, and I'm going to make you come again while you are sucking me. Is that clear?"

"Yessir, it's clear," he gasped, and sucked me down to the root.

I pushed on both of the tightly puckered holes, wondering which one would give way first. Oddly enough, I couldn't feel a difference in their tightness. The asshole eventually began to feel as if it was encouraging my finger to explore its nooks and crannies. The other hole was permitting me to enter, but it didn't feel as enthusiastic. So I focused on his butt. Two fingers fit it quite nicely, and I pumped him, thinking that it would feel great to be in here, even with a condom. I made a few dirty comments to that effect, and his throat began to tighten around my cock.

I pushed his head down once or twice, growled a bad name at him and then came abruptly, before I knew I was on the edge. He tried to swallow my come, but there was just too much of it, so we had to settle for wiping it up with a towel and exclaiming over the distance it had flown. By the way, come on a hot lightbulb has a very interesting smell.

As soon as I could, I distracted him from cleaning up by getting him back on the bed. We wrestled for a few minutes, then I wound up with my arms and legs twined around his body. He had his hands free so he could touch my face. "Kiss me," he said, and I was happy to oblige.

"You're the best thing I ever got for Christmas," I told him, tugging on his earlobes. I wondered if he'd like to have his back tattooed. I hadn't brought my sketchpad or colored pencils with me. But a design was forming in my mind, a dragon hatching from its egg, already fully formed and a fierce warrior.

"It isn't Christmas yet," he told me, playing with the ring in my left nipple.

"Not officially," I admitted. "Maybe I should say you're the best solstice present I ever got. What do you want for Christmas, little cub?"

"I want you to sleep with me tonight," he replied.

I thought of a few reasons why I should go home to my parents' house, but they all seemed rather petty when I looked at his serious face with its freckles and his blue eyes. "Okay," I replied. "But you have to know that I talk in my sleep."

Owen shrugged. "I sometimes have bad dreams that make me sit up and scream."

"Great," I said sarcastically. "You won that contest."

"Sorry. I shouldn't have said that. TMI. Do you want to go?"

"No, I called my folks and let them know I was out with friends. I can call them first thing in the morning to let them know I'm okay. Why not? I can put up with wearing my bar outfit until I get home to change."

"You just look like a biker," Owen shrugged. "We get a few

of those coming through. Not many in the winter is all. I even have a clean toothbrush for you."

We got up and puttered around, getting ready for bed, the dog dancing around, demanding a little attention. Owen went to the kitchen to let him out of the house. Sparky happily did his business and came back in, reporting that it was cold outside, and that weird white stuff was still all over the ground. When was someone going to fix that? It was hiding a lot of good smells. We tussled with the dog, who gave me the ultimate kudos by rolling over and letting me pet his belly. Then all of us were tired.

Before we fell asleep, I told Owen about the tattoo I had imagined doing on his back. He listened and said he was very flattered. "So what are you going to do about your dad being sick?" he asked me, not wasting any time.

"I don't know," I sighed, twisting my pillow into a supportive lump for my head. "I don't have very good memories of this place. But I don't know who else is going to help my mom. I can't even imagine how hard it must have been for Pops to ask me for anything. He's not the kind of man who's ever admitted that he needed help."

"Seems like it's always the gay kids who wind up taking care of the elderly," Owen commented. He was on his side, facing away from me, and sounded like he was about to pass out.

"That's true. But in my case I'm an only child. So there isn't anybody else. My dad's brothers and sisters all have problems of their own. And my mom was a refugee. Nobody else from her family came over from England after the war."

"Would you move in to their trailer?" Owen asked. "Is it a double-wide?"

"Yes, but there still isn't really room for me. I'd probably want to open my own shop here. Rent a storefront. Maybe live in back of the shop."

"I've got a spare room," Owen said. I could barely hear him. "You could crash there till you got your business up and running."

We both fell asleep before I could even consider the offer.

The next day, I called my mom and dad. It was the day before Christmas. They wanted to know the name of my new friend. In the spirit of glasnost, I told them. "Oh," my dad said, "he's the guy down at Christensen's Auto Body. Took on the business when his dad retired."

"He's always so nice whenever we take the Chevy in there," my mom interrupted. It drove me crazy when they shared a call with me. "He doesn't have any people of his own. You should bring him to dinner on Christmas."

"Mom, I don't know, I barely—"

"You know your mother will make more food than the two of us can eat," Pops rumbled. "Invite him out of self-defense if nothing else. We can watch *It's a Wonderful Life.* I've got it on videotape."

I thought about the beautiful boys of San Francisco. I'd lived there for ten years, most of them without a relationship. I wanted a boyfriend, but it was always so much easier to be friends with benefits. If I really wanted a relationship, was it ever going to happen in a city with that many opportunities for casual sex? Owen was making himself available. My parents were even urging me to bring him home to meet them. Could it be that by moving back to my home town, I'd find the love I longed for as I watched everyone else escort their dates onto the dance floor at the senior prom? That would be ironic. My post-gay friends who made a big fuss about being queer and deconstructing the gender binary would pee themselves if they knew I'd found a tranny in my little hometown. That was ironic, too. But I didn't want to tell them. I felt protective of

Owen's privacy and I felt like he had a right to be just another cub with a daddy bear. Hmm. One more thing to talk about with him.

It wouldn't be easy to accept the limitations of small-town life. I could still conjure up the bartender's vitriolic insults. "She's a girl!" I knew what kind of shit a man could get for being a faggot. What did you get for being a faggot who slept with a tranny? It was something new for people to wrap their heads around. The haters would find a way to come at me, to try to make me pay.

Well, I did know that Owen was good enough for a second date. I wasn't going to do all this future tripping until I'd put my cock in him. If I fucked him and he called me Daddy, we might have a deal.

"Did you fall asleep?" my dad asked me. "Have a late night?" I came to with a start. I had been so far into my head that I had forgotten what I was doing. And had Pops just made a joke about me having a one-night stand? My *father*?

"Just a sec," I said. "I'm trying to get his attention. Owen!" He turned around, ignoring the stove for a second, and I passed on my folks' invitation. Owen asked me if it was okay with me. I said it was, and so he said yes. "But if you're going to be my Christmas present, I'll have to wrap you up like one," I said, flirting and threatening him.

"Go look in the drawer under my side of the bed," he said.

I went.

The drawer contained a small selection of kinky toys, some of them handmade. There was a neatly coiled set of black nylon ropes. The ends had been finished with whipping, done with a smaller black cord. I picked them up so I could admire the knot work, then took them back to the kitchen to wave in Owen's face. "Time hangs heavy on your hands," I repeated.

"Not today," he replied. "I'm not going in to work. Do you want pancakes or waffles?"

After I'd fed Glenn, I had a chance to think about what I had done with him. The morning after sex was supposed to be full of regret and bad memories. Instead, I felt energized, happy to be alive and foolishly optimistic. It wasn't too hard to talk Glenn into going back to bed. He seemed a little more confused than he'd been last night. But he was every bit as handsome. I thought that once we got started, his naturally dominant personality would probably assert itself.

I peeled off the covers and reached for his cock. With one hand, I kept his balls hanging low, right on the edge of discomfort. I felt a sympathetic ache in the pit of my stomach as I firmly tugged them down. With my other hand, I put a bit of lube on his cock and squeezed, twisted my hand and went up and down. When I got to the head of his cock, I would stop and run my thumb over it, tickling the lips of his piss slit. Then it was time to move my hand back to the base of his dick, mimicking the way I would retract a foreskin, if he'd had one. It didn't take long before his cock was as hard as it had been last night, and his body was arching and coming off the bed, begging for release.

But I had something more controversial in mind than a hand job. So I grabbed a condom, tore it open and rolled it over his cock. I gently pinched it to put a bit of an empty pocket at the end. Touching him had gotten me excited. I was slick between my legs, and wanted to know what it would feel like to put him in my front hole. He was worried about not being able to keep it up. So we'd just have to find out if that was true. If he could fuck me there, it would somehow prove to me that he saw me as another man, despite my strange plumbing. If he had a problem, I could just take it up the ass. It would be nice to have a cock there, with its combination of hardness and softness, instead of a toy.

I put a hand in the center of his chest, to let him know he should hold still, and swung one of my legs over his hips. It took a bit of gymnastic posturing to get him inside of me. It felt so good, I had tears in my eyes. I just sat on him for a while, enjoying the feeling of complete fullness, rejoicing in my own power to enjoy an act that used to leave me cold, alienated, and in pain. There was no pain at all with Glenn. I wanted him.

Using my fingers on his nipples, I began to rise and fall on his hard cock. He moaned and tried to get deeper inside of me. Eventually I let him put his hands on my hips. With his help, I could fuck myself a little faster. I let go of his nipples and jerked myself off, fingers moving in time with his swollen sex. He watched me through half-closed eyes. Was he thinking about tying me up and doing this? Great! But I was glad that we were doing it this way first, so I could be sure I was okay.

We became like two parts of one organism, moving in sync, pumping each other, working up toward a release that we both needed. I felt as if I would never get enough of this man. I wanted him so badly. You could argue that I would have felt that way about anybody who had been willing to come home with me. Not so. Glenn was smart enough to understand my story, and he didn't bullshit me. He told me if he was scared or didn't have the answer. That was fine.

The power to think rationally disappeared. We were only bodies, hands that groped at one another, genitals that burned and pleaded for orgasm; taste, smell, feel of his skin, nipples; biting his neck; licking the sweat—oh! We jerked together, and being able to come was such a blessing. Such blissful prolonged pleasure. My toes curled as I took his come, knowing he was responding when I squeezed him with my pelvic muscles. I wished that I could keep him inside of me for a little longer.

Glenn reluctantly separated from me and took the condom off. Then we went into each other's arms and cuddled, not needing to be under the blankets just yet. His big teeth nibbled at my ear with the delicacy of a deer tasting new growth on the trees. His hands moved slowly over my backside, then stroked down the crack of my ass. "I'm showing you a good time there next," he rumbled.

"Please do," I whispered. Then I noticed that there were small tears coming out of his closed eyes, running down his cheeks to get lost in his beard. I moved up so I could lick them. "Don't cry, I said. "Don't be unhappy. Not when I feel this wonderful."

He smiled without opening his eyes. "Not unhappy," he yawned. "I feel pretty wonderful too. I feel so at home with you. What the hell do you call what we just did, anyway? That was awesome."

"Sodomy," I said firmly.

Glenn laughed so hard it brought him out of his sleepy state. He grabbed me and began to tickle me. I hate this, so I attacked in turn. I wasn't sure where this would lead, but I didn't care. Let the shop stay closed for one day. I was opening up much more important things.

ABOUT THE AUTHORS

RAHNE ALEXANDER (rahne.com) is a musician and multimedia artist from Baltimore. She is guitarist and vocalist in The Oops and the art rock power trio The Degenerettes, who were featured in the 2010 documentary *Riot Acts*. Her film and video work screens frequently in festivals and galleries across the country.

TONI AMATO (toniamato@writeherewritenow.org) has been a teacher, editor and writing coach for over twenty years. His fiction has appeared in several anthologies and journals, including *The Underwood Review* and *Food and Other Enemies*. He is the editor, with Mary Davies, of the anthology, *Pinned Down By Pronouns*.

LAURA ANTONIOU (lantoniou.com) is a long-time writer, activist and teacher of sexuality relationship classes, known for her groundbreaking Marketplace books, the first S/M erotica series featuring a transman as the romantic hero. She is always working on new projects and invites friends on Facebook and Fetlife as long as you don't bother her.

S. BEAR BERGMAN (sbearbergman.com) is the author or editor of three books (most recently the anthology *Gender Outlaws: The Next Generation* with Kate Bornstein), four solo performances and numerous contributions to anthologies on all manner of topics from the sacred to the extremely profane.

KATE BORNSTEIN is an advocate for teens, freaks, and other outlaws. She tweets incessantly at twitter.com/katebornstein. When she was a boy, she wanted to be Huckleberry Finn.

HELEN BOYD (myhusbandbetty.com) is the author of *My Husband Betty* and *She's Not the Man I Married*. She has spoken at numerous gender conferences and has been running various community forums for transpeople and their partners for over a decade. She is a happy and visible—and happily visible—trans partner.

RACHEL KRAMER BUSSEL (rachelkramerbussel.com) is a New York-based author, editor and blogger. She is senior editor at *Penthouse Variations* and hosts In the Flesh Reading Series. Her books include *Best Bondage Erotica 2011*, *Orgasmic*, *Fast Girls*, *Passion*, *The Mile High Club*, *Bottoms Up*, *Spanked*, *Peep Show*, *Tasting Him* and more.

PATRICK CALIFIA (patrickcalifia.com) writes about sex politics and queer culture and he counsels sexual minority members. He has edited many anthologies and is the author of fourteen books, including *Boy in The Middle: Erotic Fiction*, *Speaking*

Sex to Power: The Politics of Queer Sex and the classic *Macho Sluts*, rereleased in 2009.

IVAN COYOTE (ivanecoyote.com) was born and raised in Whitehorse, Yukon territory, Canada. Ivan is the author of seven books, four films and three CDs. You can find out more about Ivan and hir work on hir website.

KIKI DELOVELY is a queer femme performer/writer who has lived and performed all over the United States, as well as internationally, and now calls Durham, NC home. Her work has appeared in *Best Lesbian Erotica 2011, Gotta Have It: 69 Stories of Sudden Sex* and *Salacious* magazine.

GINA DE VRIES (ginadevries.com) is a genderqueer femme, a queer Paisan pervert, and a writer, performer, cultural worker, and activist. Recent publications include *The Revolution Starts at Home* and *Bound to Struggle*. Founder and facilitator of Sex Workers' Writing Workshop San Francisco, she's currently pursuing her MFA in Fiction Writing at San Francisco State University.

ALICIA E. GORANSON (themaskofinanna.com) is a Boston author, playwright and screenwriter. Her first novel, *Supervillainz*, was a 2006 Lambda Literary Award finalist and winner of the first Project QueerLit Award. She is writing and producing The Post-Meridian Radio Player's flagship audio drama, "The Mask of Inanna."

MICHAEL HERNANDEZ loves being a big ole hairy fag. He lives with his long-term husbear, grandkid, and a little brown-eyed beauty named Sugar (i.e., the dog). Mike's previous work appears in *Best of Best Lesbian Erotica 2* and *Doing It for Daddy*, among others.

ARDEN HILL is a PhD student and teacher out on the prairie where ze writes about gender, sexuality and disability. Hir erotic work has appeared in *Best Gay Erotica 2008*, *Boys in Heat*, *Best of the Best Gay Erotica 3*, loveyoudivine.com, and justusroux.com.

TOBI HILL-MEYER (nodesignation.com) is a trans activist and writer. She started writing to fill the utter void of diverse trans characters in media as well as to offer an alternative to the overwhelmingly exploitative and exotic ways that trans women's sexuality is often portrayed.

JACQUES LA FARGUE is now a name twice used to grant safe passage to a Canadian Jew. This Jacques appreciates a good historical reference, has a total fetish for books and the printed word and excels at the esoteric. Jacques enjoys both gender and genitals in many combinations.

PENELOPE MANSFIELD is a transwoman in California. She's still finishing up her electrolysis.

SANDRA MCDONALD (sandramcdonald.com) is the critically acclaimed author of the story collection *Diana Comet and Other Stories*, which Lambda Literary Review calls "joyful, poignant, silly and clever," and *The Outback Stars* trilogy of science fiction novels. Her short fiction has appeared in more than forty magazines and anthologies.

SKIAN MCGUIRE is a working-class Quaker who lives in the wilds of western Massachusetts. Skian's fiction has appeared in many anthologies, webzines and print periodicals.

Eroticist **GISELLE RENARDE** (gisellerenarde.webs.com) is a proud Canadian, supporter of the arts and activist for women's and LGBT rights. Ms. Renarde lives across from a park with two bilingual cats who sleep on her head.

DEAN SCARBOROUGH (hobbitdragon.livejournal.com) is an aspiring sex educator who writes and illustrates erotica in his spare time. His artwork has been published on the front cover of the queer speculative fiction magazine *Collective Fallout* and in the queer feminist porn magazine *Salacious*. He lives in the Bay Area of California.

JULIA SERANO (juliaserano.com) is an Oakland, California-based writer, performer and activist. She is the author of *Whipping Girl: A Transsexual Woman on Sexism and the Scapegoating of Femininity*, and she has also penned pieces in numerous anthologies, magazines and blogs. Her writings have been used in colleges across North America.

SINCLAIR SEXSMITH (mrsexsmith.com) runs the personal online writing project, Sugarbutch Chronicles: The Gender, and Relationship Adventures of a Kinky Queer Butch Top. With work published in various anthologies and websites, including the *Best Lesbian Erotica* series, Mr. Sexsmith writes, teaches and performs.

EVAN SWAFFORD (jnicole58@yahoo.com) is a genderqueer queer currently living the dream in Oakland, CA. He is a

Daddy, a dom and a boish soul. Some of his passions are BDSM, polyamory, transmasculine folks and smut. He was previously published in *Best Lesbian Erotica 2009*.

SHAWNA VIRAGO (shawnavirago.com) is a celebrated transgender songwriter and cultural activist. *The SF Bay Times* said Miss Virago is "a transgender songwriting goddess who manages to channel Joe Strummer through a Candy Darling-like persona." She is the Director of the San Francisco Transgender Film Festival.

ANNA WATSON (femmebibliography.blogspot.com) is an old-school femme living in the Boston area with her butch husband and two sons. More of her writing can be found in *Best Lesbian Erotica* (2007, 2008, and 2009) as well as *Visible: A Femmethology, Vol. 1* and *Girl Crazy*, among others.

RACHEL K. ZALL (radiosilent.org) is a poet, performing artist, activist and graphic designer living in Somerville, MA. She has published two books of poetry, *The Oxygen Catastrophe* and *New Problems*, and is currently working on a third, tentatively titled *Naming*, about overcoming transphobia. This is her first published work of erotica.

ANDREA ZANIN (sexgeek.wordpress.com) is a gender-fluid queer poly pervert who lives in Toronto and spends her time being a blogger, journalist, community organizer, educator, translator, editor, writer and PhD student while trying to keep up with her two partners and her leather family and do enough yoga to stay sane.

ZEV is a fresh-faced, innocent-looking young man with a dirty, dirty mind. An inveterate globetrotter, he has explored back rooms and bathhouses on three continents and counting. Despite his peripatetic lifestyle, he feels most at home at the feet of his fabulous Owner, who keeps him firmly in line.

ABOUT THE EDITOR

TRISTAN TAORMINO (puckerup.com and openingup.net) is an award-winning author, columnist, editor, sex educator and feminist pornographer. She is the author of seven books: *The Big Book of Sex Toys, The Anal Sex Position Guide*, *Opening Up: A Guide to Creating and Sustaining Open Relationships*, *The Ultimate Guide to Anal Sex for Women, True Lust: Adventures in Sex, Porn and Perversion*, *Down and Dirty Sex Secrets* and *Secrets to Female Ejaculation and Great G-Spot Orgasms* (forthcoming). She was creator and original series editor of sixteen volumes of the Lambda Literary Award–winning anthology *Best Lesbian Erotica*. She runs Smart Ass Productions, and has directed and produced more than twenty adult films, from sex education to reality porn. She was a syndicated columnist for the *Village Voice* for nine and a half years and writes an advice column for *Taboo Magazine*. She has appeared in hundreds of publications and on radio and television. She lectures at top colleges and universities and teaches sex and relationship workshops around the world. She lives with her partner and their dogs in Upstate New York.

TO OUR READERS:

For more than thirty years Cleis Press has been among the vanguard, publishing books that reflect our mission to help create a world in which we are all free to live our authentic lives.

Whether you've been a loyal Cleis Press reader or are just now discovering our list, we thank you for supporting our press.

Your purchase of this book helps us thrive.

Visit us at www.cleispress.com.